A Noble Cunning

The Countess
and the
Tower

Patricia Bernstein

ISBNs:
978-1-7364990-5-4 (pb);
978-1-7364990-6-1 (hc);
978-1-7364990-7-8 (eBook)

Library of Congress Control Number: 2022938664
First Printing: 2023
Printed in the United States of America

Names: Bernstein, Patricia, 1944- author.
Title: A noble cunning: the countess and the tower / by Patricia Bernstein.
Description: [Roseville, Minnesota] : [History Through Fiction], [2023] | Includes bibliographical references.
Identifiers: ISBN: 978-1-7364990-5-4 (paperback) | 978-1-7364990-6-1 (hardcover) | 978-1-7364990-7-8 (ebook) | LCCN: 2022938664
Subjects: LCSH: Countesses--England--History--18th century--Fiction. | Rescues--England--History-- 18th century--Fiction. | Women--England--History--18th century--Fiction. | Catholics-- Persecutions--England--History--18th century--Fiction. | Great Britain--History--1714- 1837--Fiction. | LCGFT: Historical fiction. | BISAC: FICTION / Historical / General. | FICTION / Christian / Historical. | FICTION / World Literature / England / 18th Century.
Classification: LCC: PS3602.E762857 N62 2023 | DDC: 813/.6--dc23

Also by Patricia Bernstein

Ten Dollars to Hate: The Texas Man Who Fought the Klan

The First Waco Horror: The Lynching of Jesse Washington and the Rise of the NAACP

Having a Baby: Mothers Tell Their Stories

This book is dedicated to the glorious young women of today,
Katherine, Jessica, Rebecca,
Alexandra, Stephanie, Gennifer,
Caitlin, Laura and Alyssa
And of the up-and-coming generation, Kiera Rachel
...And to one splendid young gentleman, Emry Weston

"Fortune's blows, when most struck home, being gentle wounded, craves a noble cunning."

Coriolanus, William Shakespeare

Portrait of Winifred Herbert Maxwell, Countess of Nithsdale, the
inspiration for Bethan Glentaggart in A *Noble Cunning*.
By permission of the Traquair House Charitable Trust

Portrait of William Maxwell, Earl of Nithsdale, the model for
Gavin Glentaggart in *A Noble Cunning*.
By permission of the Traquair House Charitable Trust

Portrait of King George I, circa 1714, the first German king to rule
Great Britain.
By permission of the © National Portrait Gallery, London

Table of Contents

Chapter One – No Safe Place 1

Chapter Two – Lucy and Gavin.................................. 17

Chapter Three – The Fate of the Wicked 31

Chapter Four – War Comes Closer............................... 47

Chapter Five – The Uprising Begins 61

Chapter Six – Letters from the Field 69

Chapter Seven – A Household is Broken...................... 79

Chapter Eight – A Winter Journey................................ 87

Chapter Nine – A World Turned to Snow.................... 97

Chapter Ten – In the Lair of the Beast........................ 111

Chapter Eleven – The Wayward Sister 127

Chapter Twelve – Rebels at the Bar............................... 143

Chapter Thirteen – Painting the Lily............................ 153

Chapter Fourteen – Plea to a False King...................... 169

Chapter Fifteen – A Plot with Many Parts 181

Chapter Sixteen – The Uses of Chocolate 201

Chapter Seventeen – The Curtain Rises 211

Author's Historical Note 241

Appendix A – Bethan's Family in *A Noble Cunning*..... 245

Appendix B – Chart of Stuarts and Possible Heirs
    to the Throne of Great Britain 246

Appendix C – Timeline of Events............................... 248

Bibliography 250

Acknowledgments.. 253

About the Author 254

Chapter One
No Safe Place

Heath Hall, Scottish Lowlands, 1710

"...we shall do our utmost endeavor to have the land purged of Popish idolatry... particularly the abomination of the mass... We shall never, consent, for any reason whatsoever, that the Penal Statutes, made against Papists should be annulled; but shall, when opportunity offers, be ready to concur in putting them to a due and vigorous execution."

The Auchensaugh Renovation of the National Covenant.
Reformed Presbytery, July 24, 1712.

I had gone to bed early and slept soundly until I was awakened by a wild noise of cries and shouts almost under my windows. I rose and peered out. As if one of my most troubled dreams had come to life, at least one hundred men were gathered below, waving smoky torches and brandishing pikes and hammers and other tools they had probably seized from our smithy.

One night in London many years earlier, when I was a child of nine, I had witnessed a raucous anti-Catholic parade made up of London rowdies disguised as grotesque parodies of priests and bishops and the pope. Ever since then, I have feared mobs at night, faces distorted by flickering torchlight.

I looked down from my window upon this motley crowd of bedraggled sowers and reapers, my senses assaulted by the sting of smoke and the writhing fingers of flame. For a moment I swayed and felt that I might fall. Gavin, my husband, was many leagues away politicking in the back-street coffeehouses of Edinburgh. How could I face this crowd without him?

But I could not fall. I am Bethan Carlisle Glentaggart, Countess of Clarencefield, a Catholic amid the heathen Protestants, I thought, and must show neither fear nor weakness. Unruly crowds of this kind feed on the terror they engender in their betters. I repressed an involuntary shiver and vowed to demonstrate that they were dealing with a woman of spirit, in full command of her household, not a mere drawing-room ornament. They would not smell *my* fear. My heart banged violently in my chest, but I would smooth my features as I had seen my mother do when our family was threatened.

The boldest of the leaders—a ragged bunch with tousled hair, mismatched garments and broken-down shoes—hallooed up at me.

"Mistress, you are hiding a Romanish priest, a servant of Satan, and we will have him! Bring him out or we will come in, as is our right by law!"

Oh yes, of course, I thought but did not say, your "legal rights" are meant to be exercised in the dark of night with a mob at your back, against unprotected women and children.

My brain, still a little sodden with sleep, churned and brought forth no response for a moment, but then clarity broke through. "Hold there, sirrah. I will come down to you," I cried.

I tossed an unlaced gown over my shift and wrapped a cloak over the whole. Leaving my hair loose, I ran down the stairs, as the storm of bangings and knockings on the front door grew louder and more insistent. Despite the noise, I paused for an instant at the foot of the stairs to run my hands over my face, trying to forcibly soften lines of worry and subdue the pinch of anxiety around my eyes and mouth.

My companion Lucy had also risen. Shocked and pale-faced, she came running to me barefooted. For once, she, also abruptly jerked from sleep, had no advice to give. But I was beginning to feel more confident that I could maintain at least the outward appearance of a woman who was unruffled by scares in the night, even though my legs were trembling.

"I have read this chapter before," I told Lucy. "When I was

only seven, soldiers came to our home in Wales for this self-same purpose, hunting an illegal priest. I believe I can manage these vermin as my mother once did. None of these men are fit to kiss the hem of Father Jerome's shabbiest robe."

Then Lucy and I looked at each other. She gasped. The fact was we *had* been hosting Father Jerome, a secret missionary priest from France, traveling disguised as an itinerant shepherd and sleeping in the shielings or shepherd's huts used during summer grazing.

Somehow the priests who came to Scotland knew where the Catholics were and who would welcome them. Father Jerome, diminutive and elderly—but sinewy and strong enough to climb goat paths from glen to glen—once acknowledged to me that he knew his ultimate fate would be exile, prison or perhaps death at the hands of a mob.

"We all believe that at some point we will be caught, my lady, and we are resigned," he had said with his gentle smile. "When that time comes, I will be grateful for my years spent comforting a scattered and persecuted flock." I had knelt and asked for his blessing. The itinerant priests were the holiest men I ever knew.

Father Jerome was supposed to have left us at dusk, but neither Lucy nor I had actually seen him go. He had a way of slipping away into the dark without making a sound. But what if he had not yet left and was still somewhere in the house? I had to hope he would take heed of the commotion and make himself scarce.

I could hear the leader of the mob yelling, "We will not give you time to hide him. Open this door or we will break it to..." I managed to raise the iron latch and pulled open the heavy oak door, just in time for him to screech the end of his sentence in my face, "...splinters."

The night was cold. It was close to Christmastide and, though there was no snow, the wind was sharp. I gathered my cloak more closely around me.

This spokesman was of medium height and spindly, his coat torn and half off his shoulder. His long, greasy, gray-brown hair crept back from his forehead as if it were running away from his face, embarrassed by his actions. His linen was soiled, and his jacket sleeves were too short for his knobby-boned wrists. Ah, but he carried a Bible and proceeded to wave it in my face.

"And you are...," I asked quietly.

He hesitated, thinking perhaps to hide his identity, which was absurd. A shorter, even grimier man standing next to him—this one wearing a shapeless hat jammed almost down to his eyebrows—punched the leader's arm.

"Minister Adam Goodnow," the leader declared, and immediately tried to seize the offensive again by brandishing the Bible in my direction. "Bring us the priest and we will trouble you no further tonight: 'For your priests have violated My law and have profaned My holy things; they have put no difference between the unclean and the clean and I am profaned among them.'"

"Ezekiel 22:26," he concluded with an air of satisfaction.

"There is no priest here," I said, forcing a calm tone into my voice that I did not feel. "We would bring no man into danger."

"Your *souls* are in danger," he spit at me, "if you follow the Whore of Babylon and pursue the Antichrist into darkness..."

I pushed my palm out towards him, intent on holding it steady. I had to find a way to keep a horde of wild men from rampaging through my home. I remembered that, when the soldiers came to Castle Banwy in Wales, when I was seven, my mother took control by telling them they could search for a priest if they left their muddy boots outside. Something about the foolishness of marching upstairs and down in their dirty stockings full of holes took the edge off their eagerness to find the priest. Perhaps I could keep most of these men outside if I gave way just a little.

"It is late," I said. "My babies are asleep. I desire you not to wake them. Three of you—no more than three—may come in and search the house...if you do it quietly and do not wake the children."

It was almost comical to see some of those in the front ranks lower their crude weapons and turn to hush each other. I do not believe they were all wicked men, but the press of the crowd and heated rhetoric lead so many weak souls to doom.

Minister Goodnow appointed himself and two others of his ilk to undertake the search, Minister Walter Cleeves and Minister

Joseph MacGurk. Cleeves was the squat little man with his hat pulled low. Now I knew who they were. I had heard their names before. They were so-called "Covenant ministers," the most extreme of the Scottish Protestants, who had undoubtedly riled up this mob of dullards to frighten women and children in the dead of night.

Minister MacGurk, I observed, was unlike the other two who, for all their bluster, seemed ready to agree to my proposal that only three would enter the house. MacGurk was tall and very lean with a long, thin face, a low forehead and eyes so close together and crossed towards each other that I silently named him "Cyclops." His hair was cropped very short. Yet even the stubble somehow managed to look uneven and patchy as if he was going bald by random sections.

With a close-shaven head and no cap, there was a look of a skeleton about him. Something I could not place disturbed me about this man. Goodnow and Cleeves seemed to cover up a natural timidity with loud talk. Somehow I did not think this MacGurk was timid.

He grinned at me, revealing his brown and broken teeth, but it was not a mirthful smile, rather a gleeful, secretive one, as if he knew something I did not. He had an odd way of carrying his arms raised in front of him with his hands dangling from the ends of his wrists. His long, bony fingers ended in ragged nails rimmed in some black, greasy substance like tar. Once I had really noticed him, I shuddered slightly and drew my cloak more closely around me. I wanted this midnight violation of our hearth to be done.

I led the three men through the house as Lucy and our steward, McClaren, brought up the rear, raising candles to light our way. Most of the servants had gone home to sleep with their families. But I was glad of the presence of our stolid McClaren and would come to be gladder still before the night was over.

Upstairs and downstairs and in my lady's chamber we went, as the old nursery rhyme has it. I really wished the last lines could come true: *There I met an old man/Who wouldn't say his prayers. So I took him by his left leg and threw him down the stairs.* But, even with the help of Lucy and McClaren, I didn't think we could throw all three down the stairs at once. And, if we did, we might have the whole mob rushing in upon us.

In any case, this rhyme was an unlucky thought. I remembered I had once heard that the lines had become popular in the time of Henry VIII as an anti-Catholic verse. They were meant to describe hidey-holes where priests, once discovered, might indeed be thrown downstairs.

I kept moving quickly to finish this ordeal as soon as I could and to suppress the quivering in my legs. As we entered each room, I threw open cupboards and chests where a priest might hide and allowed my unwelcome visitors to rummage through our clothing and other goods. It was, to say the very least, unpleasant, watching those filthy hands paw our white linens and coverlets trimmed with point d'Alençon lace. Lucy and I glanced at each other as if to say, everything they've touched will have to be washed.

The fear I felt thrumming in my breast, forcing me to keep my hands clasped together so they would not shake, was beginning to meld with a growing anger. How dare they! These men were hardly better than beggars, eking out a bare living, preying on the ignorant and selling them perdition in the guise of salvation.

MacGurk seemed to take particular pleasure in tossing our petticoats, stomachers and waists, ribbons and laces, linens and headdresses, on the floor. When he could, he trod heavily upon the delicate, embroidered linens and silk velvets. After he had stepped on and torn a petticoat, Minister Goodnow hesitantly put a hand on his arm and shook his head as if to rebuke him.

"Minister MacGurk, we are looking for priests," he said mildly, "not seeking to despoil possessions. We are here neither to steal nor destroy."

MacGurk shook him off.

"These are papists who live here," he hissed, not seeming to care that we heard, "all of them and their brats, too. No matter their station in society, they should have all been driven out with their snake-tongued, Pope-loving king twenty-five years ago. Why are they allowed to lord it over the Saved?"

Goodnow merely shook his head again, wrinkling up his high forehead anxiously. He looked as if he was ready for the night to be over, as well.

We even tiptoed into the rooms of our sleeping Gareth and

6

Moira—oh, my babies!—who were undisturbed, thank the Blessed Virgin. And here Goodnow and Cleeves did prevent MacGurk from throwing the children's things on the floor.

The last chamber was almost empty. It held simply a bed without hangings and an old wardrobe. My fear rose once more, and this time I was afraid I might be sick. I turned away from the three men for a moment, trying to calm my innards and school my countenance again to remain utterly smooth.

I hoped they would be content with simply regarding the room from the door—or perhaps, if they saw that this wardrobe contained only empty hooks, they would not pry further. There were no goods here for MacGurk to rend. When I saw MacGurk was not content with a cursory examination, I feared to look at Lucy. She knew what I knew.

MacGurk approached the bed and kicked it, discovering the shelf hidden beneath. I could not completely suppress a slight shudder. Fortunately, MacGurk was too busy examining what he thought might be a triumphant discovery to notice any change in my expression.

He knelt and pulled the shelf out with a flourish. Thanks to all the saints in Heaven, it was empty. He stared at me as if to demand an explanation.

"My sister-in-law comes to visit us. If she brings any of her children, they may sleep there," I said as indifferently as I could manage, but it came out in a bit of a croak. The truth was that Father Jerome had been sleeping there for a fortnight. But at least I could now trust that he was gone.

I clenched my hands together, nails digging into the softness of my palms, hoping MacGurk would not decide to pull the shelf all the way out and crawl under the bed. For then he might perceive that, despite the piles of coverlets laid on top, the mattress was a thin one set high on a tightly knotted layer of ropes. There was plenty of room for a grown man to sleep on the shelf under the bed. I held my breath.

But perhaps MacGurk was too ungainly to fold himself into such a space and not imaginative enough to see that a smaller man than he might do it easily. He left the shelf tilted onto the floor and

7

turned away with a black look of disappointment.

As the preachers were leaving the room, and I exhaled, Lucy came close and squeezed my hand. Pray God, I thought, that this be the end of it.

But once we emerged into the hall, MacGurk fixed his close-set eyes on me and perhaps he sensed my momentary relief. His chilling grimace returned, as if he knew how frightened I really was—and how angry. He had me in his grip and would not yet release me. This sudden, rare power to torment the family of a Catholic lord was irresistible to him.

"There must be a topmost floor to this house," he declared.

"Yes," I said, biting off my words, angry at him and even angrier that I was allowing this degraded, false preacher to unnerve me. "There are cobwebs and broken furniture up there. No priests."

"I would see for myself," he insisted, coming too close and bending over me. Again I saw his broken and rotted teeth and felt a little spray of spittle on my face as he said, "Women are ever deceitful."

The stench of him overwhelmed me as much as his brutality. Minister Cleeves smelled of horse dung like many peasants. Minister Goodnow smelled of illness, a sourness that suggested to me that he might be meeting his Maker in the austere, gray-washed Heaven of the Covenanters before long.

But this man MacGurk stank of the grave—of putrefaction, of rotting teeth and oozing, blackened flesh, as if he were a gravedigger (which perhaps he was) or a grave robber (he might have been that, too).

I gave him no more words, thinking we would soon be done.

Goodnow and Cleeves, Lucy and McClaren waited below while I squeezed my cloak and skirts up the narrowest of stairs and MacGurk followed close behind.

We emerged into an open space just as empty of hiding places as I had described. But I had forgotten the great wooden chest, covered with a lacework of dust and spiders' webs, in a corner of the space. My eyes fell upon it, I remembered what was in it, and I knew I had made a mistake.

I turned, just as the light of the torch I held reflected a sharp gleam in MacGurk's eyes. "Open it!" he ordered, pointing at the chest.

"That will be difficult," I said. "It hasn't been opened in many a year. There is nothing in it, I believe, but an old cloak and a featherbed from the last century."

"Or a priest," he said with one of his grim smiles.

In the end it required a crowbar, brought by McClaren from the smithy and handed up the stairs to MacGurk, who wielded it to break the rusted lock, which should have told any rational man that a priest who had hidden in the chest would be long reduced to bones by now.

MacGurk tossed away the crowbar, threw open the lid with a squealing of hinges and looked inside and it was just as I had told him. There was nothing but a musty, flattened feather bed and a velvet cloak that had once been fine but was now somewhat deteriorated from close consorting with moths.

MacGurk, in a fit of frustration, pulled both items out of the chest and tossed them on the stone floor. He then peered so deeply into the chest, still searching for a priest who might have hidden beneath the bed, that he almost fell in. I should have tipped him over the edge then and there and slammed the lid.

Once again, I thought we were finished, and I could now usher MacGurk and his companions out of my home. But MacGurk proceeded to turn over and examine the feather bed and then to pull a small knife from the rope around his waist and slice it open. Predictably, slightly damp feathers flew everywhere, filling the air around us like a heavy snow and coating Minister MacGurk from head to toe.

This—and his failure to find a priest—seemed to enrage the man. He slammed the lid of the trunk so far back, I thought the entire structure would topple over backwards, but it did not fall. He next seized upon the deep crimson velvet cloak, picked it up and threw it down again. I had not seen the cloak before, but I knew what it was and could only hope that he did not. I was just daring to catch my breath when he grabbed it up once more and looked more closely at the sleeve, where a large patch of embroidery represented in gold and green the curious figure of a tortoise climbing a tall palm tree. These were the very items Gavin had mentioned to me more than once that had been left behind at Heath Hall by Mary Queen of Scots during her feverish flight through Scotland.

The odd figure of tortoise and palm tree had once been the symbol of Mary's second marriage to Lord Darnley. In the first, short-lived happiness of this marriage, Mary was known to have embroidered the image on many of her bed linens and items of clothing. As she flew from refuge to refuge, heading south, perhaps belongings that reminded her of the wicked Darnley were the first she discarded.

A moment passed and MacGurk's lips slowly parted in the same mimicry of a smile that had made me so uneasy before as he turned to look at me.

"Vessel of temptation!" he cried. "For so are all women...you have sought to hide from my view an object of disgust to all good Christians, a relic of that wicked adulteress and murderess, Mary of Scotland, who was so righteously executed. Yet you preserve it as a valued memorial."

"A robe is not a priest," I said, "no matter whose robe it was."

He began to rip the fabric, intending, I saw, to tear it to shreds. I thought of all the long years during which my husband and his ancestors had kept this remembrance of poor martyred Mary Stuart.

There was more to this story of the doomed queen and the Glentaggarts than Gavin had originally told me. It had come out, little by little, over time. One of Gavin's long-ago grandsires had supported Mary Stuart to the end of her star-crossed reign, and it was to Heath Hall she had fled after the battle of Langside, which was her final undoing. This decayed robe was, in some sense, almost sacred to Gavin because it represented the unstained honor that was part of his family heritage, come down to him along with his estates. The Glentaggarts had always supported the Stuarts.

I grasped MacGurk's arm, unable to contain myself any longer.

"You shall not destroy the property of my husband!" I cried.

Minister MacGurk responded by dropping the robe and

slamming into me, pushing me up against the dusty wall, seizing my jaw in his grip, stretching my neck up until I thought my head would come unhinged from my body. A multitude of feathers lifted from his body and flew into my nose and eyes.

"*Where is the priest, woman?*" he whispered hoarsely, pressing the full length of his body against me, his long head towering above me. His grimy nails bit into my neck. I felt I *must* vomit but with my jaw in his hard grasp, I might choke on my vomit.

Because all conflict in Scotland, it seems, comes from ancient feuds and old battles that often began before man made records, somehow it was no surprise to me that, at this exact moment, MacGurk should choose to justify himself by calling on an old hatred that had nothing to do with me or mine.

"My grandfather Campbell was killed by papists at the Battle of Inverlochy," he spat directly into my ear as he squeezed my jaw until it seemed he would simply snap the bone. "I despise all the tribe of ye, all ye Romanist sinners with bloody hands. *Where is the priest?*" He pressed his free hand, and its claws, into my breast.

Infuriated that this appalling monster should lay his hands—and his fetid odor—on me, I tried to push his arms away. I wriggled. I kicked his instep but my soft slippers did little damage. I reached up to scratch his face. The thought of my children roared in my mind though I could not speak. What would become of them if this creature murdered me?

I could not reach his eyes, so I gouged at his nose, causing him to whimper and loosen his grasp of me a little. Then he had me again and was slowly forcing me to the floor, clawing now, not at my breast, but at my skirts. My head hit the floor and bounced—two painful clangs.

Had he not been so frenzied by the failure of his expedition to catch and punish a priest, he might have made short work of the little resistance I could offer. As it was, he seemed not to quite know where to tear at me first. He would grasp and rip the collar of my gown and then reach down and scrabble to get under the cloak, the gown, the shift.

The blows to my head had dizzied me. His weight pressed me

to the floor. How could such a gangly skeleton of a man be such a weight? I hit at his face with my fists, hooked a finger in one of his ears, pulled and gashed it. He had released his hold on my jaw when we fell, so I bit his chin, which led him to rear back to hit me with a closed fist. Clearly I was losing the fight. You may overcome me, I thought, but I have laid marks on you that will linger. I raked a broken fingernail across his neck, pushing as deep as I could into his flesh.

I heard the sound of boots banging up the stairs. Lucy, having heard the commotion, came thundering into the room with McClaren and Ministers Goodnow and Cleeves right behind her. I could just see their heads as they came into view over MacGurk's shoulder—Lucy's mouth pursed with fury, McClaren expressionless as ever, the two ministers with mouths agape.

Have I mentioned how much I had come to love my devoted companion Lucy, who had followed me hither and thither and was always nearby to quiet a whining child, bring fresh scones to heal fatigue or discouragement, listen to my daily worries, or...follow me into battle?

Lucy marched right up to MacGurk and stomped on his foot. Unlike me, she had stopped during our odyssey through the house to put on her shoes. McClaren—bless him—followed her, brandishing a besom made in the old way with a bundle of sharp twigs bound together and began beating MacGurk on his back, his buttocks, his legs, his head.

"Minister MacGurk!" cried Goodnow in a thoroughly horrified tone of voice. Cleeves, behind him, stared at the tangle of the two of us on the ground with his mouth gawping.

"Remember yourself!" Goodnow admonished. "'Know ye not that the unrighteous shall not inherit the Kingdom of God?'"

"1 Corinthians 6:9," he added.

In the effort to evade McClaren's blows, MacGurk drew himself up to a sitting position and finally half stood, crouched, blood seeping through his tattered coat, leaving me to collect myself as best I could with my head ringing, my garments disarrayed and my throat gagging. Even stunned and hurt as I was, I would have sprung at the wounded man if I had had the strength. Rage had buried my fear. But I was in such discomfort I could barely move and did not know how I would stand.

For a moment there was so much tension in MacGurk's bent posture, it seemed as if he might charge McClaren. But McClaren coolly pulled a flintlock pistol from beneath his shirt, pointed it at MacGurk and pulled the cock halfway back.

MacGurk, it seemed, was not so maddened as to charge a man pointing a pistol at him from the distance of an arm's length. He opened his mouth to rain more curses on our heads, but then closed it again and merely glared. Slowly he turned toward the narrow staircase, showering feathers in all directions and limping with each step he took. I was angry that he was not more damaged and tried to rise, but sank back, letting a wave of relief and exhaustion wash some of the fury from my heart. I would live and my children were unhurt and unknowing.

Lucy helped me up, brushed off my cloak and skirts, tried to smooth back my hair and shake out the feathers, and gently touched my jaw where a bruise was beginning to bloom. I could already feel my cheek swelling where he had struck me. I cried out at her touch.

I also moved in a halo of floating eiderdown. Incongruously, it seemed as if two angels had wrestled there, losing masses of feathers from their wings as they struggled together.

McClaren and Goodnow, close on MacGurk's heels, forced him back down the stairs. Lucy and I followed slowly, me leaning against her, all the way down through the darkness to the front door once more. I heard no children crying, thank the Blessed Virgin for small mercies in this awful night.

The crowd outside was much smaller than it had been. The men had waited so long in the deepening cold that some had simply lost interest and drifted back to the road and away to their homes. What must those who remained have thought when they saw two apparitions emerge from the house clothed in feathers?

Goodnow paused and turned to me, as if to apologize. I tried to speak and coughed and choked instead. The bile I had tried to hold down suddenly came out in a rush of dark liquid and feathers—falling onto the packed earth, fortunately, not on a Heath Hall carpet.

"You see," I finally choked out, "*there is no priest.*"

"Mistress, we had not meant to..." Goodnow stammered, while Cleeves drifted shadow-like behind him. But then the stack of Bible verses stuffed into Goodnow's head overcame him again and he could not stop himself.

"'Repent ye therefore and be converted,'" he warned me, shaking a trembling forefinger, "'that your sins may be blotted out...' Acts 3:19."

And my own Lucy spoke up—from whence this came I know not—and declared in a strong voice: "Hypocrite! 'Not everyone that saith unto me, Lord, Lord, shall enter into the Kingdom of Heaven; but he that doeth the will of my Father which is in Heaven'... Matthew 7:21." She cast a glare towards MacGurk, who was crab-footing away into the darkness, white feathers swirling up in the wind around him, runnels of blood trailing behind him, muttering in a kind of low growl to himself.

"'Woe unto you, scribes and Pharisees!'" cried Lucy, as she stretched out her arm and pointed at Goodnow in turn. "'For ye are like unto whited sepulchers, which indeed appear beautiful outward, but are within full of dead men's bones, and of all uncleanness...' Matthew 23:27."

Goodnow looked entirely shaken. He had clearly not expected to have Biblical quotations flung at him like arrows in a house where followers of Rome resided.

"This was not my doing," he pleaded, shivering a little all over. Had it occurred to him at last that this evil night might have consequences?

His pale eyes watered. He looked back towards MacGurk, who had almost disappeared into the shadows. "Some are too zealous in the service of the Lord and are o'ermastered by the Spirit."

"And some are driven by hatred and cruelty and *call* it the Spirit of the Lord," said Lucy. "Did our Savior not command us to love one another?"

Goodnow looked confused. Altogether, the night had been too much for him. He had only a few more words to spare for me.

"I hope you will be well, Mistress. We did not mean...we were only looking for...we...," he said and turned to leave. But one more thought came to him.

"'If ye forgive not men their trespasses, neither will your Father forgive your trespasses.' Matthew 6:15," he murmured, eyes downcast. It was not entirely clear whether he was asking me to forgive them, or whether the ingrained habit of compulsive quotation was just running ahead on its own, without any mental engagement.

"'Judge not, and ye shall not be judged. Condemn not, and ye shall not be condemned,'" said Lucy firmly. "Luke 6:37."

Goodnow also drifted away into the dark with Cleeves following behind like the remnant of a shade. But we all remained standing at the door until we were sure they were gone, and the night had returned to itself, to the stars and the occasional sleepy bird song. Pain came over me, growing more intense—especially the throbbing in my cheek and my head and bright strands of pain across my lower back where MacGurk had thrown me down. I could think of nothing but pain.

Lucy helped me up the stairs, rinsed my wounds, put a cold, vinegar-soaked cloth on my bruised jaw and cheek, and laid me down in my bed, where I stayed for the following three days, every part of my body aching. While I recovered from the attentions of Minister MacGurk, Lucy busied herself with the maids, putting the house to rights, cleaning and washing and mending whatever could be mended, and discarding what could not be repaired.

I must have been a little feverish during those days. I was thinking on the majesty of the Roman Catholic Church as compared to the frenetic scufflings and squabblings of those who had broken away. I thought I had a vision of the clear path of the Catholic, like Jacob's ladder, leading upward in measured steps, rung by rung, as we are lifted along by priests, by saints, by the sacraments, until our final confession and ultimately, perhaps after a period of time in Purgatory, through the golden doorway to Paradise.

But these stubborn Protestants ramble, noses deep in the Holy

Book, going, often as not, in circles or into dead-end eddies, sliding downwards more often than upwards. If any ever attain Heaven, it is by way of miraculous accident or God's pity.

That is the difference between us, I whispered to myself. We follow what has been ordained over centuries while they wander in their own prideful ways farther and farther from Truth. How dare these miserably lost souls of Covenanters and Dissenters and every manner of Protestant believe that *we Catholics* are the cursed ones who must be exterminated?

Yet the vision I had dimmed and dispersed when the fever left me, and I remained as always in my way of believing sometimes, and not believing other times, and sometimes I felt both belief and non-belief at once, clinging to the Virgin Mary as my only constant. But never did I long to be among the fractured crew of Protestants, and never did I want to bring man or woman to my faith, such as it was, by force.

Chapter Two
Lucy and Gavin

"Above our life we love a steadfast friend."

Hero and Leander, Christopher Marlowe

"If ever two were one, then surely we.
If ever man was loved by wife, then thee."

"To My Dear and Loving Husband," Anne Bradstreet

On the third day after the search of Heath Hall, Lucy came and sat on my bed. I felt a little better, was sitting up and sipping a dram of our good Scotch whisky, and it suddenly occurred to me to ask my Lucy where on earth she had learned all those Bible verses? Was she a secret Protestant? Would she tell me the truth if she was?

"You are a learned woman, Lucy," I said. "I am well aware of that. I am never surprised to hear you quote Shakespeare...or Molière or even Dante on occasion. But...Holy Scripture?"

Lucy flushed and stared downward at her knitting so that her face was hidden by her prim, spare little white bonnet.

"Lucy?" I said.

She then told me a story I had never heard before. When she was a companion/governess in one of the houses where she had stayed for a time, the eldest son of the household, a young man of nineteen or twenty, quietly converted from the Roman Church to the Church of England and then to one of the Dissenters' sects.

"He seemed to feel that I, young as I was," she said, "was a ripe target for his proselytizing, where his family members were not. He knew I could not readily escape him...and he also suspected...that which was true..."

17

She paused and seemed even more intent on her handwork.

"Yes?" I said impatiently.

"...that I had fallen into an overwhelming longing for him, as young girls do."

"Lucy!" I cried, as startled as if she had told me she once roamed England with a troupe of roving players, playing Desdemona one night and Juliet's Nurse the next. This was not the cool Lucy I had always known, unruffled by even the most extraordinary human dramas, unmoved by the customary human passions.

Now she looked at me with a little flash of anger, so rosy that I could see that she must have once been almost pretty.

"Oh?" said I. "In what other ways did he take advantage of your youthful worship?"

"None," she declared. She laughed, a soft sound between a wry giggle and a cough. "More's the pity. You see, his longing to save my soul was sincere."

I did not ask what she meant by "more's the pity," though I found that too surprised me and left my fond image of my strait-laced friend a little frayed around the edges.

"What happened?" I asked. "Did his parents find you out?"

"No, he left England. He went to Germany to study with the Protestant theologians. The children I was teaching were nearly grown, and I moved on. I never heard what became of him. But some of the verses he taught me have stayed with me to this day—and done me no harm."

She recited with a slight smirk that was speedily gone: "'O give thanks unto the Lord; for he is good: because His mercy endureth forever...' Psalms 118:1."

We moved on to other topics, but that story of her early, un-requited love in the end rounded and deepened my view of Lucy a little and reminded me that she did not merely exist for my convenience but had had her own secret desires and dreams. I wondered if her womanly longings would cause her to leave us in time—or if her flights of sentiment were all in the past.

Lucy Dunstable had first come to our family twenty-five years earlier, when we were living in our town house at Lincoln's Inn

Field in London, awaiting the coronation of King James II. My parents had served James and his queen, Mary Beatrice, when he was the Duke of York and heir to his brother Charles' throne. They would be powerful advisors in his new court.

Lucy was my mother's distant cousin who came to teach us four sisters (Marged, Aelwen, Glynis and me) the intricacies of French, Italian, embroidery, music, and dancing. I can still hear her in my mind admonishing us: "The gavotte requires intricate leaps and jumps, but you may not land flatfooted with full force as if you have just fallen out of an apple tree. And if you make a mistake in the pattern—or, God forbid, twist your ankle in the landing—your expression must betray nothing. You catch up in the steps, or you limp gracefully to the nearest chair, but you are always in perfect command of yourself."

Lucy must have been quite young then, though she always conducted herself with an air of authority. I was only thirteen. To me, she seemed to be of a great age, lean as a rail and pinning her reddish hair up severely in tight coils rather than teasing and plumping it around wire frames into the stylized ringlets of the day. She was not a pretty woman but neither was she homely. She had clean, spare features with a little droop at the corners of her mouth. She was not unkind but a reserved soul, disappointed early in life by her lack of a dowry. Instead of a husband and children, she had acquired an impeccable command of the French and Italian tongues.

Lucy had given me a greater gift than dancing and French though—a love of books, especially of Shakespeare and John Donne and the Cavalier poets. I was an indifferent seamstress but, under Lucy's tutelage, was rarely without a book, slipped into the pocket of my petticoat—a habit that has continued to this day. Books opened new worlds to me and saved me from being like many of the noblewomen around me, ruminating only on menus and furnishings and fashion and society gossip.

In fact, our mutual love of books eventually became one of the close bonds between Gavin and myself. He too loved the Cavalier poets and Donne, and, as for Shakespeare, the first gift Gavin ever gave me was a new edition of *A Midsummer Night's Dream*.

When William of Orange invaded England and my family escaped to France with the queen and infant prince, I thought I had lost Lucy forever. But she came to me in Paris and remained my closest companion and a substitute of sorts for the loss of my dearest sister Glynis to a convent in Bruges.

It was Lucy who had the idea of telling the children, who could not help but see some of the wreck MacGurk had made, that "naughty men" had come into our home but had been made to go away. Nine-year old Gareth accepted that brief explanation for the broken crockery and garments on the floor and went straight to the kitchen to see what Ainslie our cook was preparing that smelled so irresistibly of baked apples.

Moira, only five, lingered and looked up at me with her deep gaze and a single tear resting on one pink cheek. "But, ma mère..." she said, (Lucy had taught the children a little French) "what if the bad men come back?"

"That will not happen," I told her with an assurance I did not feel.

It tore my heart but also gave me enormous anger that such young children must know the sensation of being in danger. How I loathed our persecutors. I wished them all imprisoned in a dank cell where there was nothing but an enormous Bible...with all of its pages pasted together so it could not be read.

Lucy and I were both starkly aware that Gavin would be returning soon. We had to decide what to tell him. I was emerging from my torpor enough to be overcome with fear as to what he might do—and the harm that might come to him—if we told him the truth.

I tried to remember when I had last seen him most enraged. Was it when the young daughter of one of our tenants was abducted by a village lout and forced into a mummery of an overnight "wedding"? I remembered Gavin's anger when he heard the story, and how quickly he had organized servants and tenants to search for the girl. They found the poor child in a low inn, half-clothed on a dirty straw mattress, weeping uncontrollably.

Rather than force her to stay with the villain who had taken her, as another lord might have done, Gavin had the kidnapper beaten and banished and the girl returned to her parents. The Blessed Virgin must have heard her prayers because the girl did not bear a child. A year later, she married the boy she truly fancied and no more word was spoken about her ordeal. We helped to fit out a neat cottage for the two of them.

But this situation was much worse. Gavin's wife and home had been assaulted and his children endangered. I imagined his comely face darkened with rage as I had never seen it. As I lay in bed, I could foresee Gavin pleading for a justice which he would not be granted, not here in the Scottish Lowlands, overrun as it was with Covenanters. If he was denied justice, what would he do?

We could not hide the fact that *something* had happened. Gavin would certainly observe my injuries. In any case, if we did not tell him, we could not be sure that one of our tenants or a neighbor would not mention what he had heard of rumors and gossip, if only to offer sympathy.

"I must tell him the whole story," I finally said to Lucy. "I have no choice. I cannot deceive him in something as important as this, even to save him from himself. If I don't and he finds out elsewhere, the fabric of our marriage may never be mended."

"You must tell," she said, "but perhaps you can modify it a bit, trim off the worst of the rough edges?"

"Oh, but, Lucy, I am so afraid for him."

How it broke my heart to see my husband arrive the next day during a rainstorm, bursting through the front door and flinging his hat and cloak off with his usual vigor, spraying raindrops in all directions, full of smiles with his pleasure at seeing us. He came straight to me and lifted me off the floor in a sodden embrace, which normally would have pleased me. I smiled up at him...but then winced at the sharp pain in my back.

He gently set me down, looked at me with a quizzical raised eyebrow and then noticed that the entire family was sitting stock still and staring at him. Lucy's blue eyes, the pale blue eyes of our very blonde Gareth, and the deep, dark eyes of Moira—her father's eyes—all these were trained on Gavin.

Alistair of Wamphray, Gavin's cousin and business agent,

was also present. He too knew what had happened at Heath Hall. Normally he would have eagerly leapt up to welcome Gavin, but on this day he was very carefully studying a ledger on his lap and offered no greeting when Gavin came in. That may have been the telltale giveaway.

"Tell me quickly," said Gavin, no longer smiling. "What has happened?"

"First you must sit and have a homecoming dram," I replied, hands folded in as near a posture of calm as I could manage, though my voice shook a little, much to my disgust. "As you can see, we are all here and well, so you need not fear the worst."

"I will not sit or drink," he said, "until you tell me."

We sent the children upstairs with their nursemaid, and Lucy and I took turns offering an abbreviated account of the attack on Heath Hall. All this time Gavin stood very still and heard us out.

Then he looked at me with his brow knotted, and I noticed that the inner edge of just one of his heavy, dark eyebrows was beginning to turn gray. This will age him further, I thought.

My husband was no longer the radiant youth of twenty-three I had first met at the court of James II in exile in Paris. Yet I thought he was even more handsome than he had been then. His face was careworn and bronzed from his many hours on horseback or in the field with his tenants. But the indentations across his forehead, the laugh marks around his eyes, the leaner cheeks and graying stubble, gave him character.

He looked like what he was, a man of authority and determination who took his time in great matters, considering and analyzing before he made a move. But I also knew his love of his family and his allegiance to his heritage were intense beyond the norm. I feared he might be impulsive, even reckless, if either was threatened. This attack had threatened both.

"There is more," he said, looking hard at me. That inescapable gaze was so like Moira's. "You are hurt."

"Yes," I admitted. "One of the three men became very angry when they could not find a priest. He threw me against the wall and then to the floor. Lucy and McClaren forced him off. McClaren, bless him, beat him until the man ran blood all over."

"Amid the feathers," said Lucy. So we had to explain the ruined feather bed that had exploded all over us. It was an absurd image but no one smiled.

I had thought Gavin might lift his voice and demand to know where these miscreants—especially MacGurk—might be found, but at first he was too angry to say anything, so angry that his face paled and his lips turned white. My fear for him rose, when it seemed for a moment that he might break from his stillness, seize his hat and cloak, and leave us without another word to track down the men who had so insulted us.

Instead he embraced me with the lightest of touches, trembling slightly himself, and kissed the top of my head. I put my hand on his arm and urged him again to sit and drink and give thought to what action should be taken. This time he did as I asked. After he had downed two whiskies, though I could still see the slight tremor in his hands and could hear it in his voice, he began methodically, bless him, to gather the details of the damage that had been done.

"I will go to the magistrates at Dumfries. We will need to take down all the evidence. I will make a record of every mark on you," he said, though he choked a bit on the word *mark*. "Lucy," he went on, "please give me an inventory of every bed linen, every tablecloth, every garment, that was ripped or soiled. I will ask McClaren to review the tools stolen from the smithy, and I will talk to every servant who was here."

At these words, I allowed myself to exhale and untwist the handkerchief I had knotted into a tiny, damp ball in my palm. He had not gone flying forth, sword in hand, to take immediate revenge on those who had attacked us. He was still my high-tempered Gavin, and I could see what his restraint was costing him, but he had realized in a flash that if he indulged himself in extravagant action, it could hurt us even more.

I also loved him the more because he thought of us, not just his own outrage. He gave me, and later the children, an extra round of embraces and kisses with thanks to God that we were all sound. He even kissed Lucy's cheek and thanked her for her help and defense.

McClaren received a little purse full of Scottish merks and a warm clap on the back. The besom, somewhat battered from its dance on the back of Minister MacGurk, was put in a place of honor by the great fireplace, and a new one made for humbler household use.

It had taken me a little time to warm to McClaren when I first came to Scotland as a new-wed bride. He spoke very little and his face never betrayed what he might be thinking, much less how he might be feeling. He was a stout, solid man, so reserved that it ultimately gave me comfort because I believed he would be little prone to gossip about our private affairs in the local taverns. He had a square face and a solemn expression.

When, occasionally, Gavin would offer him a taste of whisky to celebrate some holiday, he would toss it down and flush slightly, but his essential solemnity did not waver. It had taken some time, but I had learned to appreciate his devotion to our family when it mattered. On that terrible night I had come to value his loyalty more than ever.

In the next few days we spoke at length with Alistair about how he and Gavin could best present claims for damages to the magistrates in Dumfries. But whenever we came to speak of MacGurk, my husband's sweet face, usually so cheerful, became as wrathful as when he had first heard the news.

On one occasion, Gavin asked the stable boy to bring his fastest steed. Without a word to me, he leapt on it bareback and rode off at such speed that I feared for him. But, an hour later, he returned unhurt.

He saw me standing in the doorway watching for him. He dismounted, handed the horse over to a stable boy, came to me and put his arm around me. His face was deeply flushed, but his expression had eased. He saw the tears of relief in my eyes, which I wiped away before they spilled.

"I have frightened you," he said. "I'm sorry. I have not ridden a horse in that way since I was a boy, and I promise you I will not do it again. Will you forgive me?"

"Only if you mean it. We have enough troubles and soon you

will be off on your mission to the magistrates. I beg you, give me no unnecessary cause for more tears."

"As you please, but..." he began, stopped, started again. "This was once my only way to cool my overheated brain and exhaust myself when I was angry."

He could see I did not understand. He beckoned to me. I fetched my cloak and we walked out together along the allée that wandered under overarching trees from our front door to the ivy-covered gate marking the entry to our property. Halfway along, there was a very old stone bench, cracked and blackened, where we sometimes sat when we wanted to talk privately.

I spread my cloak around me, lifted my face to the cold, fresh air and tiny, spitting pellets of light rain, and then laid my head against his shoulder. He took my hand in his and tried to make me understand.

"After my mother died," he murmured, "my father and I sometimes quarreled. If I knocked over a pitcher at table, or if my tutor criticized my lack of devotion to Latin, my father would furiously berate me as if my youthful mistakes were proof that I was not fit to manage the estate after him.

"Rather than attack him in kind, I used to ride off alone without waiting for an ostler to apply saddle or bridle. I was far too angry at my father to speak my thoughts aloud. I did not think he had been kind enough to the mother who was always kind to me."

He went on. "I know you have said your parents loved each other through all that they suffered. But my father and mother were formal and dry towards each other. It was never a love match, and I think it cooled further when my mother bore no more children after my sister and I were born. He always wanted another son.

"My mother had her little dogs and her shopping expeditions to Edinburgh and London and the dignity of her title. My father had a barmaid at the Heath Arms and a 'cousin' he was fond of at Douglas Manor in Shawhead. But he was not a cruel man by nature. I think he brooded on his failures towards my mother after she died, and it made him irritable."

"I am sorry for the distance between your parents," I said. "Marriage is a very long game when there is no closeness of spirit."

But, pitying the bereft boy he had been, I could not help but add, "I think your father was very lucky to have you for his heir instead of some careless young wastrel devoted to hunting, claret and compliant women."

I was so relieved at the promise he had just given me to ride out no more without stirrups or reins that I felt inclined to tease him a little. I wagged a scolding finger at him: "You have mentioned this 'barmaid' and this 'cousin' of your father's before, and I will remind you once again that no barmaids and no cousins will be permitted to interfere with *this* marriage."

At that he laughed and responded as he always did.

"As if the comeliest barmaid or the rosiest 'cousin' could compare to you, who, in your tartan and brogues, would still out-shine all of the Sun King's favorites at Versailles!"

"How would you know!" I said, laughing with him, "You never saw the beauties at Louis XIV's court."

"No," he agreed, taking my face in his hands and kissing me. "When I was in Paris, I was otherwise occupied, courting and mar-rying the famous beauty who appeared once at Versailles, awed all the courtiers with her exquisite dancing, and never was seen there again."

The legend of my single appearance at Versailles had become greatly exaggerated over the years. My sister Marged had even written me that some believed that my dancing and the sparkling shoes I had borrowed to wear at Versailles, were the inspiration for Monsieur Perrault's charming fairy tale about a mistreated girl, a fairy godmother, and a glass slipper.

My husband's compliments always gave me a little thrill of pleasure, nonsensical as they were. Gavin had the idea that he had somehow carried off a treasure when he married me. I would not disabuse him of that fantasy, though I knew he had actually rescued a penniless refugee of twenty-seven with no prospects, who was en-tirely dependent on the dwindling largesse of an exiled king.

I was not sorry that I was living in the Scottish Lowlands with a beloved husband and children and no longer haunting the Grande Gallerie and the Salon de Mars of Versailles!

That night we sat by the fire with the children tucked away and Lucy up in her chamber with a new copy of Alexander Pope's *Pastorals*.

I sat with a book in my lap, which always soothed me—rather than some poor piece of embroidery that seemed to cringe at every poke of my blundering needle. I have never been a seamstress. Often Gavin would also be reading, perhaps Jonathan Swift's *A Tale of a Tub*, one of his favorites. But this night he was too restless to read.

"In the old days when we were all good Catholics," Gavin said, puffing intently on his pipe, "before that gorbellied knave Henry VIII decided to sell his soul to the Devil to get a son...I would simply have had one of my men horsewhip this MacGurk until there wasn't enough flesh left on him to cover his bones.

"And who would have dared to complain? I am a lord and you are my lady. Or I would have taken him to the magistrate, told the story, and he would have been unceremoniously hanged after a brief proceeding."

He placed his pipe on the table at his elbow, leaned forward and took both my hands in his and squeezed them gently. He had thrown off his peruke, but his own short auburn curls fell against his face on either side, a few strands of silver catching the light, and threw his features into partial shadow. His dark eyes glinted angrily.

"But nowadays we must be careful because the heathens and the fanaticals have taken over my dear land, and we are the strangers here. So I am going to follow the law precisely and hope that the law at least is still our friend."

As he sat back again and crossed one long leg over the other, picking up his pipe once more, he mused aloud, "Once we all believed the same Truth. You would think all these advocates for the Bible and every man his own pope, would see that, in the splintering of religion lies the evidence of its delusion. How are we mere humans to find our way to truth through this motley maze of sects and factions?"

"In all this confusion," I said. "It is even more important for us to cling to our ancient wisdom and belief and teach our children to do the same." I was at least to that degree my mother's daughter, though I have never achieved her utter certainty in her faith. I believe when I can because I must. Else what is all this suffering for?

Through all I cling to the Blessed Virgin because she understands the lot of women and, though she can be stern, she is always Love and Mercy. But I must admit I have wondered what her honest thoughts are of the many ways in which men subject women to their will and cause them pain.

I do not believe, as the priests would have us, that Mary was sublime because of her purity and her docile submission to suffering. I believe Mary must have been a strong woman indeed to keep her remarkable son Jesus alive and safe for thirty-three years. I glimpse ferocity just beneath the surface of that meek expression. Her eyes are downcast because she will not show us her strength and her anger. The Mary we see in images made by men is not the Mary who was.

Within a week, Gavin had compiled everything he had learned about the late-night attack on Heath Hall into a detailed report. Before he left, he arranged for more of our menservants to spend the night in the house for the time being for our greater safety.

Taking along Alistair of Wamphray, who had calculated and totaled the value of all the items the preachers had despoiled, my husband planned to go first to Dumfries and then on to Edinburgh, if necessary, in their search for justice.

Alistair had become much more presentable than he had been when I first came to Scotland. The first time I ever saw him, he was emerging from my husband's little library in a rush, mopping his brow with an oversized handkerchief and pushing his wire spectacles up on his short nose. Startled at the sight of me, the new bride, he had dropped the large leather ledger he was carrying. His papers flew up and landed everywhere—one in the butter dish on the table and several in the fireplace which, fortunately for him, was not lit.

He wore no wig and his hair was as unkempt, thin and colorless as an overblown dandelion. He was scrupulously clean—even his fingernails devoid of a speck of dirt—and yet entirely disordered with buttons undone and one cuff hanging by a few threads. He tended to fluttery gestures with arms akimbo, but, when he did not stutter, I found he often had something intelligent to say.

On this day of their departure to see the magistrates, I saw that Alistair now wore a small wig pulled back with a black ribbon (a new style which was beginning to replace the heavy peruke). His clothes were neat—no dangling buttons or cuffs, no twisted cravat. He seemed a bit calmer, as well, and hardly stuttered at all anymore.

I noticed without paying much attention that Lucy and Alistair exchanged a glance that seemed to contain some personal meaning between them, just before Alistair mounted his horse. They sometimes appeared to communicate without words, to express paragraphs with a quick nod and a smile. It pleased me that these two people, who were so important in our lives, got along well. But I was too worried about Gavin at the time to think what this might mean.

I could spare few thoughts for Alistair while I was admiring my husband who always looked so imposing on horseback in his glossy black boots and voluminous dark green cloak. Sometimes for fun I called him "Chiron" after the centaur who tutored Hercules, Achilles and Jason. His brown cheeks always flushed russet out of sheer excitement when he was about to begin a journey by horseback.

The last thing I said to him before they rode off was, "I am safe and well, my dear. Now look to your own safety. I will not have my revenge bought by putting you in danger."

Chapter Three
The Fate of the Wicked

*"Heav'n is just, and can bestow
Mercy on none but those that Mercy show."*

"Written in a Lady's Prayer Book"
John Wilmot, Earl of Rochester

While Gavin was gone, I comforted myself spinning tales and reading books to Gareth and Moira, these story sessions broken up by bright winter hours in which they ran through the fields and gardens in the sunshine. Days when a freezing rain fell, sheeting down the windows and turning the walkways among the herb and flowerbeds into fast-flowing streams, were especially suited for fireside expeditions into long "fairy tales" of the kind concocted by the women storytellers I had met in Paris.

Lucy was mildly aghast at the amount of time I spent with my own children. But my mother, despite the nurses and governesses, had kept her children close to her as much as she was able, even with all of her responsibilities. I informed Lucy that I intended to do the same.

I was beginning to sense the possibility of a new baby within me, which I confided to Lucy, wondering aloud if the new child might have Gavin's auburn hair at last—or my own sandy brown hair and brown eyes. Moira had heavy dark curls and deep, dark eyes, as I've said. Those eyes, always watchful, followed and closely observed those she loved. Gareth had the white-blonde ringlets and pale blue eyes of my sister Aelwen, who was truly the great beauty of our family. Gareth's coloring had worried me at first, it was so like to Aelwen's, but he was a placid child with no trace of my sister's vanity, meanness, and hunger to be always center stage.

On the surface, Lucy, the children, and I all appeared to be peaceful enough, but some nights while Gavin was gone, I thought I could feel a rumble under the earth when the heaviest rain fell, or the morning birdsong was jangled and out of tune, and I would sense an evil time, still far away but always coming closer. The attack on our home had banished all sense of comfort for me at Heath Hall. Were we not an island of believers floating amidst a turbulent sea of renegades who might storm ashore at any moment, seize us and drown us all?

Or, if the mob did not come again...I feared war—a war between religions—would come instead. I already anticipated and dreaded a long separation I foresaw, during which I would try to discern in the shape of clouds or the scent on a breeze whether my husband yet lived or had taken leave of the earth on a Scottish battlefield.

War might even come to us here at Heath Hall, though we were far from any large towns. Instead of hedge-preachers, we could have redcoats rampaging through our home—not looking for a priest this time but simply breaking, destroying, stealing, setting fires... How could I bring another child into such a world!

I was sitting near the fire with my slippers up on the fender, brooding on all the possible catastrophes that could envelop us. The book I had been holding, pretending to read, had fallen to the floor and I hadn't even noticed. I reached down to pluck it from between the folds of my gown and noticed with a little surprise that for some reason, I had pulled Shakespeare's *Julius Caesar* off the shelf, though I had read it many times before. Blood and doom, evil portents and civil war, what could be more appropriate! This would not help my mental state. I resolved to exchange it for *A Comedy of Errors*.

The longer Gavin was gone, the more my fears intensified, to the point that I was afraid my distress might cause me to lose the baby. Lucy used every nostrum in her considerable store to try and calm me. She and Ainslie conspired to balance a regimen of red raspberry leaf, dandelion and nettle tisanes with an occasional dram of the local whisky.

When Gavin finally arrived, at the end of six endless weeks, during which I spent most of my time at the window, he came alone. Alistair had stopped at Wamphray and would come to us the next day.

My husband's banging on the door just before dawn awakened McClaren, who went to see to him, and Lucy, who came to wake me. I ran barefooted to greet him and slid, almost falling on the stone floor of the entranceway, which led Lucy to express such alarm that Gavin, windblown and coated in the dust of the road, looked at me suspiciously. But I said nothing.

I clung to him for so long, that the dust on his cloak soiled my nightdress, but I did not care. There would be a tale to tell. I could see that in his dark gaze. But not yet. My husband lived and was free. For the moment I just wanted to look at him and touch him and rejoice in his presence.

Ainslie, who rose with the first cock crow anyway, threw her bonnet on haphazardly with the strings left untied, baked some oatcakes and cooked up a mess of eggs to celebrate Gavin's return. Lucy took his road-stained cloak away, and I brought him a basin of water and helped to scrub the grime of the road off his face and hands. A dram of the best whisky cleared his throat of dust.

But after these ceremonies had been completed and Gavin had been fed and I was dressed, I wanted to hear the news—all of it—before the children rose. Gavin said he had gone straight to the magistrates in Dumfries and told them about the nighttime raid on Heath Hall, the willful destruction of our property and the assault on my person, "so opposite," Gavin had said, "to the spirit of the gospel." When the ministers were questioned, they did not deny the attack. The ruling came quickly: the ministers were judged guilty and were to pay a fine of five thousand Scottish merks.

I heard this, all the while holding my breath, with my palms pressed against my stomach. When he finished, I released my breath and smiled. I almost thought I would not even ask him what had become of MacGurk. But he raised his hand for us to listen. There was more.

This was not the end of the case. The ministers and their congregations fought back, filing their own complaints that Lord

Clarencefield was breaking the law by hearing mass and harboring priests. They claimed further that the Act of Parliament for the Prevention of the Growth of Popery gave them leave to search Heath Hall just as they had done, although they acknowledged that the attack on the mistress of the manor by one of their own should not have happened.

Gavin rubbed his palms over his face and suddenly I realized that his eyes were watering and his eyelids were drooping. I rose from my chair to urge him to go straight to bed.

"You can finish the story later," I said. "Just assure me that you still own Heath Hall and no king's officers will arrive to seize our home and possessions."

He gave me a tired smile.

"No," he said. "Our lands and home are still ours, except..."

I sat down again with a bump that disarranged the cushions. "Now you *must* tell us. What do you mean?"

"The magistrates did not know what to do. They agreed that there was some truth in the reference to the law, but they still believed the assault on our home—and on you—was not to be tolerated. Especially since no priest was discovered. No one could prove that I *was* hearing mass or harboring priests."

"So they dismissed the charges?" I said.

"Not exactly. Judge Tollybridge took me aside and told me—he could hardly look me in the eyes—that, times being what they were, and feelings being so high in this matter, I should seek to come to a compromise with the Covenanters who *broke into my home and assaulted my wife.*"

When he explained this, the fatigue seemed to slip from him. His anger brightened his eyes and reddened his cheeks, and he could no longer sit still. He rose and walked to the great oaken table to pour himself another whisky, and then slammed his fist down, making the bowls hop.

"I chose the least sacrifice I could think of and agreed to give up my office of heritable steward of Kirkcudbrightshire."

I was puzzled. I knew almost nothing of Kirkcudbright except that it was a port town finely situated on the River Dee which had little business other than the smuggling of tobacco, tea, rum, brandy, and Geneva gin—and the punishment of smugglers, who were often summarily hanged in town if they were caught. Gavin was the Earl of Clarencefield and Baron of Cleughbrae, and held several other titles, too many to remember. Why would this haunt of outlaws and the ghosts of outlaws be a loss to his estates?

But I knew any diminishment of my husband's lands and rights wounded him, and the injustice of it hurt him even more. He sat down again, slumped deep into his chair, head hung down. I rose, stood behind him, draped my arms around his shoulders and kissed the curls on the crown of his head.

"I am so grateful, so grateful, that you are returned to us and have suffered no more than the loss of an insignificant town," I said.

Gavin was satisfied that paying the fine had damaged the three ministers who had come with MacGurk, and their little "societies" of malcontents who held services in open fields. They would not be eager to engage in another nighttime excursion to assault the home of a lord.

But MacGurk was another matter. No fine would pay off his debt to us. Gavin told us that Alistair had discreetly queried the villagers in Kirkton, where MacGurk preached, and discovered that MacGurk had developed a local reputation for the delivery of sermons in such a frenzied manner that he was beginning to frighten his followers.

In the past year or so, his preaching had come to rest exclusively on fearful tales from the Book of Revelation. MacGurk raved, not about the heavenly rewards promised to those who were true to their faith, but about the burning sulfur that would torment those who fell prey to the worship of beasts and the trampling of infidels' souls whose blood would flow from the "winepress of God's wrath." He would linger on the image of festering sores that would disfigure those who worshipped the beasts. And he would describe these tortures in such vivid details that children whimpered and women fainted.

Above all, MacGurk spoke of the... Here Gavin paused,

searching for a suitable phrase that could be spoken before gentle-women— "Scarlet Woman." She who comes "arrayed in purple and scarlet color, and decked with gold and precious stones and pearls, having a golden cup in her hand full of abominations and filthiness of her..." her *misdeeds*, he finally said.

"It seems that MacGurk conceived a particularly powerful dislike of women," said Gavin. "He sees Satan in the poor, tattered women of his 'society' and hates the comfortable wives of burghers even more and, most of all, women of the nobility who *do* some-times bedeck themselves in purple and scarlet and gold and pearls."

Our Catholic priests had always offered us comfort. I could hardly conceive of a creature so foul that his purpose in preaching was to terrify his flock, whose lives as laborers were already hard enough. I poured another dram of whisky for Gavin, which he downed in a gulp, wiping the back of his hand across his mouth. His words had slowed as he tried to express what he now under-stood of a preacher whose faith was not a thing of God but a license to fill his heart and his words with hatred.

"MacGurk fell into the habit of singling out particular women and girls in his small group," said Gavin, "and fixing them with his glare while he railed at them for their sins. He had seen one woman smiling pleasantly at a stranger in the village, and another walking homeward alone at sunset when, he ranted, all righteous women should have already been home behind closed doors. Women were formed to entrap men and destroy them, he said, and men must always be wary, even of their own wives.

"At last the husbands and fathers of some of these women—very strict, godly creatures, most of them, who barely stirred abroad— began to resent these unjust accusations. Most were ready to be rid of their minister, no matter how well he knew his Bible." For a moment Gavin fell silent.

I listened to this tale, with wide eyes and complete attention, but also with an uneasy sense of premonition. I could stand it no longer.

"You would not have returned if you had left this matter un-resolved," I said. I nodded toward Lucy, who seemed intent on the pattern of roses and green stems and leaves she was embroidering on a child's white woolen gown. "Should I send her away?" I asked Gavin with a glance. Gavin shook his head.

"Did he become entirely mad at last and drown himself in the river?" I asked. "Did his 'parishioners' hound him into the wild or do away with him?" In softer tones, I asked, "Did *you*?" Did he now have that sin upon his soul because of me?

Gavin continued to regard me and puff on his pipe. He picked at and rearranged the folds of his trousers, crossed his long legs and pulled his dressing gown more closely around him. He rose and dumped the contents of his pipe into the fireplace, then slowly added a pinch or two of new tobacco from the tin and relit his pipe with a paper spill pulled from the spill jar and thrust it into the fire.

Finally he said, "I think I should *show* you what I did, my dear."

That was too much. "What are you going to show me?" I snapped. "A graveyard? A tombstone? The wretched man's cottage burnt to cinders?" I shuddered again at the thought of MacGurk's sharp-clawed hand on my throat.

"*He may yet live*," he said cryptically. "Let us go tomorrow. Kirkton is only a few leagues away. We can return by way of Dumfries and spend the night at the inn."

We left the next morning, just the two of us in the carriage with our coachman, a miniature of a man named Angus with a mop of flaming red hair, usually kept in order under his hat. Angus wore no livery but a plain frock coat and pantaloons, good, warm woolen stockings and heavy boots. We intended to travel quietly and without display.

There was no snow but the road, like almost all roads in Scotland, was appallingly primitive, with deep ruts and pits. We were shaken and tossed from side to side, despite instructions given Angus to keep to a stately pace. Sometimes we drove straight across a meadow, a gentler ride than proceeding on a much traveled and mangled roadway. I did worry for my baby during some of the worst jolts and began to think I should not have come. But I had to know what had happened to MacGurk.

The countryside was beautiful as we rode in sight of the Lowthers and the Scaurs, rows of brown hills streaked with green, humped up, one on top of another, with the next mound beyond half flung over another and on and on into the infinite distance. To the South was the broad River Nith, spilling like the flow of a silken shirt into the Solway Firth, with deep green land all around the V shape of the opening.

At the very mouth of the Nith was the Glentaggart family's castle Glencaple, built in the thirteenth century and drifting into ruin, which we had not visited in all the years I had been in Scotland. Gavin pointed to it, but from the carriage window it was no more than a bright dot in the far distance. Gavin said that golden eagles often wheeled up the river to the hills, and I thought I glimpsed one tiny golden spot in the air. The masses of white beads we could clearly see were waterfowl floating on currents of air above the Nith and the Irish Sea glinting beyond.

But as we came over the highest rise and began to go downhill again, and I knew we were nearing Kirkton, my enjoyment of the Scottish landscape drained away and a touch of gloomy foreboding overtook me. What did Gavin mean when he said that the man MacGurk *might yet live*? Surely Gavin knew whether he was alive or dead. I could not imagine what to expect.

Gavin seemed to partake of my growing discomfort. His expression darkened and his lips pressed together. He seized my hand and kissed my palm but still told me nothing. We came rattling into the village of Kirkton at last and drew up before a rather large, thatched cottage with an outbuilding or two. We were met by a lean, gray-haired maid who ushered us into the neat, uncluttered parlor where a middle-aged woman rose to greet us.

"This is the Widow McPherson," Gavin said. "You might say she has solved our problem."

I didn't quite know what to make of the Widow McPherson. Her person was well-ordered like her parlor, her gray hair tucked neatly under a lace cap. She was dressed in a long, dark gown and a clean white apron. The room had one small window, which meant the light was rather dim. But from what I could see of her, the widow appeared to be a respectable woman, even to possess a kind of severe handsomeness.

I noticed that when she spoke, she only opened her mouth a little and she did not smile at all, even in welcome. This usually meant, in my experience, that the individual in question had bad teeth and did not want to display them. She curtsied to the two of us and offered ale and the ubiquitous oatcakes and rowan jelly. We sat and Gavin urged her to explain to me how she had come to set up her establishment.

What "establishment?" I wondered. But I sat and smiled and listened to this soft-voiced woman who spoke placidly with serious thought, but with very little movement of her lips, almost as if she had a bit of bread in her mouth and was trying to keep it from spilling out.

"My husband died suddenly of the ague three winters ago," she said. "He was a wheelwright and, as we had no children to support, we managed with just the two of us. He was skilled but he was a quiet man, not a pushing-forward sort of man. He had no son and did not have enough business to hire an apprentice. When he died, his trade ended with him as I had not the skill or strength to continue it."

Here she looked down at her long-fingered, pale hands laying open in her apron, as if to observe how useless they were. She went on to explain that a neighbor, taking note of her isolation and her plight, knew that she had a little extra room in her home and asked if she could take in their simpleton, the youngest of a large family, who would never be able to apprentice to a tradesman or support himself. They would pay her a small monthly fee to cover his room and board.

"And so," she said, spirits seeming to lift a bit as she looked up at us, "I took in young Jock who was just nineteen. He was very simple but sweet and biddable. I taught him to do some cleaning and washing up and a bit of laundry, and he was company for me... until he died of a fever. He was always fragile and often ill."

After young Jock came Nicholas Crimmen, also unwanted by his family, also a paying guest. He was not simple but so melancholic that he could barely drag himself from his bed and complete any task over the course of a day. He had been a sad child who became a man mired in black thoughts.

"He wasn't much company at first," said the widow, "but I would go into his room every morning and sit on the chair next to his bed, and just talk to him for a while about goings-on in the village, and then bring him a bowl of porridge and leave him alone. He did just manage to eat. One day he answered me back a little. And another day he began to get out of bed, and we would sit by the fire, and he would speak sometimes."

"But that is wonderful," I said and reached out to touch her cool fingers. "You helped this poor man just by passing the time with him when no one else would."

She sighed and looked down at her hands again. "I only helped him gain enough strength to complete his original purpose," she said. "He took himself to the river, loaded his pockets with stones and threw himself in at the fastest flowing point of the current. I believe he was swept rapidly into the Firth and out to sea."

And so it went. Her home became a refuge for the mad and the simple, whose families wanted to be rid of them and were willing to pay for the privilege.

Then the widow looked at Gavin and hesitated. He nodded and she continued. She flushed and became more animated.

"Some also came who were not so biddable. Wild men, you might say. For the safety of all, I could not keep them as I kept the rest."

She slowly rose—reluctantly, it seemed. She put on her cloak, lifted the lantern and led the way out the back door to one of the outbuildings. Gavin held my elbow and guided me over the cobblestones. The building might once have been a stable but I neither smelled nor heard horses. We entered a dark enclosure, and the widow hung her lantern high on a hook by the door. The circle of pale, yellow light illuminated the corner of a pile of straw on the floor. I began at last to suspect what I might see there.

There was a long leg, thin as a bone, clad in some threadbare, dark material stretched out across the straw, and I saw a long, narrow foot, naked and smeared with layers of dirt, the ankle encir-cled by an iron ring. The skin of the foot was blistered and bleeding. A sturdy chain stretched away from the iron ring into the darkness. The smell of ordure and unwashed flesh was very strong. I put a gloved hand over my mouth and nose.

A low muttering rumbled up in the darkness as if a spigot had been turned on and the water ran out and splashed on the pave-ment. I caught a few phrases in the mash of words: "Lord, how are they increased that trouble me...Thou has broken the teeth of the ungodly...The heathen are sunk down in the pit...Break thou the arm of the wicked..." All the misshapen verses he babbled turned on prayers for the punishment of his enemies.

There was a rattle and a clank and the glimmer of malevolent eyes in the darkness beyond the reach of the lantern. I knew at once that the chained creature must be MacGurk, and he had caught sight of us despite the dim light. Right away he set up a screeching and howling as if he were being tortured with hot irons. His face—what I could see of it in the darkness—was wholly distorted, mouth wide open, eyes bulging.

More words began to emerge from the yowls. A quivering finger, lean as a reed, appeared out of the black pointed directly at me.

"Throw her down," he cried. "So they threw her down...her blood sprinkled on the wall...on the horses." His voice fell and rose again: "...and he trod her under foot...dogs shall eat Jezebel...there shall be none to bury her." This last phrase rose to a shriek like an everlasting malediction. "Dogs shall eat Jezebel," he cried again.

He seemed wholly mad. My heart quailed within me. As I have said, I never liked the sight of torchlight against darkness and now this lost creature who had assailed me was hurling curses at me from the deep shadows.

The Widow McPherson and Gavin walked a little way from me and spoke to each other in low tones. I think Gavin was asking if she had a strong man on the premises who could handle MacGurk if he should somehow manage to break his chains.

I continued to stare horrified at this creature whose madness had burned away the human part of him. He was still gabbling and pointing at me, and then, so quickly that I could not have anticipated it, he rose and came at me, a black mass scrabbling across the fetid straw and heaving upwards, screeching curses all the while.

Of course, rationally I knew he could not reach me. He was chained. But perhaps, I thought, his violent lunge would break the chain.

I did not even pause to scream. I turned, almost crashing into Gavin as I ran past him and around Widow McPherson's house. I did not stop until I had reached our carriage where I threw open the door, startling our coachman Angus, who had crept inside, out of the wind, to nibble on an oatcake the widow had given him.

Angus cried out and his oatcake went up in the air and landed on the carriage floor.

"My lady!" he said. "What is the matter?"

I fell into the seat, slammed the door behind me, and began to sob so uncontrollably that I could not speak. Angus grabbed up his bit of bread, climbed out of the carriage at once, and went running to fetch my husband. Gavin came soon after, climbed in and put his arms around me, apologizing over and over for subjecting me to the sight of the chained creature who had once been Minister MacGurk.

For a long time I was not able to respond. It was as if all the tears I had not cried when the man first attacked me were pouring out of me now.

"I thought you would be glad to see him brought down and tethered," Gavin murmured as he pulled me close to him. "I did not take into account that your fear of him might be greater than whatever satisfaction you would feel. I am so sorry. I have only hurt you the more, which was the furthest thing from my purpose."

"Please let us leave this place at once," was all I could manage to say. Gavin signaled to Angus that we were leaving.

"I will write to the widow," he muttered, "and warn her that she needs to keep more strong men about. I will send her more money. She's already told me that MacGurk will not accept so much as a bowl of gruel from a servant girl. He upends it. Only men can come near him without provoking ravings and howlings that they are unclean."

Gavin and I did not speak to each other during most of the short journey to Dumfries, as my sobs gradually subsided, and I continued to try to dry my eyes with my damp handkerchief. Gavin sat, shoulders hunched, the collar of his cloak turned up around his ears. He was staring out the window, but I don't think he was really seeing the hills or the rolling, spreading Nith as we rode alongside the river on our way to Dumfries. He kept a tight hold of my hand and patted it abstractedly.

Finally he said, "I was so filled with fury, I wanted to erase him from the earth. I wanted to break his bones and drain his blood. The idea that this loathsome thing laid hands on you...But, as things are..."

"And as God is," I said. "I never wanted you to carry the sin of murder on your conscience for my sake."

"But I feel cheated of my revenge," he said. "He is now so mad that he doesn't know where he is or why and recognizes no one."

"I believe he knows *me* well enough," I replied dryly.

"Perhaps I should have whipped him into more complete submission," he said. "Or I should instruct the widow to starve him."

But I knew Gavin well enough to know that he would not do these things. Brutality was not a natural part of his character, though it seems to come easily to many men. He was capable of great anger but not of studied cruelty.

I did not say more until much later that night when we lay next to each other in the upstairs bedroom at the Dumfries Inn, listening to the barmaids and their patrons below—bursts of high-pitched giggles alternating with the low rumble of men's voices.

All the time I was thinking of MacGurk and the insult he had visited on me, the disruption of the whole household, the blood and the pain. And then I thought that the madness that had seized on him was a judgment from God, and perhaps it was enough. He had been cast out by men for good. He would never know the Love of God, only the Wrath of God that had caused his own rage to redound upon him and destroy him.

"If I were to see him again with his wits restored and as strong as he was when he came to our house, perhaps I would still want a murderous vengeance," I said slowly, as I tried to put my thoughts in order.

"Maybe he brought about his own doom by using his faith only to do evil. But as he is now, he is no worse than a rabid dog. The dog cannot be blamed for its condition, can it? But it is dangerous, nevertheless. The important thing is to make sure, absolutely sure, that he will never get loose, and his lunacy will never harm anyone else."

I turned over towards my husband and placed my hand on his arm.

"I ask you to tell the widow that she must always keep all women away from him and out of his sight, if possible," I said. "Let him never know a womanly kindness again...But I think he could have porridge sometimes instead of gruel and maybe something wrapped around his shackles to ease the chafing. His ankle looks like that of a wolf that has tried to gnaw its leg off to get out of a trap. Still... the men who take care of him must always be sure new shackles are applied before they remove old ones to clean his wounds."

A silence.

Then Gavin kissed me and said, "I will write a letter to the widow tomorrow and have a boy take it to her with just those instructions. And we will never speak of him again."

I doubted, however, that this last would be possible. After all, Gavin would have to continue to send money to the widow. And who knew how long MacGurk might live on, even in his degraded condition?

I also knew that Gavin's anger would remain with him and would continue to grow, now that he had seen such a vivid demonstration of the hatred of Catholics abroad in his own country, abetted and encouraged by barbarous laws. Everyone we most dearly loved was in danger every day.

Gavin slept, but I did not for many hours, long past the time when the voices had subsided below and all the customers of the inn had either gone to their rooms, staggered home, or fallen asleep in their chairs below, heads on the table, dreaming perhaps that they were frolicking with the prettiest of the barmaids.

I was thinking of everything Gavin and I had endured and all that my parents and brother and sisters had endured before that. English law forbade Catholics to hold office, buy land or serve in Parliament—not because they were unfit but because they were Catholic. We were forbidden to own any items associated with Catholicism, such as rosaries. The Catholic mass was forbidden; everyone was required to attend Church of England services or pay a fine, which was ever increasing. But that was just the beginning.

My sister Glynis and I, when we were children, sneaked out of the house one day, went exploring in the great city of London, and encountered, as I have mentioned, a ghoulish, anti-Catholic parade that left us with nightmares for years. My parents, highborn though they were, had each known the inside of a cell in the Tower of London, accused of crimes they had not committed. The ascendancy of our family to the court of our good, Catholic King James II, when we thought Catholics were all safe at last, had endured only three short years.

We had been forced to flee from England with the queen and baby prince when William of Orange invaded England. During that upheaval, a London mob had cut off the hand of a young priest carrying an altar candlestick.

My parents had both died in France, bereft of their home and possessions. I had married and come to Scotland, thinking it would be a peaceful haven, only to find that in the Lowlands, Catholics were caught in a roiling jumble of intense religious animosities that never seemed to subside.

It wasn't just Catholics against Protestants. There were Dissenters like the Covenanters who hated the Church of Englanders almost as much as they hated the Catholics. And the dissenting groups themselves were splintered into many pieces, each group despising all the others.

Even if there were no more attacks on our home, I felt that the possibility of war was inching its way towards us. Catholics were wearied to their bones of being beaten down and angered beyond caution.

45

As for me, the black mass hurtling toward me from a fetid straw bed, the clanking of a chain as it drew taut, that skeletal face so stretched and distorted by rage, the shriek that dogs would gnaw my bones...that creature would reappear in my nightmares for months to come.

Sometimes I awoke and soothed myself back to sleep without disturbing Gavin, but other times my cries woke him. Even as he held my hand in both of his and murmured kind words—once he sang me a snatch of a lullaby we sang to the children—I knew by the grim set of his jaw that he had not forgotten the attack on our home any more than I had.

I came to think sometimes in the depths of the night that the image I saw lunging at me in my nightmares did not represent a danger that was past, but dangers that were coming—the worst dangers yet, that were almost upon us.

Good fortune was with us in one thing though. The next morning, as we breakfasted in the Dumfries Inn, I told Gavin that I was with child again. The following summer our daughter Elspeth was born and lived.

Chapter Four
War Comes Closer

1710-1715

"Therefore take heed how you impawn our person,
How you awake our sleeping sword of war:
We charge you, in the name of God, take heed;
For never two such kingdoms did contend
Without much fall of blood."

Henry V, William Shakespeare

A few more years passed after the attack on Heath Hall before our fate fell upon us.

I resolved to treasure every blessed moment I had been granted to awaken to no sound more threatening than the warbling of chiffchaffs, throstles, and blackcaps. And so equally to savor eating breakfast porridge across the table from my husband and watching our children grow in health and heartiness.

The years of rain and cold and bad harvests in Scotland of the 1690s had passed. Our tenants looked contented—some were even a bit stout! It was a pleasure to watch the fields around our home full of barley, oats and wheat, and the tenants' cottages in good repair.

I was so grateful for this time of peace that I even took pleasure in walking out on a fine day to the washhouse and the bleaching green where our two household laundresses Fiona and Davina spent their days cleaning our clothing and our table and bed linen. Fiona was a big, bluff woman with round, red arms and a thicket of curly hair that would never stay tucked away under a kerchief. Davina was more delicate and liked to adorn her hair with ribbons or flowers. As different as they were, the two of them got along like loving sisters, and I liked to hear them laugh and chafe each other as they worked.

Nearby was the dairy where two other maids, Una and Morag, churned butter and made cheese and the Brew House where ale was made. Tenants brought us fresh partridge, salmon, trout and chickens. Our house gardens had expanded. We now had onions, leeks, parsnips, cabbages, three kinds of peas—Hotspur, Haston and sugar—cucumbers, cauliflower, melons and asparagus, each emerging in its proper season. The harvest from these gardens was often so bounteous that we could share it with our tenants and neighbors. We sent to Edinburgh for cinnamon, ginger, mace, cloves, capers, prunes and olives.

We had also finally acquired a few luxuries better suited to our station than the heavy, old furniture Gavin had inherited from his mother—a fine walnut dining table and chairs, crimson velvet hangings for the little study where Gavin and Alistair wrangled over the accounts of the estate, new featherbeds and silken quilts, and a new wardrobe for my best clothes.

One evening, at dusk, dinner was done and the children were settled upstairs. We had left Lucy inside, ensconced in one of the new armchairs with a book.

Gavin and I sat on a bench in the garden amidst the mingled fragrances of herbs that rose and drifted around us. It must have been late spring because I remember particularly the thick, green smell of new parsley, which would have emitted a thinner, more incisive aroma by summer.

Gavin was humming a tune and it sounded familiar to me. Then all at once we began singing together,

Thou art my life, my love, my heart,
The very eyes of me;
And has command of every part,
To live and die for thee.

It was a verse from a Robert Herrick poem, "To Anthea, Who May Command Him Anything." Gavin, as a young man in the Scottish Lowlands, and I, as a young woman in London, had somehow learned the same tune for the verse and both of us remembered it. I squeezed his hand and put my head on his shoulder, and no one disturbed us for a long time. That memory is very sweet to me.

As for the children, Gareth was in constant motion and loved nothing better than riding out with his father, but we had little luck getting him to settle to books and study. Moira was quieter, very industrious and a lover of books like her mother.

I saw that she would be a beauty, a dark-eyed and winsome lass, but I did not intend to marry her off young. I was convinced that the success of my marriage to Gavin was partly due to the fact that I had not been bartered away as a child bride, although I did not want Moira to wait until the great age of twenty-seven to marry as I had!

Elspeth was a sprite with a head of pale golden hair, as spiky and unruly as yellow gorse, and great hazel eyes like my favorite sister Glynis who had left us long ago for the religious life and was now the abbess of a convent in Bruges. Elspeth loved her poppets and played with them in the herb gardens, but she was too young yet for me to see what she might become.

We were of necessity more and more concerned with political matters during this time, as it appeared that Queen Anne was failing in health and nearing the end of her reign. After King James II was forced off his throne, Parliament in its wisdom had passed a wicked act requiring that no king or queen of England could ever again be a Catholic or be married to a Catholic. This meant that, when Anne succumbed at last, the nation would pass over more than fifty closer relatives and bestow the kingdom on the Elector of Hanover for one reason only, the fact that he was the closest *Protestant* relation.

We all knew that Anne's death would be the best chance the Stuarts in exile would ever have to regain the throne of England and end the persecution of Catholics before the kingdom was utterly stolen by the German rustic George, Elector of Hanover. George knew little of England and probably even less of Scotland.

On August 1, 1714, Queen Anne died. Alistair had been to Glasgow on business and hurried back to bring us the news. He arrived on a bright, cloudless afternoon as I was playing a game of tag in the garden with the children. I had just "tagged" Elspeth and we had fallen on the grass, laughing, as I clasped her around her tiny waist.

I caught sight of Alistair and Gavin striding towards us across the lawn and knew at once by their stern expressions that Alistair's news was grim. I pushed Elspeth away and stood up so abruptly, brushing tendrils of grass off my skirts, that she began to cry, and I had to stoop to comfort her while Alistair waited.

"Anne is dead," he said, when he had my full attention. "George of Hanover is already on his way to London to be crowned."

Over dinner that night, Alistair reported all the gossip he had heard among the coffeehouses of Glasgow. According to rumor, this George, this interloper, this thief, was unworthy to govern his own negligible fiefdom, much less rule a mighty nation!

To begin with, unlike the royal Stuarts, George of Hanover entirely lacked a kingly appearance or bearing. He was stubby and stout with coarse facial features, heavy-lidded, bulging eyes, an excessively long, pointed nose and cheeks so red that they appeared to be inflamed. (I can confirm the truth of this report myself, having later seen him up close.)

An ill-favored man may yet be an intelligent, or a witty, or even a good man. But in George's case, his outward appearance, it was said, accurately reflected his inner nature. He had neither wit nor conversation nor any sort of style. As for his capacity for goodness or evil...I believe the tale of George and his wife Sophia Dorothea reveals the truth. I now remembered hearing some version of the story from the gleeful gossip of courtiers when I was a young woman in Paris. Serving a king in exile was a dreary job. Any scandal was noised about with much enthusiasm.

Sophia had found her husband dull, Alistair told us. It was reported that she fainted upon first setting eyes on her future husband and referred to him among her familiars as "Pig Snout." She was a woman who preferred her pleasures and entertainments to her duties. In short, Sophia was a flibbertigibbet married to a block of wood. But the block of wood had a capacity for malevolence that was not yet fully known.

After bearing George two children, Sophia told herself her obligations to Hanover were done and took a lover more to her liking, a handsome, dashing Swedish count. But, alas, as Shakespeare observed, "Love is a devil. There is no evil angel but Love."

Sophia and her count planned to run away together, but too many people knew. George heard of the affair. Just as the Swedish count was leaving the castle where he had spent the last night of his life with Sophia, a group of ruffians murdered him and threw his corpse into the Leine River. George then divorced Sophia and sent her to live for the rest of her days in dreary Ahlden House, a drafty chateau on the edge of one of those sinister, dark German forests where hobgoblins are said to abide.

The allotment of firewood for the house was strictly limited and George made sure the only foods and wines allowed were those Sophia detested. Sophia was never allowed to see her children again. George's son never forgave his father for banishing his mother when the boy was only eleven years old.

A month or so after the death of Queen Anne, we learned that this George of Hanover, this Bluebeard, had arrived in England for his kingly coronation speaking no English and accompanied by two grotesque mistresses, one tall and emaciated, known as "the Scarecrow" and the other short and corpulent, who was called "the Elephant." These harpies and George's other attendants then proceeded to strip England bare, acquiring land and offices and demanding huge bribes from anyone who approached them for any sort of favor.

No wonder Catholic Englishmen and Scotsmen and many who were *not* Catholic wanted to overthrow this "King Troll" and place a true Englishman, the exiled Stuart prince James Francis Edward Stuart on the throne instead as King James III. It was long past time for the relentless persecution of Catholics to end.

The first clear sign that Gavin would be pulled into the maelstrom that was coming was the visit to Heath Hall of three of the most active plotters against George and in favor of our beloved James, the "king across the water." I am not sure I ever saw around our great table an odder, more mismatched group of men.

Lucy and I spent most of a day preparing for their arrival, supervising a thorough cleaning of our great hall, dusting off two of the most distinguished bottles of our local whisky from the cellar, and making sure that Ainslie and her staff prepared several baked delicacies in addition to the ever-present oatcakes. We had a very presentable array of meat and onion pasties, Aberdeen butteries, and shortbread.

My stomach was fluttering to such a degree all day that I had to depend on Lucy to sample the breads. I could not eat and found it was wisest not to even look at the set table. I was so torn in my head, I couldn't tell if my indisposition was more a matter of excitement or fear, or a confused mixture of the two.

I was almost afraid to ask myself what I wanted. Well, of course, I wanted George off the throne and young James, whom all were calling "the Chevalier," on it. I wanted freedom for Catholics to pray and live as they wished throughout the land. But I also wanted my husband safe at home and our peaceful, sweet life to go on without interruption.

I am not a fool. I could see perfectly well that freedom could only be bought with blood spilled, and that a rebellion against George was unlikely to be a swift campaign of a summer's day. But then I would purse my lips and remember all the cruelties my family had suffered and my anger grew until, yes, I could almost imagine carrying the banner into battle myself. And yet again, I would think, Oh! I do not want my husband to suffer pain, to be maimed, to die.

I was in this bemused state of mind when our first guest arrived. The "first among equals" was John Erskine, Earl of Mar, a tall, lean man of middle years, wearing an elegant sandy-blonde peruke and fine red frock coat, with cascades of Flemish lace falling from his cuffs and down his breast. His wig was of the most exaggerated type with curls halfway down his back and above his forehead, the fashionable twin humps or peaks that were as absurd, I thought, as the tall, narrow, *fontange* worn above the forehead like a unicorn's horn by fashionable French ladies.

Mar's long, thin face seemed almost lost, peering out from the surround of his immense crop of false curls like a fox peeping out of a bramble thicket. Mar always, I noted, stood self-consciously with one foot pointed forward in a posture that seemed to demand that all admire his well-rounded calves.

The Earl of Mar had already changed sides several times, alternating between the Whigs who had brought George to the throne, on the one hand, and the Tories, who were aligned with supporters of the Stuarts, on the other. Because of his history of changing allegiances, Mar was known behind his back as "Bobbing John," though I doubt anyone ever said it to his face as he was a skilled swordsman. Mar was now styling himself as the man who would lead the revolt against George of Hanover and replace him with James Stuart.

Lucy and I saw to it that our guest was served bannocks and pasties and Ainslie's strawberry jam, along with a dram of whisky, while I observed that, whenever he began to try to explain and justify his revolving loyalties, his right eyelid started twitching.

We had heard that Mar had changed sides this time only because the new King George had rudely rejected his service. I had expected to find Mar slippery and to dislike and distrust him at once. But I had to admit the man radiated sincerity like a fume. There was nothing oily or evasive in his manner. Whatever star he had followed before, whatever his motives, he admitted his mistakes so openly and spoke so plainly of his enthusiasm for young King James-to-be, that it was hard not to believe that he was now devoted to the fortunes of the Chevalier. Yet even so, that twitching eyelid would set off little bursts of doubt in my mind.

While we were waiting for our other guests, Mar withdrew a little painted snuffbox from one of his deep pockets, wiped it off with a lace handkerchief and displayed it to us.

"I bought it in Edinburgh," he said. "There are many such items in the stores and sold on the streets. They show you the heart of the people."

The snuffbox depicted in miniature a notorious, rumored incident in which the maladroit "King George" had fallen out of bed while attempting to have congress with both of his mistresses at once, the Scarecrow and the Elephant. George's rotund, naked body was rolling over the edge of the bed towards the floor, while a toothpick woman and a great barrel of a woman, similarly undressed, were reaching over the edge of the counterpane, trying to catch him. I would not have exposed this item to the gaze of my children, but I have to admit that Gavin and I had a good, guffawing *lachan gàire* over it, as Ainslie would have said in the Gaelic.

The next to arrive was the famously eccentric George Seton, Earl of Winton, whose estates lay in East Lothian, just to the east of Edinburgh. Winton was a bit younger than Mar and not quite as tall, but a well set-up man, powerfully built with broad shoulders.

I was very curious about this Winton, whose behavior had caused many rumors to spread about him. He was said to be an irritable recluse, a misanthrope, a madman even. As a youth, he had gone abroad and returned to find his father and brother dead and evilly disposed cousins making off with his property and attempting to claim his estate. He had to face them in court and prove that his parents *had* married (although they did so rather late in their lives) to recover his own. Perhaps it was no wonder he was distrustful of everyone.

Winton's eyes were unusual—large and green and staring. I once saw a drawing of a mysterious African animal with enormous, specter-like blue eyes that appeared to be lidless and wild. Winton's eyes reminded me of the fearsome gaze of that creature. Winton had a way of turning his head and fixing his stare upon you abruptly.

He also had a high-pitched laugh, more like a whinny. When he looked at me and erupted into his tinny laugh, it was unsettling. But most of the time he was quiet. He would idly pick at a loose button on his coat or twist his neck and pull at his cravat as if it irritated him. Often he did not even seem to be paying attention to what was being said by the other men.

In his defense, however, when he did speak, he came straight to the point and seemed to see circumstances more clearly than others. He knew devilment when he saw it and it angered him greatly. I gradually saw that he laughed his odd whinny when he was angry.

The last of the three was the most appealing by far, young James Radclyffe, Earl of Derwentwater, who was only twenty-six years old at the time. James Radclyffe was a bonny young man, much like my husband when he and I first met in Paris at the forlorn Court of King James II in exile.

Derwentwater, it was said, was a true nobleman by nature—plain in his speech and considerate of all, from his noble friends to his aged relations to his servants to his dogs. He had taken on the task of raising up the needy on his estates as his personal crusade. His loyalty to his religion and to his Stuart lord, the young Chevalier, never wavered for a moment. He was that singular creature, someone of whom nothing bad could be said and of whom no low act was ever reported. Everyone loved him.

I observed Derwentwater and a small voice inside me seemed to say, "Tell him to run away and live. The rebellion does not need him." But I knew I would scandalize everyone there and the young man would insist on doing his part anyway. His honor would demand it.

When all were present, Mar began again with his explanations and excuses—and his eyelid twitching—while Derwentwater listened intently and Winton seemed lost in his cups, until Gavin finally broke in with, "Accepted, Mar. We understand that you are with us now and will keep to the cause. What exactly do you propose to do?"

In the midst of this group of conspirators, my husband appeared to be the most admirable and also the most sensible. Gavin was close to forty at this time, but, on this fine summer afternoon, he was blooming with the health and strength of a much younger man. He was neither foppish nor careless of his appearance, but dressed in a simple, elegant fashion that suited him. He had taken to wearing the shorter, shoulder-length peruke and had put on his best tan-colored frock coat trimmed in silver gilt embroidery. He wore indigo breeches, ivory stockings and boots polished to a bright sheen.

How my heart yearned towards him. My fear for him had been partially smothered under, earlier, by the busy thrum of our many preparations to receive company. But now, as I was gazing at Gavin and heard Mar begin to talk plainly of war, anxiety seized me. This was no longer only a frustrated, long-repeated tallying of grievances. These men were going to take action.

"I am prepared," Mar was saying, with intense passion, "to return to Braemar Castle, gather our supporters, and declare our intent to restore King James to his rightful throne. Then we will begin to seize key points, including Edinburgh Castle, moving gradually south to join with the English supporters of James, led by you, Derwentwater." Here he gestured toward James Radclyffe.

Derwentwater's rosy face was troubled, clouded. I thought he seemed terribly solemn for such a young man. I saw that, although he had raised his glass for a toast to our hoped-for King James III with the others, he had only taken a sip and put it down again.

"But what of our king? Where is James?" Derwentwater demanded. "We have nothing if we do not have him. What news is there? When will the Chevalier come with troops and money from abroad? Are we to leap into the darkness without any knowledge if or when he will be with us?"

Winton spoke last, and I knew why this man had never married and why he laughed when he was irate. He did not expect either joy or good fortune in his life and thus did not trouble himself to seek it.

"King or no," said Winton, turning his green gaze first on Mar and then on Derwentwater, "this uprising is foredoomed. We all like to say that this will be just like the restoration of Charles Stuart to his throne in 1660 after the reign of Oliver Cromwell. But at that time Cromwell had just died, the nation was leaderless, and everyone was heartily sick of the repression of the Puritans.

"When William of Orange invaded England and took the throne from James II in 1688, the circumstances were quite different. William arrived with money and troops and easily overwhelmed a king whose people mistrusted him because he was a Catholic."

"You mean you will not join us, Winton?" Mar declared, rising.

"You do not see how the people despise this German infestation—this pestilence—overrunning our country? You are defeated before you have even come to the fight? I say, let the brave join our cause and let cowards skulk at home!"

I gasped inwardly: Would this newborn rebellion perish in a duel between two hotheads? I started to rise from my seat and saw that Gavin also had lifted an inch or two off his chair.

"Patience, Mar," said Winton and then laughed his odd snicker, threw back his head and quaffed another dram of whisky. "Do not insult me. You have only been with us a little while. It is... unbecoming of you to accuse a man who has loved the Stuarts all of his life."

Mar's lean cheeks reddened and his eyelid twitch returned. He placed a hand on his sword and made as if to pull it from its sheath, but Winton was already holding his hands up, palms out, trying to explain his meaning:

"I did not say I was not with you," he said. "I will bring my men, and I will fight. I just do it frankly, I tell you, without hope. I agree with Derwentwater. Where is the young king? Have you had any message from him or his people? Does anyone even know where he is now or what resources he has...?"

Mar cut him off before he had finished.

"When he hears that the people have risen, he will come," he said. "He cannot deny us. This German George has been on the throne for almost a year. The longer we let him enjoy the trappings of royalty, the harder it will be to dislodge him."

Then all of them turned to look at Gavin and there was silence while he appeared to come to a decision. He motioned for Mar to resume his seat.

"Should we not wait until we know what James Stuart can do and when he will come to us? What if we rise and gain ground and he is prevented from coming?" said Gavin.

Gavin was only speaking aloud what we all were thinking. We knew the aged Louis XIV, always a great friend of the young Chevalier, was dying. When the Sun King died, the Duke of Orléans would become regent for Louis' great-grandson, the five-year old who would reign as King Louis XV. The Duke of Orléans would not risk war with England to put a Stuart back on the English throne.

Who then would give James treasure, weapons and troops to take back his kingdom? Even with all the courage in the world, his Scottish and English supporters alone could not seize the throne for him.

It was also quite plain that none of these men assembled here, despite their determination to challenge the reign of German George, had any military experience to speak of. They would be opposed by an army of redcoats whose very business was war.

I had welcomed the men and said little but observed them closely. But, now with the prospect of fighting so close to hand, I wanted to seize Gavin's arm and hold him back.

I wanted to kiss Radclyffe's cheek and send him home to his young wife. I even wanted to urge Winton to run from battle, to marry and raise children and live a long, comfortable life in defiance of his melancholy nature. As for Mar, somehow I did not fear for him. I suspected that, even if he meant well now, the Mars of this world would always survive, though they might lead others to their graves.

But what could I say, though my heart misgave me? I knew as well as any that our best chance was now, when we could offer England a fine young English king to replace a German lout. Once the English had learned to live with alien rule, another King George would follow this King George and then another and another, and these Georges would learn to speak English and to feign Englishness. The people would become accustomed to them—and the persecution of Catholics would continue and perhaps even worsen.

More silence. Winton helped himself again to the whisky decanter. Gavin and Mar joined him, and even young Derwentwater threw back a glass.

Gavin broke the silence again. Now he smiled, though ruefully.

"Of course, I will join you," he said. "I have been anticipating this day all of my life. You awaken in me the memory of stories I was told as a child, of the burning cross, the *Crann Tara*, that was carried from village to village in a time of danger to rouse the clans to fight.

I cannot deny the call. Whether we succeed or fail, we must seize our best chance yet to restore our rightful king."

He looked at me, filled another glass and invited Lucy and me to join them.

"My wife is an even more passionate supporter of the Stuarts than I am," he said. "She fled England with King James II and his queen and lived in exile with them in France for many years. The fortunes of our women will rise and fall with ours. I ask her—and her companion—to share this pledge with us."

I knew he needed me to signal my willingness to stand with them. I came to them and Lucy came with me. We each swallowed our dram, and I added a hearty toast to James Stuart, forced a smile and downed another glass, although I had to fight to keep the tears down as I did it.

Two weeks later, my husband went off to war.

Chapter Five

The Uprising Begins

September 1715

*"Your brother kings and monarchs of the earth
Do all expect that you should rouse yourself,
As did the former lions of your blood."*

Henry V, William Shakespeare

Gavin took with him a handful of the servants, fifty or so of his tenants, and a string of the best horses. He had been quietly buying up horses for some of his men. Two hundred or so additional tenants would meet up with this group in Moffat.

It is not true, as some have whispered since, that Gavin forced his tenants to join up. Each man was left to his own conscience and, if some stayed behind, all the better, because otherwise who would tend to the harvest?

One of the horses, a large bay, was ridden by the stable boy, young Callum, son of Angus the coachman, a freckle-faced child with a wild mane of sun-bright, red hair who was ecstatic with delight. He had spent his life grooming and feeding our horses and mucking out the stables, but almost never got to ride the beasts. In his great elation, he kicked his heels against the sides of his mount and yelped continuously, even when they were not moving.

Callum was the only one who was happy that day. The other men had their women and children swirling around them with tears and last-minute additions to their packs of woolen mittens and scarves, turnips, onions, hard-baked bread, salted meat and cheeses.

Words were few among these folk. The women knew the odds

that their men would not return or would return without an arm or a leg. They had all heard stories around the fire or over the kneading of bread of the many wars that had come before—wars between clans, wars against the English, all vicious and bloody.

Some couples clasped hands. A few, husband or wife, had last words of instruction for each other, usually delivered in the heavy Gaelic that I could not understand. One man knelt to hug his wee-est child, a little girl of two or three with a mass of light brown curls. Angus clapped his son on the back and then quickly walked away so that Callum would not see the tear winking in his eye.

That was enough. I could not watch anymore. I went inside and Gavin and I embraced in the dark hall. I buried my face in his heaviest cloak, which he wore though it was still high summer. Before he came back to me, the weather might turn cold, and he might need the thick cloak for a pillow or blanket.

"Promise me," I said, "that you will *not* be brave. Swear to me that the minute you spot the standards of the English in the distance, you will turn tail and run."

That made him laugh, which was my purpose.

He held me closer. "You do not instruct me then to return 'with your shield or on it'? What kind of Spartan wife are you?" he said. "Have you ever heard the story that Spartan women once freed their husbands from an enemy prison by sneaking into the prison and switching clothes with them so the men could escape and return to the fighting?"

"What happened to the women?" I asked.

"No idea," he said.

But I already knew the answer. That was not part of the story. The point was that the men were freed to fight. No one cared what happened to the women.

"Clearly I am no Spartan matron," I said. "I want you to come back to me, and I really have no mind for what happens between now and then, so long as you return."

At that he bent down to see my face.

"It is a matter of indifference to you, is it, whether the Stuart king is restored or not? You surprise me."

"I would prefer that the young Chevalier recover his throne—of course, I would. After all that my family suffered? After what *we* have suffered at the hands of our tormentors here? But my first care is that you be alive and well.

"The truth is, now that the time has come, that I am a wicked, selfish woman," I said, "I would see acres of valiant men slaughtered and young King James drowned in the English Channel if it meant you would come back to me."

That was true, too, but it did not mean that I was not mindful of all the other mothers and wives and sweethearts and daughters farewelling their own men. Or that I would not weep over the careless, bootless loss of lives that I knew would come in this war.

"Yes, that is wicked," he said, "but I cannot scold you for it." He laughed and held me close. I wanted him to remember that we had laughed when we said goodbye. I wanted him to ride away smiling, at least for a few moments.

I kissed him and made him swear to write me, but then again *not* to write if he needed his sleep more urgently. And yet again, to write, because that would be the only way I would know of his condition and circumstances.

"Now," he said, "keep in your mind what I told you last night." For he had read to me by the fire one of his favorite poems by John Donne:

> *All other things to their destruction draw,*
> *Only our love hath no decay;*
> *This, no to-morrow hath, nor yesterday;*
> *Running it never runs from us away,*
> *But truly keeps his first, last, everlasting day.*

I was thinking at that moment of the end of the poem, though not speaking it aloud, and how much I wished it would come true:

> *True and false fears let us refrain,*
> *Let us love nobly, and live, and add again*
> *Years and years unto years, till we attain*
> *To write threescore...*

I pushed him gently towards the door and said I would not watch him ride away. But when he had gone out and closed the door behind him, I changed my mind and ran up the spiral stone staircase of Mosstroops Tower, which had been built to protect the Glentaggarts against Borderlands "mosstroops," marauders who wallowed in mossy bogs.

Gavin had taken me to the top of the tower when we first arrived at Heath Hall, but we had seldom gone there since. At the top, out of breath, I climbed onto the battlements, stood on my toes, and peeped through one of the crenels.

I saw Gavin in the lead on his great black stallion followed by the hostler and Callum on their mounts and then a series of men, some riding at ease, others bumping along awkwardly, followed by a long, straggling line of walkers, carrying scythes and pikes and even a rake or two. Ten or twelve of the more successful tenants with some small acreage of their own, carried muskets.

In the little town of Moffat, Gavin would join with the rest of his tenants, the forces of Lords Kenmure and Carnwath, and other loyal Catholics—and other Jacobites. (They had begun to be called Jacobites because they were supporters of James, which is *Jacobus* in Latin.) I only knew the names of these lords; they had come from some distance. I knew no more than that Kenmure was an older man and Carnwath was quite young, something of the age of Derwentwater.

The day was soft and warm with a light breeze and few clouds, a lovely day for a long march. I wondered if the weather would remain so forgiving and how many Scottish seasons might pass before Gavin came home again. If he came home again.

I saw Gavin and his men march away on a road that led over a low-sloping hill, across a stream on a narrow bridge, and around a birch copse. Just as they reached the trees, Gavin stood in his stirrups, twisted around and vigorously waved his plumed hat towards the tower where he must have guessed I was standing, even though he could not see me. The tears I had sworn I would not cry began to leak from my eyes. As I watched, a gust of soft summer air shuffled the birch leaves and turned them silver in a silent fanfare. Then the men rounded the copse and were gone.

I had made a plan for the afternoon and evening. I would make sure that Gareth spent at least an hour with Alistair, going over his figures, and another hour reading the massive, dusty volume of Shelton's *History of the Glentaggarts*. I would read more fairy tales to Elspeth and take a long walk with Moira while I tested her French vocabulary.

And we would have an excellent meal that evening with everyone's favorites. I had discussed it with Ainslie. There would be roast venison for Lucy, red grouse for Gareth, marmalade pudding for Moira and Elspeth and for me, blaeberry pie, though I knew I would eat little of it. There would be no haggis, which I could not abide.

Gavin had often teased me that I would never be a true Scotswoman without acquiring a love of haggis.

"Then I despair," I would say. "A true Scotswoman I will never be."

But instead of doing all the sensible things I had planned, I simply lay on the stone floor of the tower and wept. The most terrible thing about sending a husband off to war is the sick sensation of helplessness for those who stay behind.

What could I do? I was no Maid of Orleans. I had no troubadour's view of battle—flags flying, brave marches, acts of heroism and derring-do. I sensed that war, if it got any way beyond small feints and skirmishes, was a disgusting business made up only of blood and pain and ugly, random death.

I swore a vow in my heart that day, that if there ever was anything I could do other than waiting—if I could feed and care for wounded men, if I could hide men escaping from an English rout, if I could do anything to stand against the forces that were crushing the Catholics, I would certainly do that thing, whatever it was.

After a little while, Lucy came up the stairs. In her careful way, she brushed away some of the dust and dirt clinging to my gown and hair with a rag she had brought with her and then sat down beside me on the floor. For a long time, she just sat and stroked my hair and said nothing. She seemed to have a supply of fresh handkerchiefs because as soon as I drenched one, she handed me another.

At last she encouraged me to rise to a kneeling position and together we prayed to the Blessed Virgin to keep my dear one safe and all the men who rode with him. We proceeded together through Our Father, Hail Mary, the Apostles Creed and the Acts of Faith, Hope and Charity.

But Lucy brought me most comfort with a little prayer of St. Francis she had learned as a girl. She loved it for its very simplicity, she said, but thought that it had great power to still a troubled mind. Holding my hand and beating the words softly with her forefinger on my palm, she taught it to me:

> Most High, glorious God,
> Enlighten the darkness of my heart
> And give me
> True faith,
> Certain hope,
> And perfect charity, sense and knowledge,
> Lord, that I may carry out
> Thy holy and true command.

Then I remembered another I had learned long ago at Castle Banwy in Wales where I spent my early childhood, a prayer composed by Saint Teresa of Ávila, that my mother loved for its simplicity. She had said that this prayer blew away the dust in her mind by reminding her what was most important. I had liked the beauty of the words but never really understood it. I thought I understood it better now. I spoke it aloud and tapped the words on Lucy's palm with my finger:

> Let nothing disturb thee,
> Nothing affright thee,
> All things are passing:
> God never changeth.
> Patient endurance
> Attaineth to all things
> Who God possesseth
> In nothing is wanting;
> Alone God sufficeth.

These two prayers were dear to me, even in the dimness of my uncertain beliefs, because they asked God for nothing but simply expressed belief and hope.

When we had had enough of praying, when our knees were cold and bruised, and we had cried all of our tears, we went down from the tower and prepared for the long wait of women whose men have gone to war.

Chapter Six

Letters from the Field

*"Scotland hath will to help, but cannot help;
Our people and our peers are both misled,
Our treasures seized, our soldiers put to flight,
And, as thou seest, ourselves in heavy plight."*

Henry VI, Part III, William Shakespeare

The only news we had after my husband left us were his letters—other than occasional reports from Alistair's trips to nearby towns which brought us only a wild mélange of contradictory rumors. But, in truth, I did not receive many letters from Gavin during the time that he was gone. He was engaged in battles and campaigns and was up early and on the move almost constantly in the first weeks.

We were far from the battle sites. The royal mail was not to be relied upon. Gavin feared officials might open letters directed to Heath Hall. He trusted to messengers he knew—not strong men needed in battle but youngsters who could ride fast. They would deliver his messages and then return and try to find the army again.

Despite our misgivings, at first letters did come and it seemed that all was well...

The beginning of the first letter I received read only "September." Gavin would not put in writing exactly where he was in case the letter was seized by an enemy to the Rebellion. He always wrote in haste in a loping scrawl that allowed only five words or so to each line, which meant he covered a page quickly.

Sometimes he wrote on the back of a pamphlet or a notice, and often down the middle, around the margins of the page on both sides and even diagonally across what he had already written. I could see that he had already used up the paper he had taken with him and was struggling to find more.

The effort to decipher what he had written would have been a joy, had I not been so eager, with the children scrambling into my lap and looking over my shoulder, to find out what he had to say.

September

My dear Wife,

Be of good cheer. All is sunshine so far. Was I wrong to mistrust of this brave venture?

At first only sixty of us were gathered at Mar's Braemar Castle. But before long our sixty men were joined by the entire Mackintosh clan, distinguished by their red and green plaid, and other clans came with them until we had an army of 1500 foot soldiers and 1000 horses milling around in the mud. Then Mar held a great ceremony at which the blue and gold standard of the Stuarts was raised.

Such a brave sight, my dear! On one side of the flag, the arms of Scotland wrought in gold thread, and on the other, the Scottish thistle with the famous motto, *Nemo me impune laccessit*, which means, as you know, "No one harms me without punishment." White ribbons unfurled from the standard with other mottos: "For our wronged King and oppressed country" and "For our lives and liberties."

But the day was full of rain and wind and lightning, and the gold ball was blown off the top of the king's standard. The men began muttering that this was an ill omen. You know the Highlanders, full of strange beliefs in portents and premonitions, especially before battle.

Gavin went on to tell how their little army began to march across northern Scotland, attracting more and more men as they went, entering cities and towns without a fight to be hailed like

Caesar's finest, pelted with late-summer flowers by women and girls, and toasted in every tavern by the men.

In no time they had "taken" Kirkcaldy, Kinghorn, Dysart and all the north side of the Firth of Forth, and then the kingdom of Fife, and Forfar, Kincardine, Aberdeen, Banff, Moray, Perth, Inverness, the Isles of Skye and Lewis and all the Hebrides. It was a "summer's war" indeed with hardly a man lost.

All the while, as they marched to bagpipes and fife, they were singing the songs of the Jacobites, such as the *brosnachadh* (call to battle), "To the Army of the Earl of Mar." The song was sung in Gaelic, which I did not understand, but I knew it listed all the clans that would fight for our King James III to be. What clan would endure the shame of being left off such a roll of honor?

Gavin wrote that the hardest part of the adventure so far was convincing the men not to lift pies off windowsills or chickens from barnyards. He expended many pennies and even shillings, purchasing food from farmers and tavernkeepers and then had to keep a constant watch to see that hungry men did not divest the birds of feathers and eat them nearly raw after a light toasting over a fire. He knew enough of war to know that men with grumbling insides from hasty, ill-cooked meals are poor fighters.

Gavin's next letter described the attempt to take Edinburgh Castle, which *was* an ill omen of what was to come.

Yet September

Dearest Wife,

Yesterday our mighty army of Lowlanders and Highlanders almost seized Edinburgh Castle with all its stores of ammunition, arms, cannon and gold. I would have argued for distributing this money among the people again. Or using it to buy more arms to resist those rogues of Englishmen!

One of Mar's men had suborned a group of the castle sentries who were to lower a rope ladder down to a force of ninety of our best climbers after they had clambered up the rock. But—would you believe it!—the ladder was too short! No one above or below had thought to take a measurement of the distance from the top to the bottom of the walls.

The moment of opportunity passed. The watch changed and the new sentries were not in on the plot. Our attacking force was seen fleeing, the plan was exposed and the sentries who had tried to help us were either hanged on the spot or flogged until they would have preferred death.

Still we hold the north of Scotland and no strong force of redcoats has yet come against us. But this disorganization...it is as if we are a collection of many little armies, each of its own mind.

I am about to lose the light, my dear, as my candle gutters out, but I have a wish for you yet: "Let not the dark thee cumber/What though the moon does slumber?/The stars of the night/Will lend thee their light,/Like tapers clear without number."

I remain always,

Your loving Husband

That last I recognized as a stanza from another Robert Herrick poem, "The Night Piece, to Julia," and, of course, it touched me that he remembered even now how fond I was of Herrick. I guessed that Gavin's uneasiness was greater than he would tell me so he was trying to distract me with verse.

Yet he was still safe, and every night the children and Lucy and I thanked the Blessed Virgin for protecting him, as if we were fashioning with our prayers a starry veil to be spread over him by the very hands of the Madonna, that would repel all bullets, cannon-balls, bayonets and the myriad other dangers of war.

Sometimes I almost believed that our prayers would succeed.

Every morning of that exceptionally beautiful autumn, which passed in a glory of russet and orange, I woke with the absolute knowledge that Gavin yet lived and was well. I could see him in my mind, being shaved by the first light of day by one aide, or hastily downing half-cooked eggs and crisped toast prepared by another over a campfire. Or debating with Mar and Winton and the other lords around a table upon which maps were spread helter skelter, trying to determine where the English forces were and what moves they were planning. And, above all, everyone asking, where is our king? Where is the Chevalier?

For our young hero James Stuart apparently had not appeared and they still had no sure word of his coming. No victories in battle, no territory gained, would suffice if the Chevalier did not appear, backed by soldiers and arms. No one knew then that wind and weather, illness, betrayal, and the ill will of European monarchs following the death of Louis XIV on the first of September—all of these calamities had beaten James back again and again as he tried to cross the Channel. But men could not fight forever on behalf of a phantom.

Other letters followed from Gavin, generally cheerful, but with a discernible undertone of apprehension. While Mar led his force north, deeper into Scotland, Gavin and Winton and Derwentwater went with the party that crossed in and out of the north of England.

The latest news here is that Thomas Forster of Northumberland, a Protestant with no military background, is to take charge of our army, according to an order from Mar. Forster has been a Member of Parliament, but I doubt that his battles on the floor of the House of Commons, fierce though they may have been, have prepared him to take on the Duke of Argyll, who heads the troops of "Wee Geordie."

Some Highlanders thereupon mutinied. Hundreds of them, seeing that no King James has come to lead us, and worrying about their harvest, simply began to drift away, night by night. Others marched away openly by day. (I am thinking the British redcoats don't have the option of leaving their army whenever they wish.)

Winton was disgusted by the undeserved promotion of Forster and the meandering, listless progress of our forces so far. He took a good portion of his men and headed for home. The war council sent a messenger after him to beg him to return.

Under those circumstances, he said, he could not desert our righteous cause, but added, grabbing his own ears, "You, or any man, shall have liberty to cut these out of my head if we do not all repent it."

But do not torment yourself with concern for me. We have yet to be in any real danger. The camp life—riding all day, eating stale bread, sleeping on a hard camp bed—seems to agree with me, and it has not yet rained enough to make us long for a better roof than a tent over our heads.

Our men are doing well, too. Little Callum has grown two inches and is now quite stout. He is enjoying himself so much, I'm afraid he will run off to the continent to join the French or Prussian army when we are done. Do not look to see him back at Heath Hall.

I could read between the lines, of course, and see what he was not saying aloud. The troops were disorganized and without experienced military guidance. The little army, so brave at Braemar Castle, was already beginning to dissolve. But I knew Gavin would not turn homewards. He had pledged his honor to the cause and he would stick.

Lucy could see I was downcast. She came to me and put her arm around my shoulder.

"Every day he is alive and well is a good day," she said.

After that we heard nothing more from Gavin for weeks.

The silence continued as October slowly passed and eased into November. Already there were signs that the coming winter would be unusually cold. The barnacle geese with their black hoods flew over us earlier than was usual, headed for their winter campgrounds on the Solway Firth. Snowy owls arrived early and settled in and had already startled me once or twice, swooping by overhead to begin their hunt at twilight. Red squirrels had started gathering nuts in September, seeming to rejoice in the vast quantities of acorns that also presaged a hard winter. I used to enjoy the chittering of squirrels but now found it faintly sinister. What did they know about coming cold and doom that I did not?

I even thought the spider webs I saw in the gardens and among the trees were larger than usual. And there were halos around the moon, night after night. I would stand and gaze up at the ringed moon until Lucy came and draped a shawl around my shoulders or Moira and Elspeth came to drag me back inside.

"You won't find news of Gavin in the behavior of wild creatures or in signs in the sky by night," Lucy admonished me.

"I am remembering the tales we told each other as children in Wales," I said. "How you could predict coming storms and cold winters by watching the creatures prepare for the seasons. Last winter was rather mild. I fear the one that comes will not be so."

"And why would that concern you?" said Lucy. "We will be cozy by the big fire. And the horses will be warm in the stable. Gavin is away south where surely the winter will be softer. And men tend not to fight great battles in snow and ice."

I shuddered. "I can't answer as to why. I've never feared the winter before. There's something in it...it's not just the cold or the snow and ice." I pressed my lips together and said no more because I sounded like some addlepated crone, looking for signs in sky and earth, wind and water, that would foretell the future.

It was on one of these bright autumn days of mid-November that the news came at last. As it happened, I had climbed up into the tower and was balancing on my toes, peering through the crenels, as I often did. Then I would stoop and look through the arrow slits. I must bring a stool up here to stand on, I thought.

I told myself I was merely surveying the beauty of the fall day with the harvest nearly all in and the tree branches, having shaken off their load of leaves, traced against a blue sky—and just an under-current of frost in the air. The night would be colder.

But I was really on the heights to watch the skein of paths that came to Heath Hall for signs of a rider or a cart driver or anyone coming to tell us *something*. And so it was that I saw a black form rounding our cove of birches—a horse with a bright ginger-head-ed rider. It was Callum on Gavin's horse, riding him too hard, I thought. And I wished all at once that he would gallop faster and that he would slow to a trot and then to a walk.

If it was the worst news, I wanted Callum to turn and go back the way he had come, no matter how hard he had ridden to bring it to me. I did not want to hear those words. I felt as if a curse had fallen over me and I could not move. Yet I could feel my heart banging against my breastbone.

Callum was riding faster and coming up to the house quickly, his red hair, much longer than when he had left, streaming behind him in parallel to the horse's tail. And as they came closer, I could see plainly that horse and rider were layered with a heavy paste of dirt and sweat.

The curse broke. I spun around and almost fell down the spiral staircase, calling for Lucy and the children. All of us ran in a mass to burst through the great front door and confront Callum before he even had time to dismount.

I did not mean to say these words, but they just came up from my heart and out of my mouth before I could muzzle myself: "Is he hurt?" I cried. "Is he...?" I could no more than mouth the word "dead."

"No, no, my lady," Callum managed to croak out as he seized on the cup of ale Lucy had thought to bring him. "He's taken."

He thrust me a torn paper he had plucked from his pouch. I could barely read the broken scrawl.

Preston

Wife, we were defeated here and I was taken prisoner, along with the five other peers and hundreds of men.

My money is gone, spent on provisions for the men.

Please send more with Callum as I have nothing for
necessities. He will meet me at Barnet.

Come to London as soon as you can. We will be held
in the Tower, and I will have no way to petition for my
release if you do not come.

Yours in haste, G

When I had had a moment to recover from my shock and saw
there was yet hope...although the reference to "the Tower" stirred all
the nightmares stowed in the back of my memory...I hardly allowed
poor, exhausted Callum to get off the horse before I began haranguing
him, trying to get him to tell us what had happened. He had no
powers of narration, but Lucy finally elicited some sort of picture by
asking questions that he could answer with single words or simple
sentences. And he told us what he could with gesture and mime.

The southern Jacobite force under Forster had marched into
England down through Cumberland and Westmoreland, past
Penrith, Appleby and Kendal, and at last into Lancaster to the town
of Preston. Callum counted the towns off on his fingers. By that
time there were about 2000 men in the force altogether, and, as
they approached Preston, two troops of English dragoons, seeing
they were vastly outnumbered, made haste to leave the town.

The rebels were greeted with great enthusiasm in Preston,
largely by local Catholics, and perhaps, young Callum said, "There's
was a mite *ól an iomarca*."

Lucy looked at me. "Too much drinking, I'll wager."

"And dancing," Callum said. "A fiddler played. All danced."

"And pretty young women?" I asked. Callum grinned and
nodded.

It did not occur to me then to squirm at the thought of Gavin
dancing with some rosy-cheeked English maiden in Preston. Only
much later, during my endless journey to London, that thought did
bob through my mind, one spinning image among many.

Amid all the celebrating, Forster did not think to barricade the
bridge over the Ribble River, though the river was not fordable on
either side for some miles. Blocking the bridge would have stopped

the English cold.

Nor did Forster block the narrow pass that led from the bridge to the town, or even close up all the entrances to Preston. When a large force of dragoons arrived and attacked the next day, the besieged still had the advantage of cannon and the cover of the town's buildings, but the redcoats managed to get in through an unguarded entrance on the south side.

While the Jacobites were fighting gallantly from street to street, Thomas Forster nursed a headache in his bed with a posset of curdled milk, sugar and ale. By the next morning, with both sides still engaged in hand-to-hand combat throughout Preston, Forster decided it was time to surrender on the promise from the English that King George would be merciful.

Forster rode out of Preston under guard in a large, commodious carriage. He offered to take the other nobles into the carriage with him, but Gavin and young Derwentwater refused, saying they would prefer to walk to London than to ride with Forster, who had been so quick to insist on surrender.

Once we had extracted what we could of the dismal story from Callum, we fed him and gave him a fresh horse and a fat wallet and satchel packed with food. Lucy admonished him sternly to conceal the money on his person and never take it out where anyone could see him until he reached my lord. I also scratched out a note of encouragement for Gavin with a promise that I would soon see him in London.

From then on, I had no time to indulge myself in grief or to allow my great, pounding fears to overpower me. I had too much to do. I knew I must go to London and somehow save my husband's life.

That night the first snow fell.

Chapter Seven
A Household Is Broken

"Fare thee well:
The elements be kind to thee, and make
Thy spirits all of comfort! Fare thee well."

Antony and Cleopatra, William Shakespeare

I was up all night but the children slept, thanks be to the Blessed Virgin. I kept tiptoeing back and forth to their rooms to pull the covers over them, kiss their damp foreheads and brush back their curls. But they never stirred. Elspeth had dried tear tracks on her cheeks, though she had not cried in my presence.

I believe my agony at knowing I must leave them would have been unbearable, had I not been so intent on saving Gavin. My first duty to them was to ensure that they did not lose their father to the executioner's axe.

The next morning, after a quick breakfast before dawn, I tried to explain to the children that McClaren would take them to their aunt and uncle, Mairi and Dougal Carruthers at Talla Mathan. Talla Mathan meant "Bear Hall." The Prestwick manor bore this name because of the upright iron bears above the gates. Mairi was Gavin's sister: we knew that she and her good husband, the Earl of Prestwick, would take our children in without question and would protect them against any danger that might come.

Dougal was taking no part in the Rebellion. He had been to no gatherings that plotted war and had entertained no renegades in his home. Many families like ours left someone at home, to safeguard people and lands, who could not be accused of any action against the government.

I say I tried to explain. In the dark, torchlit hall, Gareth was affecting nonchalance, leaning against a wall with one long leg crossed over the other, apparently absorbed in cleaning his fingernails with his penknife, a habit I deplored. He knew I would not bother him with trifles that day. I choked on my words. He was so young, and, as I could see in the stiffness of his pose, so determined not to cry.

Looking at the girls was even worse. Moira and Elspeth were holding hands and staring at me, big-eyed. It struck me then suddenly that Moira, at ten, was truly beginning to come into herself as a young woman, with her enormous, dark eyes and long trails of heavy curls, only lightly bound with a blue ribbon.

She was standing erect, trying not to show her fear and worry me further. She had always wanted to be the steady child, the child I could rely on in any trouble, the child who seldom complained. Her ability to lose herself in books, her reveries, had never made her unreliable. If only she had been a little older, she could have come with me, but, young as she was, I had to entrust other duties to her. I needed her to be Gareth's wise friend and Elspeth's proxy mother, under the guidance of Aunt Mairi, for who knows how long.

Little Elspeth, now five, simply looked confused and bereft. I believe she was the one who missed her father the most. She was the youngest and he had indulged her, carrying her around the house and grounds on his shoulders for hours. When she was very small, I had to remind him on occasion that the child needed to learn how to walk on her own!

Elspeth's hair was my bane—so fine and fluffy that it never would lie smooth, no matter how many pomades and ribbons and bonnets Lucy and I applied. How foolish of me, it seemed at that moment, to have worried about something so insignificant. What did it matter if she had a head of wild golden fuzz, as long as she was well cared for and could grow comfortably to womanhood?

I didn't want to frighten them with my own fears, but I could not restrain myself from embracing each one with all my might for a minute or two, hiding my tears in their curls. How long might it be before we embraced again? When we did, would they still have a father to love and protect them?

I wanted to bless each with words of motherly wisdom, but if I attempted anything beyond, "Mind your lessons," and "Do as your Aunt Mairi tells you," I felt the tears rise and had to stop.

"They should go soon," said Lucy, with a gentle arm over my shoulder. "The weather is going to turn hard." I nodded. We knew without speaking that Lucy would go with me. Whatever transpired in London, I would have need of her.

Last night's snow had already melted and the day would dawn bright but much colder than it had been. As the sky began to lighten, I could see clouds flying eastward in long streamers. More snow would be coming. The wind blew so fiercely that it knocked down loose branches and scattered them over the grass, along with a fine shower of little sticks and kindling.

"Tell the maids to see to the packing," I said. "But I need Gareth and McClaren with me for the moment. And Moira." I nodded at the children and told the two eldest to wait for me while we sent Elspeth upstairs with her nurse. Lucy and I went into the library and began to gather Gavin's most important documents to be placed in a leatherbound oak chest McClaren had brought down from upstairs.

There was no conversation between us. We knew that if the family was gone for a prolonged period, Covenanters—or common thieves—might break into Heath Hall and seize whatever they could lay their hands on. I needed to travel as fast as I could to London and could not take all the important documents needed to maintain our claim to Gavin's estate, nor the valuable jewels, silver, and plate. Some could go with the children to Talla Mathan, but not all.

With the long years of fighting in Scotland, how many stories had I heard of fortunes buried deep and then forgotten? Or perhaps the master was lost and never returned to claim them. Or came back and could not remember where they were buried. To hear the gossips tell it, the lands of Scotland's lords were littered with caches of buried treasure, if one only knew where to look.

Our people were good souls, but who knew what kind of pressure might be applied to force them to betray us? I trusted only McClaren to help us fill the chest with documents and heavy valuables, coat it with pine tar to protect the wood against moisture, and bury it before the soil under the rosemary bushes got too frozen to yield to the shovel.

Even if the bushes were neglected and overgrown, or killed by a deep frost, I could certainly identify them. In case they were completely uprooted by marauders, I made notes on a scrap of paper that only I would understand—so many paces from the kitchen and the birch grove, and the like.

Alistair came to bid us farewell and promised to look after Heath Hall as best he could. A skeleton staff under McClaren was to stay on duty at the Hall; many of the men had already left with Gavin. But Alistair assured me that those who had been released from our service for the time being would still be on half pay. They were as good as our family.

I noticed again the odd glance between Lucy and Alistair. I saw them conversing very quietly and earnestly at the window, but when Lucy came to me and I looked at her inquiringly, she did not explain. I had no time then to pursue the matter.

Always in my thoughts was the image of Gavin, trussed on a horse and riding to prison as if he were an ordinary outlaw. It made me shudder and then my mind would run on to that great Tower of London that had loomed with almost palpable malice over my childhood—where my father and even my mother had spent brief periods of time, accused of ludicrous crimes only because they were faithful Catholics. Every charge, brought forth by the lowest rank of informers in the pay of lapsed Catholic Titus Oates, that they had threatened the life of King Charles II in some fantastical way—that they were planning to shoot the king with silver bullets, for instance, or poison his daily posset—all these charges had been laughed out of court. But each time another accusation would follow.

I refused to think of a headsman's block in Gavin's future because, if I indulged myself in horror so far as that, I would scream or go mad. If I did seem to glimpse it for a moment in my mind, I would busy myself rushing upstairs or down to direct the remaining servants to cover the new furniture with cloths or to lock all the windows and pull the draperies closed.

Soon after full light we stood in the entryway as Lucy kept admonishing the servants to bring more blankets for the carriage. The children were already wrapped in so many cloaks and woolens that they hardly managed to totter across the flagstones.

I now had to speak seriously to Gareth, even if it brought us both to tears. I could delay no longer. I put both hands on his shoulders and looked in his eyes, making sure I had his full attention before I spoke. Though he was only fourteen, we had completed documents transferring the entire Clarencefield estate to him a few days before Gavin left, to allow for just this kind of emergency.

"The estate is yours now," I said. "Your father may soon be under a bill of attainder and you will be, in effect, the Earl of Clarencefield. All your papers are in order. You have had no part in this uprising.

"I fear the Covenanters may come against you. Be stern. Show them at once that you will not be moved from this land. Alistair will help you, as will your Uncle Prestwick. Alistair is witness to all.

"That means you will be responsible for us, as well as for your sisters. I am so sorry to lay this burden on you, my son. You are too young, but I believe you will manage as your father did when he inherited his title at a very young age."

I almost thought to apologize for what we had done to him in remaining faithful to the Stuarts. It seemed our cause would always be swamped by folly. But how could I deny my whole life and my parents' lives? Young James Stuart was the true king. How could we not fight for him? When the Stuarts had need of us, we had always been loyal to them.

"Live always within your means, for our sakes as well as your own," I said to Gareth. He nodded. I had little fear for Gareth on this score. Like Gavin, he had very little interest in cards and was moderate in his love of whisky. His best days were spent in the saddle and on foot with dogs and horses and a few retainers, stalking the red deer and occasionally a boar, wolf or wildcat. Customarily he was a boy of few words, but he could tell stories of his hunting expeditions with great detail and excitement.

I thought of Gareth coming in at evening and sitting by the

fire in his muddy boots and damp coat, face all aglow, as he recounted his adventures in the forest. Meanwhile, McClaren would direct the huntsmen to take the remains of the gutted deer to the kitchen for Ainslie and her kitchen maids to prepare. I had drawn the line, however, at hanging the heads of wolves and boars on the walls of the Great Hall. This was Heath Hall, I said, not the rustic manor of some clan laird.

As I kissed and embraced my son, his expression was appropriately solemn, yet I saw a shine in his ice-blue eyes that suggested he was looking forward to this new experience. Gareth had known very little of hardship.

But what he said was, "Don't fear for me, Mother. I will be mindful of my duty to you and Father and the girls."

Then he grinned—a fine, open, guileless smile that I rejoiced to see. My heart twisted for a moment. It was so odd to see the very image of my sister Aelwen come again into my life with the same coloring and features but graced with a generous heart.

I then kissed and embraced my girls and admonished Moira in a soft voice to be ever her brother's good companion and to care for her little sister always, as tenderly as I knew she would.

"I entrust Elspeth to you," I said. "And I am sorry because you are young, but you are wiser than your years, my dear."

There was something of my gentle sister Glynis in Moira, though I hoped Moira would marry and have children of her own and not follow my beloved Glynis to the convent.

"We will pray every day for you and for Father," she said. Such an odd disparity between her womanly words and the childish timbre of her voice. "May the Blessed Virgin grant you success."

I wanted to give them rosaries to keep them safe, but I was afraid a rosary from our hidden hoard, still prohibited, could put them in danger if it was exposed on the road. Prayers could not be excised from their minds, though, so we recited the Ave Maria and the Paternoster together, with Moira helping little Elspeth over the difficult passages.

Having tied the last trunk onto the carriage, McClaren, who spoke so little, came and stood at my shoulder, and I knew he was trying to tell me they must leave. I saw, as we went outside, that snow was falling again. The bright early sunlight was being snuffed out by an advancing white shroud. Talla Mathan, where my sister-in-law and her husband lived, was at least fifteen leagues away. The longer they delayed, the harder the going would be.

I had given a letter to McClaren to hand to Mairi and Dougal, thanking them for taking in our children, and telling them that I was off to London with Lucy, in the hopes of rescuing Mairi's brother. I also begged them to send money to me in Newcastle to help pay for the expenses of the journey, a London lawyer to draw up petitions to plead Gavin's case, and the cost of Gavin's keep in the Tower. All that I had I would take with me. But so much of the funds we had on hand had already gone with Gavin to war. Alistair had even given me twenty-five pounds from his own savings.

As the carriage set off, I did not linger outside to watch them go. Seeing that heavy-laden carriage, bearing away my darlings, slowly dissolve and disappear into the curtain of snow would have been unbearable.

All sentiment must be suppressed, I told myself. Grieving is an indulgence. I swallowed down the glut of tears that rose in my throat. I tried not to think that there would be plenty of reason and time for grief and weeping with my children later if my mission failed.

Chapter Eight

A Winter Journey

"Her valiant courage and undaunted spirit,
More than in women commonly is seen..."

Henry VI, Part 1, William Shakespeare

We knew by now that English troops would be walking the streets and guarding the gates to Dumfries and Carlisle, so Lucy and I decided to travel by horseback across country to Newcastle. There we would catch the London coach. By midday we were ready to go, with the few belongings we could carry with us stuffed into bags and bundles and our oldest, most threadbare cloaks wrapped over our better woolens to make us look as ordinary and uninteresting as possible.

We need not have feared. At first the snowfall was unhurried, drifting at a leisurely pace as if it had no particular intention of covering the landscape by nightfall. During the first few hours, while we rode over the fields of our neighbors, avoiding the roads, we encountered almost no one. All were huddled indoors, grateful for whatever shelter they had. By evening the snow was falling harder and the wind was colder.

We stopped for the night in the little village of Ecclefechan, a bit worried that it was located on the high road between Carlisle and Glasgow and might see heavy traffic, but we had the small white inn almost to ourselves. The local fruit tarts in butter pastry were famous in those parts, as was the local whisky. But before we got ourselves off to share a bed and rise before dawn, the innkeeper insisted on giving us more unwelcome news.

He was a shriveled-up, little man, with greasy strands of hair falling flat on his shoulders, not the expansive, full-bellied kind of innkeeper I was accustomed to seeing in Scotland. I think he ate little because he was so busy attending to his pipe, which was constantly aglow. He came and sat with us, without a by-your-leave, as we chewed our way through the gristle of a stew that was no better than passable. At least the bread was fresh, and the tarts full of plump raisins and creamy custard.

"And who might ye be, traveling in such a *cathadh-sneachda* (severe snowstorm)?" he demanded.

Lucy and I looked at each other.

"Mrs. MacDonald," I said.

"Miss Lennox," said Lucy. We had both chosen common names. Scotland was full of MacDonalds and Lennoxes.

"From Portpatrick," I said, naming a coastal town far to the west of Heath Hall.

"On our way to Edinburgh," Lucy said.

"For a wedding," I added. I reassured myself that the Blessed Virgin would forgive deception for a righteous cause.

"Hard weather fur a wedd'n. Who weds in winter?" he asked, but I think it was an idle conversational gambit, not an accusation.

Then he added abruptly, "Ye might meet soldiers on the road."

I tried to catch his eye, but his gaze slithered towards the corners of the room or down to his pipe. Was he friend or foe? Or just a man who cherished most in life those moments when he had everyone's attention?

"Did ye na' hear word o' Sheriffmuir?" he asked, still without so much as introducing himself. His wife—I assume it was she—was a small woman as meager as he, sitting by the fire knitting a shawl so long that it trailed across the floor, paying him no mind at all.

"What is Sheriffmuir?" I asked, coolly studying my fingernails.

"There was a battle there," he said, "'tween rebels wi' Mar and king's army wi' Argyll, no' three weeks ago. Word came yesterday wi' a small company o' men going south who had been in the battle. If ye've been on the road in the snow…I thought ye might na've heard."

Lucy jumped in, trying to spare me.

"Dear sir," she said hastily, wiping her mouth on a little

checkered cloth, "if this is vagaries and rumors and tales to make all the women widows before their time, we are not in the market for such news."

I hushed her with a wave of my hand and put down my spoon along with my pretense of indifference. I looked at our innkeeper levelly and said, "Tell us what you know, sir, for we have only had tidings of the defeat at Preston. Does Mar still fight in the North?"

Now that he was sure of his listeners on this day with little custom, the innkeeper took his time taking out his tobacco pouch, carefully dropping pinches of tobacco into his pipe and then working for some minutes at setting the leaves alight with a spill from the hearth. I am afraid I cursed him silently but would not betray my anxiety by trying to hurry him into an explanation.

"Know ye Dunblane?" he asked. "Sheriffmuir is a far muir east o' Dunblane." I looked blankly at him.

"North o' Stirling," he said.

Well, yes, I knew where Stirling was, the site of William Wallace's great victory over the English at Stirling Bridge.

"The rebels outnumbered the English at Sheriffmuir three ta one," he said. He shook his head and his mouth turned down, which loosened his uncertain grip on his pipe with his remaining teeth and necessitated more tamping of the tobacco.

"Oor Scotsmen fought well," he said. "Whether wi' the rebels or agin 'em, a Scotsman is always a *gaisgeach*."

"*Warrior*," said Lucy softly in my ear.

"But they lost?" I said softly. I could not help leaning towards him till my face was almost enwreathed in the spirals of smoke from his pipe.

"No' exactly," he said. "'Tis said it was like a wheel."

A wheel? What on earth did the man mean?

He took our two empty bowls and the trencher and spoons and began to demonstrate how the rebels' right flank took the king's army's left flank, and on the other side, it was the other way round, so that the two armies wheeled around each other.

"But who won the battle?" Lucy pressed him.

"Nither a' the twain," he responded with some satisfaction.

"Some died. Some wur captured. The twa sides withdrew. Sad tales all round, they say."

He told us of the young Earl of Strathmore, John Lyon, a boy of nineteen, who was fighting with the rebels. He had been wounded in his innards, was taken prisoner and then was shot through the heart by an enraged dragoon in his cups. On the other side of the battle, Archibald Douglas, Earl of Forfar, only twenty-three, fighting for the Hanoverian, was wounded in seventeen places, lost all his life's blood and died.

I shuddered and pulled away from the innkeeper. He was too matter of fact—no, too *pleased* with himself as he shared dark news. I thought his deep-set little eyes glinted in the shadows cast over them by his shaggy, gray eyebrows.

It was too easy to imagine Gavin in the place of one of these poor souls who had died. I thought I would rather see my husband taken prisoner and whole, than with his comrades still, but suffering agonies from grievous wounds.

"What happened after the battle?" I demanded.

"They say Mar's troops withdrew to Perth," he said, "and did nae follow Argyll's men when they retreated to Dunblane. And now many o' the Highlanders are leaving him.

"You know a Highlander," said our host, pulling on what little there was of his sparsely whiskered chin and nodding sagely. "He will fight like a *cat fiadhaich* (wildcat) but niver will he sit and wait."

The next morning we left at dawn again, eager to remove ourselves from that place before our garrulous innkeeper began to fashion a story around our visit, as I guessed he would. I wondered if anything he had told us was more than a fable woven out of contradictory accounts of the battle he had overheard when that small company of rebels he had mentioned stopped at his inn on their way home. Of course they would say that men were leaving the Earl of Mar's force in droves to justify their own desertion.

As Mr. Jonathan Swift says, "Falsehood flies and the Truth comes limping after it."

We plowed on over meadows and fields, still avoiding the roads. The snow stopped falling but did not melt. In some places it iced over on top, so that our horses seemed to be stepping on patches of glass and often broke through to the powder below.

The world around us was so whitewashed that I began to imagine I saw little black spots like tiny insects crawling across the bleached landscape. Even the sky was white, overhung with snow clouds. If I spied the gray branches of a bare tree, or a single brown cottage, it was a relief to my aching gaze and made the black spots disappear.

We were wrapped warmly enough but, even wearing three pairs of gloves, two pairs of thick woolen stockings, and high, heavy boots, our hands stiffened on the reins and our feet swelled in the stirrups. Whenever we grew so tired that it seemed we might simply tumble out of the saddle and be swallowed up by a snowdrift, we knew it was time to stop at the next town at whatever accommodation we could find, whether nightfall was upon us or not.

We were also forced to change horses frequently, having sent our own horses home with the inn's hostler after that first night at Ecclefechan. Horses were quickly exhausted by this interminable floundering through heavy snow.

Everywhere we went we heard confirmation of the inconclusive battle at Sheriffmuir followed by Mar's feckless withdrawal. Mar had retreated, it seemed, just when he had the advantage of Argyll, just as Forster had surrendered at Preston when he had no need to.

Scotsmen being Scotsmen, with their love of music and ever wry, jaundiced view of their own history, there was already a popular new ballad about the battle. I heard bits and scraps of in the street and in taverns, and once sung by a boy hard at work at a blacksmith's forge:

> *There's some say that we won,*
> *And some say that they won,*
> *And some say that nane won at a', man;*
> *But one thing, I'm sure*
> *That at Sheriffmuir*
> *A battle was fought on that day, man.*
> *And we ran, and they ran,*
> *And they ran, and we ran,*
> *And we ran, and they ran awa', man!*

But now there were also new tales afloat that the Chevalier was on his way to Scotland at last, bringing with him vast quantities of men and gold.

Just as we were nearing Newcastle, the snow began to come down again. We were grateful indeed for the comfort of the Old George Inn, though I would not have taken refuge there if I had remembered that our martyred King Charles I had been held prisoner in the nearby home of Major Anderson before he was executed by Oliver Cromwell. Almost every afternoon, it was said, the doomed king had walked to the Old George Inn for a tankard of ale.

Unlike the wayside inns we had visited in small towns, the Old George was full of comings and goings, men on business but also king's soldiers. The town had barricaded itself against the Jacobites who had threatened to besiege it, but Newcastle's defenses were so formidable that the rebels had moved on and let it be. There was still an undercurrent in the town of rebel sympathizers—some had even gone to join the rebels—but the town authorities adhered to Wee Geordie.

I noticed a group of pompous, self-satisfied officers, whose waistcoats barely buttoned over their middles, regaling themselves with beer and loud tales of battle at a corner table. I also spied a man in a brown coat with slightly frayed cuffs preparing to leave the inn. He placed his coins on the counter before the innkeeper and then, when the man was distracted by another guest, he grabbed them up again, thrust them back in his pocket and quickly left. Not wanting to draw attention, I watched the innkeeper searching for the coins on the counter, even stooping to see if they had fallen on the floor, but I said nothing. At last the innkeeper shook his head, shrugged and went on to tend to the next guest.

We managed to get a small room where we slept in one bed and shared a cracked chamber pot, but at least there was a small fire burning. I told Lucy to stop even attempting to dress my hair, but just to let it hang in long straggles so that I would look like the merest country drab. At that she laughed heartily—the first time I had seen her laugh since we had news of Gavin.

"My dear," she said, wiping her eyes with her handkerchief,

"you would look like a queen in exile if you garbed yourself in sack-cloth and ashes! It's your handsome face, your uplifted chin and straight back, the way you look around yourself as if you are about to improve on the management of the establishment with a few well-chosen orders.

"You will never pass for a simple countrywoman. If you open your mouth and speak, it is worse. You might conceivably be the wife of a wealthy merchant, come to Newcastle to see if your husband's ships have arrived safely and inspect the cargo. You could not pass for any estate lower than that."

Even amidst my constant state of dread about Gavin, I had to smile at her description.

"Nevertheless," I said, "if I affect too much of a noblewoman's air or look about me too haughtily, you must kick me under the table. 'Tis true what you say. It takes more than a change of clothing to hide in plain sight."

I even suggested that we might play that *she* was the mistress and I, the companion. But Lucy thought that my bearing and her long habit of service would give her away at once.

"Besides I have never been married," she teased. "A lifelong spinster cannot master the manner of a wife overnight."

It was the merest of casual observations but I thought there was something more in it, a mild resentment perhaps, or... something else entirely. Lucy seemed too good-humored and self-satisfied when she said it to be hinting at a hidden envy.

The money I had begged from Mairi and Dougal was waiting for me with the innkeeper, whom I believe took no more than the usual skim off the top for his trouble. It was my good fortune that he was the nearest thing to an honest man in these rough times. But my relief in receiving the funding I needed for my fight to free my husband was quickly squelched.

The next coach to London was already completely booked, we were told. I had been weary from the journey, but moving always towards Gavin had helped keep my spirits up. When I heard that our next move was blocked, I could not at first see a way out of our predicament. I was overcome with a sense of panic that made me gasp for breath and fall into the nearest chair. We had already wasted so much time traveling cross-country. What if we should come to London too late?

At that moment a rather squat, broad gentleman in a blue frock coat and yellow silk waistcoat saw my tumble into the chair and observed that I could not catch my breath. He ran for spirits of hartshorn to revive me and, what with my coughing and choking, it was left to Lucy to explain our situation.

This kindly gentleman sat with me until I had caught my breath again. Mr. Phineas Thrupp, as he turned out to be, was an importer of silk and a collector and sometimes seller of books—in other words, not just a man of business but a man of some learning. Was it possible that the Blessed Virgin had sent me an angel, in the unlikely guise of a middle-aged silk merchant?

I guessed that Mr. Thrupp was near sixty or so but with a round, rosy face that looked much younger. He lived in London in Westminster with his wife Amelia, he said. A grown son, who was a lawyer, lived nearby. Lucy and I introduced ourselves once more as Mrs. MacDonald and Miss Lennox.

As Mr. Thrupp bent over me, a folded, yellowing paper fell out of the pocket of his frock coat. He stooped to pick it up, and I caught sight of the title, *The Spectator*. I had heard of this extraordinary literary journal but had never seen it before, of course, since it did not come to the wilds of the Lowlands.

Mr. Thrupp was pleased to show it to me, and I read on the front page that the writer had been so deeply engrossed in his studies at Oxford, he hardly spoke one hundred words for eight years and thus could claim, "...there are very few celebrated Books, either in the Learned or the Modern Tongues, which I am not acquainted with..." What lover of books would not wish to know more about this remarkable fellow?

Mr. Thrupp explained that the author of *The Spectator* was one Joseph Addison. The copy of the paper that I was perusing was several years old, but he had saved it and had a habit of rereading it, finding some new scrap of knowledge in it every time. At once I was distracted and calmed. Mr. Thrupp and I fell into a delightful discussion of books, news of the London coffeehouses, and the plays now being performed on the London stage, as the tromp and babble of other guests of the inn rose and ebbed around us.

But, in our present quandary, this moment of ease could not last long. I turned my head slightly and glimpsed Lucy, sitting nearby, with an expression on her face halfway between surprise and amusement that caused me to turn back to Mr. Thrupp and explain our situation.

I said no more than that we needed to get to London as quickly as possible, and the stage from Newcastle was already booked. We could not wait the several days required before the next coach would depart. I offered no further explanation.

"Oh," he exclaimed, slapping his thigh, "I am in the same difficulty! Business calls me back to London, but I too cannot get a ticket on the coach." He pursed his lips thoughtfully, and then asked if we would attempt to go on by horseback.

"I must go on as well," he said. "As I can probably cover ground faster than you, I will travel to York as quickly as I can and reserve places for all three of us on the continuation of the stagecoach's passage from York to London. Will that suit you, do you think?"

He believed we could all make better time on horseback than the coach and could catch it up in York. Some passengers would disembark there and we three could take their places. As a final gesture of goodwill, having noted my interest in the document, he gave me the copy of *The Spectator* that he had treasured for four years.

Since this was our first meeting, I did not confide in him, having no idea of his political leanings or his position on matters of faith. I had discovered before in my life that the friendliest strangers, who seemed brimful of bonhomie, could become cold and turn away when they discovered we were Catholics. It was as if they had found out that we were devils disguised as humans and would next force them to endure a Latin mass.

But something about Phineas Thrupp seemed true and sound to me, even on such brief acquaintance. I was grateful for his help and put any suspicions I might have had away in a back pocket of my mind.

Chapter Nine
A World Turned to Snow

"For never-resting time leads summer on
To hideous winter and confounds him there;
Sap cheque'd with frost and lusty leaves quite gone,
Beauty o'er-snow'd and bareness every where."

Sonnet #5, William Shakespeare

The snow had abated and even begun to melt a bit as we left the next morning for York. The roads were much better than our Lowland byways, and we made good progress. When we arrived in York, we discovered that Mr. Thrupp, who had gone ahead, had been true to his word and reserved us the places he had promised on the stagecoach to London. We all set off together on the stagecoach the next morning in cheerful spirits. For the first day or so, we made good progress.

On the second day out of York, a snow blast swept down on us, such as I had never seen. In very little time, enormous blown drifts formed over the tops of hedges and up to the roofs of low houses. Over and over the coach would limp along a league or two and then stop, stuck in a snowbank. The coachman would climb down and come to our window, so encased in snow from the soles of his boots to the top of his tricorne hat that he looked like a man of snow rather than a creature of flesh and blood.

All the passengers would then climb out and the men would attempt to assist the coachman with such tools as he had, or could borrow from nearby farmers, to shovel the coach wheels out of the drifts while the snow still fell and the wind still blew. We would insist that the coachman climb into the coach and warm himself while this work went on. This was a practical kindness. We might all be stranded for good if our coachman froze to death on his seat.

In the meantime, we women tried to help the horses, rubbing them with blankets and clearing snow from their eyes and manes. Even so, the teams had to be changed out in almost every town of any size that we passed. No beast could endure much of this furious winter blast for long.

In my extreme anxiety I wondered why we were being so tormented. I began to whisper the Ave Maria and Paternoster to myself under my breath and then worried that Mr. Thrupp, sitting next to me, might overhear and suspect that we were Catholics and thus possibly treasonous to the Hanoverian. At one point he seemed to start a bit, then turned, nodded and smiled at me, opened his mouth to speak, said nothing, and closed it again.

I glanced at Lucy, sitting across from me, and saw that she had taken notice of my whisperings and his response. She glanced from me to him and smiled slightly, then cast her eyes down and seemed to me to be thinking her own prayers.

At last, just outside of Grantham, as noon was turning to afternoon with the snow falling unabated, the coach came to a stop in a particularly deep drift on an upward incline and could not be moved. The coachman and some of the men unhitched the horses and we all trudged into town, carrying our bundles and bags as best we could. After all that struggle, we were still no more than halfway between York and London.

Most of the passengers decided simply to stay in the ancient Angel and Royal Inn until the snowstorm had passed and the snow had been cleared, but Lucy and I did not have that luxury. My worry for my husband was now almost at fever pitch.

I knew that my life henceforth would be agony to me if I dawdled and finally came to London to learn that the headsman's block had already taken my husband. But, besides that final horror, I feared that, if Callum had not reached him, Gavin would be trapped in the Tower without kindling for a fire or the merest morsel of nourishing food. Many men had died of fever or hunger in the Tower of London long before they arrived at their official execution date.

I determined there was enough daylight left that Lucy and I must go on. We would stop only long enough to drink hot tea and hire new horses. I knew Lucy was as tired and frozen as I was—or more so. But she made no complaint, only pressed her lips together to keep back any mutinous grumbles and sipped her tea slowly by the fire.

Just as we were wrapping ourselves up again in cloaks and blankets to set out, Mr. Thrupp stopped me.

"Pray excuse me, sir," I said. "We are hoping to reach Colsterworth before nightfall." I could see the snow still blowing and coming down through the small window in the door to the courtyard of the inn. The white-gray light of the day had already turned a shade darker.

"A moment's leave," he replied. "Forgive my inquisitiveness, my dear madam, but have you friends in the city? Do you know how to find your friend's house in the maze of the great metropolis? If you have not been to London in recent years, it may seem a maddening confusion of streets that ebb and flow, and twist and twine, without rhyme or reason."

I stood for a little while in uncertainty as I looked up into Mr. Thrupp's round face. His expression was so open and earnest, so concerned for us, that I thought, if he is a fanatical Covenanter attempting to expose dangerous Catholics, or a government spy uncovering hidden rebels, he is a better actor than any I saw onstage at Whitehall or Versailles.

I knew Lucy was trying to shake her head at me. From the corner of my eye, I could even see her place a finger on her lips. Nevertheless, I plunged.

"I must stay near the Tower of London, sir," I said very quietly so that he had to stoop his head to hear me. I was determined to hold back any annoying tears that might betray me to the other tavern guests.

He was silent for a moment, gathering his thoughts.

"I am saddened by your trouble," he said at last. "You must come to us, to my wife and myself. Westminster is no great distance from…" Here he looked around us and took note of other passengers nearby, though no one seemed to be attending to our conversation.

"It is no great distance, as I say," he continued. "Since our son's marriage in the summer, our house seems large and empty. Even before our son moved out, our daughter married a baronet and went to live in Derbyshire. We would be most gratified if we could offer our assistance. I am away so often that my wife, in truth, would welcome your company."

Lucy was shaking her head so vigorously that her elaborate arrangement of head coverings fell off, hood falling back on her shoulders, blankets trailing on the floor.

"You are too kind, sir," I said. "I must confer with my friend."

As Lucy and I put our heads together, Mr. Thrupp thoughtfully moved away to the other side of the room, where he perused coach schedules.

Lucy did not spare me. She spoke more sharply to me than she ever had before, though all in a hoarse whisper.

"I believe the cold and your distress have dulled your judgment," she said. "When have you ever trusted to strangers encountered in a public inn? We know nothing of this man. We do not even know if he is the silk merchant he purports to be. Our situation is precarious; we travel under false names. If we are not ourselves rebels, we are close associates of rebels. We are drawing nearer to London, the Lair of the Beast. And you...!"

"I can say very little in my defense," I acknowledged, also in a whisper. "Everything you say is true. But this one time, Lucy...I perceive goodness in this man. And you cannot deny that we are in need of assistance and have no friends we can rely upon in the city.

"Except..." I dug deep under layers of cloaks and wrappings and pulled out a letter from my oldest sister Marged and waved it at her. "According to Marged, this is where my sister Aelwen now resides, in a place called St. James's Square in London. I have no hope of my brother Gwilym in Wales or my sister Marged in Ireland—there is no way to get aid from them in time. But I have thought of seeking out Aelwen, even though I have had no contact with her for twenty-five years. That is the measure of my desperation. I can assure you, at this moment, I have more hope of assistance from this strange gentleman than I do from her."

"Would you risk your own safety," hissed Lucy, "when you are your husband's only hope of release? What if this man has guessed you are the wife of an imprisoned rebel and seeks to confound your purpose?"

Lucy's sallow face had flushed bright pink from her forehead to her chin. It was quite startling to see her so lose herself. I wondered whether it was she or I who was going astray. But I also could not help but consider her warning soberly. My life had not taught me to expect miracles around every corner. I did not know if Mr. Thrupp was a gift the saints and the Blessed Virgin had sent to us, or a razor strop to sharpen my wits and tutor my credulity.

And yet...I had a sense, as vivid as a sip of hot tea, that this man meant us no harm.

"This time I'm going to follow my instincts, Lucy," I said, as I rearranged her hood over her cap and replaced the blankets over her shoulders. "I have committed no crime. It is against no law for me to go to my husband. We need help if we are to save Gavin, and this man offers it. I will take advantage of his seeming kindness and, if I am mistaken, then I will suffer the consequences."

Lucy sniffed. I'm sure she wanted to say, "As will your husband," but instead she briefly embraced me and went to see to hiring the horses. This took some time. The innkeeper was well aware that, if he sent his good beasts out in this storm, he might never see them again. He wanted to charge us three times the usual rate, but Mr. Thrupp mentioned to him that he was a familiar acquaintance of the Chief Magistrate in Grantham and knew that this magistrate particularly disliked merchants who profited from the distress of a citizen by charging exorbitant prices for necessary goods.

Thrupp gave this advice without any show of threat or anger, as if merely offering useful information to the innkeeper for his own good. The innkeeper immediately revised his price. By so much was I confirmed in my good opinion of Phineas Thrupp.

I told Mr. Thrupp that we would accept his generous proposal. He promised to send a note at once to his wife and wrote detailed instructions for Lucy and me as to how to locate his house near St. John the Evangelist, a new Anglican church then under construction in Smith Square. He even drew a detailed map showing the path we must follow from the entrance into London on the Grantham Road, with little sketches of landmarks I might see along the way to Westminster, such as the old Charterhouse.

"We'll see Whitehall Palace as we come along the river," I said, remembering my days there during the brief reign of James II with a very small internal twist of pleasure and pain, but Mr. Thrupp shook his head.

"No," he said. "Sadly, you will not. Whitehall Palace burned down almost twenty years ago. A Dutch maid was drying linen sheets on a charcoal brazier in a bedchamber. Though the rules forbade it, she left her work for a few minutes. The brazier ignited the sheets, then the bed hangings, then the entire building.

"It was mad chaos. Servants who were trying to save the priceless tapestries, marble statues and paintings were impeded by looters who climbed over the walls. Inhabitants bolted the doors against the looters, thus impeding the firefighters. Now nothing is left but the banquet house and the gardens."

I felt of a sudden as if my time when I was a young girl at the court of King James II had been a sweet dream, even with all the falseness, the bitter struggles for power, and the dread collapse. Now, with just a few words, even that dream had dissolved like sugar in water. Perhaps, I thought, it was another young girl, not I, who passed her days in a palace in the heart of London long ago. Perhaps the story of the reign of James II was just one of those French fairy tales, which I had never lived, only read.

"Then where, pray tell, sir, does the new king, the Hanoverian, reside if Whitehall is no more?"

"At St. James's Palace madam," he said.

"That shabby old place?" I cried in surprise, and barely stopped myself from adding, "How manifestly appropriate."

St. James's had never been more than a secondary residence. I could not imagine how it could possibly serve as the primary residence of the king of England. But it was still more than Wee Geordie deserved.

If that is where the Usurper King lives, I thought, I may have to go there to plead for my husband's life. But, of course, I did not speak this thought aloud.

Lucy had returned, reporting the horses were ready and the storm had subsided a bit. She thought we had a chance of getting to Colsterworth without too much more excitement on the road. And so we said farewell to Mr. Thrupp and plunged forward.

It was less than forty leagues from Grantham to London, but it took more than a week to make the trip, and I was fortunate to arrive at all. The snowstorm had only hiccupped briefly while we were in Grantham, and then was in full force again. By the time we left Colsterworth the following morning, the snow was up over the horses' sides and, in some places, snow was piled on the roadside above the horses' withers.

When the snow stopped falling and the wind died to a whisper, the temperature fell to the coldest I have ever experienced in all my days. No matter how much I wrapped my hands and feet, fingers and toes lost all feeling as we rode. With every breath, I seemed to inhale ice until my breast stung. My moist exhalations caused tiny icicles to form on my lashes like little diamonds.

But I soon realized that Lucy was worse off. She had not spent as many hours on horseback as I and was never easy in the saddle. She was simply exhausted. When we stopped for new horses at the old Bell Inn in Stilton, I nibbled on samples of the local cream cheese with toast, and more hot tea, with a bit of brandy mixed in. Slowly I became aware that Lucy was sitting very still, staring straight ahead, touching neither food nor drink, as the snow melted around her in glistening puddles on the wide, wooden floorboards.

Then, slowly, almost gracefully, she slid out of her chair and lay only half-conscious on her spread cloak. When I touched her, her skin was burning. I called at once for cool clothes, smelling salts and help to lift her and get her to a bed. Of course, I blamed myself for failing to see how much she was suffering. I knew her well enough to know that, under these circumstances, she would never complain or demand that we pause longer or go more slowly.

By the time we were able to settle Lucy in a mercifully clean bed upstairs in the inn, I had bowed to the realization that, no matter how the Blessed Virgin might be praying for me, I had lost my wager with the Fates. I would not get to London in time to keep my husband from rotting in misery in the bowels of the Tower. I might not get there in time to save his life.

I had the odd sensation that my entire body up to my scalp itched and burned with my frustration. My fingers were reddened and swollen. Each time we stopped, it had taken longer to warm them, through sharp pain, at the fire. My eyes were puffed and red with the effort to search for the road or carter's path through a world of white. I was so tired that I thought if I once lay down, I would never get up again. It would have been a great relief to abandon the quest and release myself from the effort, remain at the Bell Inn, and let my thoughts plumb the depths of my failure at leisure.

Lucy immediately fell into such a deep sleep that I feared she would leave this world while she dreamed. For hours, as I watched and dozed by the light of one tall candle, she did not move. She lay with her mouth slack and her eyelids occasionally twitching, until I thought I should turn her, just to keep her arms and legs from stiffening into immobility. But when I touched her arm, even through the fabric of a thick, woolen nightdress, the heat of her fever burned my hand so that I released her and jumped back.

When she finally did begin to move near dawn, it was only to twist and roll, muttering incomprehensible strings of words that would sometimes congeal into a meaningful word or phrase. Once she cried out, "*Ma pauvre dame!*" (my poor lady). I thought surely she had awakened, but she was still asleep and subsided at once into more soft moans and the muttering of random syllables in French or English without any pattern.

In the late afternoon I had fallen asleep myself with my head on Lucy's coverlet when I felt her hand very gently on my hair. My cap had fallen back on my neck with only the strings that were tied under my chin holding it on. I started up, not knowing where I was at first. Then I saw her gazing at me, and I could see she had become herself again. Her cheeks were ghastly pale, but the fever had subsided.

"You must go on, you know," she croaked.

I shook my head frantically. I could not leave her in this strange place. Besides, the thought of continuing to brave the storm alone chilled me as deeply as the cold we had felt outdoors.

She drifted away again, but when she came back to life at twilight, we had a longer conversation. There was a small window next to Lucy's bed and, as the daylight shimmered briefly through the snow and faded, we both stared at the blowing eddies of white and the icicles dangling from the overhang of the roof.

"You know you must go," Lucy said. "I will get better and follow behind you. As you see, I'm already better." At this, she tried to push herself up into a sitting position, but her arms gave way and she fell back on the pillow. "Well, maybe I'm not a great deal better yet," she said, closing her eyes again.

I could not decide. I was drawn to stay and care for my Lucy, who had cared for me so many times, almost as fiercely as I was drawn to go after my husband. My thoughts tumbled over each other, biding me to stay and then again to go. Tears came into my eyes, but I would not let Lucy see me weep, so I put my head down on the coverlet with my face turned away from her and dabbed at my eyes where she could not see.

"You know I am right," said Lucy with her eyes closed. "I am always right."

That almost made me laugh. "Not about Mr. Thrupp," I muttered softly. "I hope." And then I knew I must go on. The reasons for my forced journey in all this winter misery had not changed.

"I will leave you money for your keep here," I said.

"Just take my little purse from my bag and put it under my pillow," she instructed. "It will be enough. I do not intend to stay more than a day or two."

"I will leave more for you and will make sure the people here care for you," I said.

Lucy opened her eyes and spoke to me as she would have if she were well. Her voice was just as firm, though soft.

"You will *not*," she said. "You need every ha'penny you have to save His Lordship."

After giving the innkeeper's wife a thousand instructions the next morning, I went to tell Lucy goodbye. Her fever was gone, but I could see that she was far too weak to sit astride a horse, even if it had been a glorious May morning. I pushed the lace trim of her cap aside and kissed her softly on the forehead, then went downstairs and prepared to set off again.

The beginning of my solo journey was as harsh, if not harsher, than the last day's travel. I don't believe any woman has ever made such a journey alone as I made that day. The snow still blew hard and the drifts gathered and shifted so that I was in terror of missing the road, even though the surface of the high road seemed to be improving bit by bit as I got closer to London. The ground seemed a little more solid under the coating of iced-over snow and then more snow. But there were still deep ruts to stumble through.

My most urgent concern, other than freezing to death, was that my poor horse would slide on one of the icy stretches and fall, and there I would be, stranded on the road with a horse in dire straits as night came on. I took careful note of every cottage we passed in case I had to turn back to one of them to seek help.

Every time I rode through a village, I recited another series of prayers to the Blessed Virgin and all the saints. At the time I thought these might be the worst days I would ever know, and I think, in terms of sheer physical labor, I was right.

By the time my horse and I stumbled into Biggleswade, I had come to believe that neither the snowfall nor this journey would ever come to an end. I could not even tell you the name of the inn where I fell into bed and could have slept till the Day of Judgment, had I not given instruction to the innkeeper's boy to wake me at sunrise.

The only way I managed to endure the last two days was to keep my head bowed and my face far down in my wrappings while I hummed to myself little snatches of Scottish songs and songs Lucy had taught us, and recited passages aloud from Shakespeare, which I'm sure I mangled fearfully. I spoke only lines uttered by the proudest of Shakespeare's maidens. I needed their strength. I thought of Rosalind, Miranda, Kate.

"My pride fell with my fortunes," I muttered to myself as Rosalind, and then thought of, "Who ever loved that loved not at first sight?" and remembered my first meeting with Gavin, that devastatingly handsome young sprig, as he was then, when I first saw him at the faded palace of Saint-Germain-en-Laye in Paris.

All of a sudden, a windblown drift of snow brought me a clear memory of Gavin on our wedding night. My mistress Queen Mary Beatrice had arranged a small but pleasant feast for us, with rare delicacies. I remembered the unaccustomed succulence of oysters with whipped cream, and the melting crumbles of a veal kidney and a lemon rind soufflé. But that night I had little appetite to do more than take tiny tastes of each dish.

We had been given one of the best bedrooms at St. Germain-en-Laye, thoroughly cleaned and aired and laid with fresh linens for us. The queen had also given me a silk robe to wear over my new, embroidered linen nightdress. I was so cold that I kept it on as I scrambled under the covers.

My lovely young husband came to the bed and lay down on top of the covers, where he turned toward me and stroked my hair, which was spread out and draped over my shoulders like a scarf. I had such hair then when it was let loose! Thick and honey-colored and full of waves.

I lay my head against his white shoulder, his skin so soft with a faint aroma that put me in mind of my favorite Calville Blanc d'Hiver apples, the little yellow ones with a red blush that taste like champagne. His eyes were deeper and darker by firelight. His own hair beneath the wig, as it turned out, was a tangle of short curls that were colored a deep auburn.

I said, "Why do you lie on top of the covers, my dear?"

And he said, "Because I want to be patient with my bride. We will spend these nights together for many years to come, so I thought I would do well to begin gently." He did not say, you are a maiden of twenty-seven and the very idea of being with a man probably frightens you, but that is what he meant.

But he had misjudged me. "I am a maiden indeed, sir," I said, "and not a young one. But I have no fear, and I want to embrace my husband. God knows I have waited long enough." I lifted up the covers and helped him scramble underneath them, and that is how we began. Our son was born within the year.

My tears came, first warm then cold on my cheeks, but I wiped them away. Tears would not save Gavin, but sturdy resolve that he would not die, absolute determination to find a way, might save him.

I remembered all at once lines spoken by Portia, heroine of *The Merchant of Venice* to the man she loves, "Live thou, I live: with much, much more dismay/I view the fight than thou that makest the fray." "*Live thou, I live,*" I repeated to myself over and over as I pressed on through the storm.

In truth, I think, in my extreme fatigue, I was meandering in my thoughts and did not know quite where I was or what I was thinking about.

It was only as I came to the top of a rise on the second day and saw the spires of London in the distance, all clothed in white against a late afternoon sky, that I realized all at once three things: the snow had stopped falling at last, the wind had died down, and the air was not so bitter cold but had come up a little in temperature so that I could take in bigger breaths.

I followed Mr. Thrupp's directions as best I could through the maze of crowds and noise, which were both welcome and somewhat stunning to my senses after my long solitary ride. London seemed so much larger and louder than in my youthful time there. It was so much grown that I almost thought I had come upon a city that was entirely strange to me. But then, other than one day when Glynis and I, children who had run away to explore the great city and gotten ourselves entirely lost, I had only seen the city from the safety of a carriage window. Riding a horse through its twisted lanes was much more intimate.

Everyone seemed in a great haste to get home through the cold before full night came on, women hurrying from the market, men from shops and the courts, boys rushing to finish sweeping away snow and horse droppings, and burly men in livery bearing sedan chairs hustling by, their elegant patrons hidden behind curtains as boys ran before them bearing torches. In a few cases, I saw, with some astonishment, that the top of the sedan chair had been pulled back and a concoction of high-piled wig studded with jewels or feathers could be seen peeking out, but the identity of the occupant was still a mystery.

It was almost full dark when I arrived at Smith Square and found the first row of houses newly built near the ghostly frame of an enormous church that was to be called St. John the Evangelist. The red brick house on the corner with a green door recessed in white columns under a wide ledge, fit Mr. Thrupp's description, and also bore a gold name plate that read "Thrupp," in case I had any doubt.

As I eased off the horse and tried to stand, I almost fell against the fence and must have made a clatter because a petite, young maid opened the door a crack, just enough for me to gasp hoarsely, "My name is Mrs. MacDonald. I believe Mrs. Thrupp is expecting me?"

"Oh yes, oh yes, do come in please!" she said.

A whirlwind of servants ensued that carried away my half-frozen horse to be tended, brought me indoors and settled me on a citron velvet couch in a front parlor, stoked the fire, and served me hot tea and then a glass of the finest claret I had ever tasted. At least I think it was so. In my dazed extremity, warmed whey might have been just as welcome.

The little maid who had opened the door gently removed my sodden boots and rubbed my feet until they began to warm, and then removed my gloves and rubbed my hands as well. I was entirely passive through this operation, so sunk in fatigue that it took me some time to comprehend that I had come to a safe, toasty haven at the end of my odyssey, and even longer, to look around and realize that I was in the most beautiful house I had ever seen.

Not the grandest house—for grandeur nothing could compare to Castle Banwy in Wales, where I had spent my earliest days. But it was the most exquisite and commodious of homes, with soft, silk velvet tapestries in large, formal floral patterns of blue, red and black hanging on the walls, furniture upholstered in velvets with a smaller, more natural floral motif, and a magnificent marble hearth large enough to warm the whole space of the room. Beside the hearth was a silk screen to protect the delicate complexions of ladies who were inclined to sit too close to the flames.

My head resting against a silken pillow, I began to drift into sleep no matter how I tried to resist, caught in a half dream of all the fairy tales I had read about glittering caves with walls made of diamonds and emeralds and magical palaces where unseen spirits provided for all human needs. I seemed to be swathed in a silk cocoon where my questions, doubts, suspicions dissipated in the luxurious warmth like little balls of spun silk lifted away on a spring breeze.

I was so near sleep that, when the Mistress of this Silken Palace entered the room, I had only the vaguest sense of her presence and could not rouse myself. I thought that she laid a soft hand on my hair, loosened my heavy cloak and draped a coverlet over me, up to my chin. I fell asleep and dreamed that my mother was alive again and was tending me, and I'm sure I smiled to myself before my dreams swept me away.

Chapter Ten
In the Lair of the Beast

"If our two loves be one, or, thou and I
Love so alike, that none do slacken, none
can die."

"The Good-Morrow," John Donne

I did not formally meet Amelia Thrupp until the next morning, and she was not at all what I had expected. I had imagined that Phineas' wife would be round and plump and exuding good cheer as he did, with graying curls peeping out from under a starched linen cap, and a good, homely face full of genial wrinkles.

Amelia in the flesh was no such creature. She was tall and comely and, I would guess, a good twenty years younger than her husband, with a wealth of thick, golden-brown hair spilling out from under her little lace cap, deep-set, green eyes, a long, narrow nose, and a full, wide mouth. She wore an understated but exquisitely draped gown of a deep ocher color with a cerulean petticoat, which somehow achieved a fashionable effect effortlessly. She charmed without intimidating or provoking envy. Her gown had been designed to grace and enhance the woman, rather than, as I had so often seen at two royal courts, the woman being overwhelmed and quite upstaged by the gown.

Amelia herself brought me breakfast on a silver tray to welcome me properly, since I had fallen asleep before she could even introduce herself. When she identified herself as the lady who presided over this silken wonderland, I, still rubbing my eyes, gaped openly and then blushed violently, having so forgotten my breeding.

"Mistress Thrupp," I said, "I am so grateful for your kindness and so humbled to come before you in such a forlorn state," as I regarded my scrambled state of dress and imagined the condition of my hair and the soiled nature of my general appearance.

"I have some understanding," she said in her rich contralto, "of the difficulties of your journey. My husband sent a message. I don't know how the boy got through before you. He reached me yesterday afternoon and told me in detail of the storm and the roads. I'm sure he was angling for a larger fee, but by the state of his horse, I believed him and gave him more than he looked for.

"Phineas was quite taken with you and your friend and was sympathetic to the urgency of your travel. I am only amazed and relieved that you succeeded in reaching our home against all odds. I also have some suspicion of the reason for your haste and beg you to believe that you may confide freely in me. With all goodwill, I intend to give you all the support that I can. You are to regard this house as your own home while you are in London. But I was told to expect you with your friend?"

I embraced Amelia at once and explained what had happened to Lucy, and that I expected her to follow me in a few days.

When I had eaten the soft-cooked eggs and fresh bread and butter that Amelia had brought me, she took me upstairs, through more wondrous rooms like a series of jewel boxes lined with silk. I'm afraid I gawped at them like any country milkmaid come to town for the first time. I had to keep reminding myself to close my mouth and stop gasping with awe.

At last we came to a deep blue bedchamber with bright windows that overlooked the square. This room was to be my own during my stay. The maids had made up the fire in the hearth, which was lined with blue and white Delft tiles depicting unicorns, windmills and flowers. I could have stayed in that room forever, until my body and mind were fully recovered. But that dream, of course, could not be. There was no time.

No sooner had I settled my poor bags and bundles in the blue bedroom than I realized that it was already midday. I had slept some twelve hours. I scolded myself inwardly. No matter the rigors of the trip, I had not come to London to luxuriate in soft surroundings. I forthrightly told Amelia that I needed to go to the Tower of London at once and seek out my husband who might be in desperate need.

She understood and did not try to dissuade me. She offered to send for a sedan chair and also to send one of her manservants on horseback to help clear the way, wait for me, and assure my safe return to the house.

"As you approach the Tower," she said, "the alleys are so narrow that it is hard for a carriage to pass. And I do not want you to walk the last distance on your own. The streets are filthy and it is not safe...Lady Clarencefield."

I started and stared at her.

She dropped me a full curtsy and explained. "Oh yes," she said. "You told my husband that you needed to visit the Tower. He was convinced from the beginning that you were a lady of very high rank despite your efforts at shielding your identity. He made inquiries concerning the nobles who were taken into custody at Preston and sent to the Tower.

"There were only seven. Some were too young or too old or unmarried. Phineas narrowed it down almost at once in his mind to the Earl of Clarencefield and thought you must be his famously beautiful bride whose family fled to France with James II."

I was too stunned to speak. It seemed to be a wild exaggeration to call me anyone's "famously beautiful bride." I was twenty-seven when I married Gavin!

"You have nothing to fear from us," she said. She took me by the hand and led me up the central staircase to the top floor of her home. There she pushed aside one of the silk tapestries that hung around the walls of a room that must have once been a nursery. She pushed a secret spring in the wainscoting and opened a small door—cut flush to the wall so that its outline was almost undetectable—to reveal a narrow, recessed niche that was made up as a chapel. There was a gold crucifix and an exquisite portrait of the Blessed Virgin with the Christ Child in a space adorned with tall white candles in silver candlesticks, and an altar cloth of ivory silk with the letters "IHS" embroidered in red.

Whatever little anxieties I might have still been feeling subsided. Amelia Thrupp was placing her life in my hands by revealing this Catholic chapel hidden deep within her home.

"You see I am trusting you with our secrets so that you may have no doubt as to whether you may put your faith in us," she said, crossing herself before the altar, as did I.

"The Thrupps," she said, "have been secret Catholics for perhaps one-hundred years. My husband and I regularly attend Church of England services to maintain our disguise. You must not despise us for that. If we are to extend a hand to help anyone, we must remove all suspicion from ourselves. Do you think for even one moment that my husband could travel the world as a British silk merchant if the king's advisors thought he might be plotting with foreign Catholics, or even with the Chevalier himself?"

When I could speak over the tightening in my throat, I asked her, "And was your family also Catholic?"

She locked the chapel and pulled the curtain, drawing me back downstairs to the blue bedchamber and closing the door so that we were incontestably alone.

"I was not raised a Roman Catholic," she said, "but my parents had no particular love for the Church of England or the Dissenters, thank the good Lord. They were too busy mastering the hustle and scramble of the wool trade. I could see, even when I was very young, that, with five brothers, they had no need of me in their business. My only future was to marry well. Phineas wooed me into the silk trade and into the Roman Catholic Church at one and the same time. My parents approved of the first and never knew about the second."

Many more questions came into my mind. Had she and her husband raised their son and daughter as secret Catholics? Had they taken any steps themselves to support the return of the rightful king? Were their servants all in on the secret? But I realized that I was allowing myself to be distracted from my one purpose for making my way to London through the worst winter weather in memory.

I admitted to Amelia that she had guessed my identity correctly and begged her to call me by my Christian name. I also told her that my friend, when she arrived, might call herself "Miss Lennox" but was really Lucy Dunstable. I left a note for Lucy to reassure her that, despite her misgivings, I believed my trust in the Thrupps had been fully justified.

Amelia pressed me to take money from her, but, for the moment, I refused, though I was troubled by the unexpected expenses incurred during my journey. I had been forced to hire so many more horses and pay for so many more overnight lodgings than I had planned. I did not have a great deal left from my original store of money. But I had another plan in mind that might permit me to rely less on the generosity of the Thrupps.

In the meantime, I set off in the hired sedan chair that was waiting for me, thoroughly enshrouded to ward off the cold and any curious looks. I would go at once to the Tower of London, though my heart was full of my fear of the place and even more intense fear of what I might find there.

I voiced none of this to Amelia before I left. It seemed to me that speaking my fears aloud might make them come even more vividly to life. Throughout that long, bone-rattling ride, during which I could see very little unless I peeked through the curtains, but could hear and smell a great deal, I recited my prayers under my breath and told myself over and over quite sternly that my childhood fear of the Tower was nothing to do with the present. I must focus entirely on how I could help my husband, not on what had happened to my parents years ago.

By means of prayers and admonitions to myself, I came to the Tower somewhat fortified in my mind and determined to betray no sign of weakness. I would *not* be a feeble vessel inclined to fainting fits and helplessness when I was most urgently needed.

Amidst all of this worry it didn't occur to me until we were almost at my destination that I had missed something. I had failed to consider the most important element of all in my plans to save my husband. What might end up counting most, if all else failed, would be the impression I made on the men who were responsible for guarding the prisoner.

I knew I must not set foot on those grounds in the guise of a disdainful and haughty Lady of the Manor. But neither could I be a groveling supplicant before these men. That would win me neither respect nor favor.

When the sedan chair stopped, I waited a moment before I opened the curtains and stepped down, wearing a most difficult mask—that is, an air of complete calm. I would appear to be concerned for my husband but in no way panicked. Above all, I would be the devoted wife, eager to reunite with my heart's love, eager to see to his needs. Would not even the meanest, the most hardened of gaolers sympathize with my plight?

I walked alone from the sedan chair to the Tower gate, nodding politely to the warders in their garish red and gold, skirted Tudor uniforms, trying to ignore the trembling in my lower limbs and keep my voice level and steady. I did not fail to notice the flecks of ice on the dark, turgid water in the moat below and thought of the cold and damp in the Tower cells.

"I have come to visit the Earl of Clarencefield," I said, "and I thank you all for your goodwill towards my lord." I dropped a few coins into the palm of each guard, without really seeming to take much notice of what I was doing. I was aware that this was expected but determined not to arouse suspicion by giving too much. I would give a little and hope to generate an expectation that more treats might be coming their way if I was accommodated.

Some of the men regarded me with mild interest but seemed to have no desire to bestir themselves. But one who was short and round and brisker than the rest—I later learned his name was Thomas Brickle—immediately bowed, doffed his flat-brimmed hat, and offered to take me to my husband.

"Follow me, my lady," he said at once, and I caught him winking at one of his fellows. Apparently he played up to visitors with a show of cheerful alacrity, hoping to win more and larger bribes than the others. His companions chuckled as if to acknowledge that he might gain by his actions, but also to demonstrate that they did not think the extra effort was worth whatever small additional rewards he might gain.

Brickle clapped his hat back on his head, turned and pumped his legs with apparent vigor as he led me across the courtyard. But I could see he was not moving with any real haste. He did not intend to tire himself out unnecessarily on my account.

"His Lordship is in Lord Lieutenant Compton's Lodgings, my lady, upstairs on the second floor," he flung back over his shoulder. I wondered if it was a good sign that Gavin was ensconced in what might be a better, less dreary part of the Tower? Or was this choice of accommodations only intended to make it easier for Compton to watch Gavin more closely?

I observed that Brickle's scarlet uniform, though clean, strained across his broad back, seeming barely to contain his bulk. I even spotted a small separation along a waistline seam, which might soon become a tear.

I also noted, with a brief shudder, the squat-necked ravens waddling about the courtyard, coarsely squawking like rusty hinges on a worn door blown to and fro by the wind. There was a legend that, when the ravens disappeared from the Tower grounds, England would fall—an eventuality about which I had somewhat mixed feelings.

I had heard that the highborn who were convicted of treason were sometimes executed in the courtyard next to the Lieutenant's Lodgings known as the Tower Green. Two of Henry VIII's wives had fallen there, Anne Boleyn and Catherine Howard.

I did not look in that direction, forcibly directing my thoughts to my immediate objective. But to me the ugly, oversized birds seemed an evil omen and their cawing presaged doom. I walked faster to get past them.

By now we were nearing the half-timbered, white and brown, gabled Tudor buildings—also known as the Queen's House, said Brickle—where Lt. Compton lived. I saw the light of a candle glimmering through an upstairs window and had to remind myself to maintain a sedate gait. I must convey the air of a woman who was always in quiet command of the world around her.

Brickle unlocked the door with one of his massive keys and we entered the lodgings. I saw a dark room with embers in the grate, and the remains of what looked like a hasty dinner of broken bread, cheese and pickle, spread over a wooden trencher on a heavy oaken table. To my relief, the lieutenant himself did not appear to be in the residence. Brickle called and looked about and then told me

Lt. Compton was probably making one of his customary tours of the grounds, which he did several times daily, but not on a regular schedule, so as to surprise any of his men who were shirking their duties.

"You may climb up to your husband, my lady," he said, nodding at the stairs. "But you may only remain for a few moments. The lieutenant could return at any time."

I offered him another little pile of coins from my purse and asked evenly if I might stay a bit longer since I had not seen my husband since before all the "trouble" began, trying to imply that I might not be in full sympathy with the rebels.

He smiled and bowed so deeply that I feared his doublet would split in back on the spot, embarrassing both of us. But he did not commit himself as to the matter of giving us more time.

I turned and could not refrain from racing up the warped, uneven stairs so fast that I half stumbled on two of the boards that listed to the right. There was a door at the top that appeared to be closed but not locked. I knocked gently. There was no answer.

I opened the door and hesitated on the threshold. The sun had already set and the paneled room was very dim except for the one candle I had spied from the courtyard. There was a wide fireplace but the fire was low and would soon gutter out.

A man stood in the darkness by a window overlooking the Thames that was divided into small squares of glass which doubled and tripled the reflection of the candle on the table so that he seemed haloed by candlelight. The door had not been locked but the window plainly was, the casements secured with a large padlock.

I tried to speak. No sound emerged. I was just about to try again when the man slowly turned. I saw that he was my husband, though gaunt and heavily bearded, his long hair streaked with gray falling onto his shoulders. For a moment we just stared at each other—each wondering, I suppose, if the other was real or just a vaporous image summoned by longing. If I spoke, would I find myself alone in the room? If he spoke, would I vanish?

And then, after all my weeks of waiting and worrying and my dreadful journey, I was so overwhelmed with emotion that my whole body was flooded with joy and sorrow, all at the same time. Despite all my resolutions, I began to cry and ran across the room to throw myself into Gavin's arms. For several minutes we simply clung to each other. There are times when words are excessive and it is graceless to speak.

I'm not sure how long we held each other, like survivors thrown up onto a beach after a shipwreck—me weeping softly and Gavin making no sound while large tears drifted down the new furrows in his cheeks.

Finally we sat at one end of a long table, arms and hands still entwined, and knew we had to begin to talk of what would come next. I did not know how soon Brickle would come to fetch me, so I asked the essential questions first. Had he received the money I had sent him? Did he need more?

"Callum found me at Barnet," he said, "and the purse you sent has supplied my needs here. But, as you can see," he added wryly, "we keep body and soul together but we do not feast in the Tower." His voice was low and hoarse as if he was unused to using it—he who had always spoken with such clarity and firmness.

"I suspect that, even before you came to the Tower," I said lightly, "most of those chickens you bought along the road went to feed your men and not to keep your own belly full."

"'Tis true," he admitted with a rueful smile.

"At any rate, husband, I have brought you more coins to purchase fruit and greens," I said, "and hot water to shave with or even a tub to bathe in. I will bring fresh clothes and new candles tomorrow."

I pressed my little purse (so light now!) into his palm, which felt warm to my cold fingers. I closed his hand around it and put both my hands around his. Then I lay my head on our clasped hands and we were quiet again.

But I soon lifted my head because my eyes were so hungry for the sight of him and I wanted to know how well or ill he was. When he spoke again, I began to understand how much his brief experience with war and defeat had taken from him.

"My dear, I must unburden myself a little," he said. "Our

captors did not mistreat us when we surrendered. But the journey from Preston to London was a different matter. I thought I might die doing battle for King James, but I did not think to be humiliated, to be displayed before the rabble..."

Now I took his face in my hands and tried to hush him with a kiss. He pulled away. "No, no, you must listen," he said. "They trussed us up on our horses with our arms tied behind us. A foot soldier led each horse by the bridle, since we could not guide them.

"And all along the way, the commoners shouted at us. They screamed, 'Down with popery!' and 'King George forever!' I felt like a captured barbarian chieftain being paraded through the streets of Rome."

He covered his face with his hands as if he did not want me to see him, he was so overcome with shame. And so I kissed his hands. He continued to mutter softly, but our heads were bent so close together that I could still hear every word.

"They wanted to throw offal at us," he said, "rotten food and such, but our guards did not permit that degradation."

Now his voice was even lower. "Some in those mobs chided us with the punishment that awaits us. They said we traitors would be served just like the lowest with no neat, swift beheadings. We would be hanged and cut down alive and disemboweled, our innards burned before our faces, and then quartered..."

I could not permit my husband to dwell on this horror. I feared it would drive him mad. I tried to draw his mind away.

"Where are the others? Derwentwater, Kenmure, Winton?"

At last he removed his hands and I could see how sunken his eyes were and how weary and red. The flesh of his face having thinned, his dark eyes appeared to be enormous.

"They are all here in the Tower," he said, "but we are not allowed to see one another. I believe that Derwentwater and Kenmure are in the Bell Tower, in the quarters once occupied by Sir Thomas More. I do not know why I am here alone.

"Lt. Compton is correct in his behavior to me, remote and cool but not unpleasant. I have not suffered in body. He has implied that he feared I would be the one most likely to attempt an escape and wanted to watch me closely. But why am I more likely to try to run than another? I cannot understand it."

"My dear," I said, trying to smile, "you are a Glentaggart. Isn't that enough reason to keep you close?" The faint ghost of a smile passed over his face and dissipated.

"Yes, I am a Glentaggart," he said. "And I believe that will be enough to doom me. My father and my grandfather fought for the Stuarts. We have been...incorrigible."

And now I knew I had to make my strongest argument. I had to convince him that he would not die a traitor's death. I seized his hands again and held them in a firm grip. I would not betray any of my qualms to him.

"I am here to save you, one way or another," I said with more conviction than I felt at that moment. "You have kept us all safe these many years. Now it is my turn and I will not fail you. Believe in me."

Gavin looked at me steadily and this time he did smile, just a little. "You will reverse the old story of Orpheus and Eurydice and bring *me* up out of Hell, will you?" he said, with a whisper of his old teasing. He had roused himself enough to try to display a bit of hope.

"I believe you," he declared, with a solemnity that I thought was feigned for my sake. But it was a beginning.

"What do you want me to do?" he asked.

"Be kind to your warders," I said, "but not too kind. Be courteous. Give them no cause to harbor anger against you or to suspect you of anything. Make their task easy."

I did not add, "Make them sorry that such a noble one as you must die," but I meant to suggest just that.

"And I," I added, "will be the noblest and most gallant of suffering wives. All will admire us and grieve for us, and we will use that to our advantage."

Soon after, Brickle came clattering up the stairs to tell us that Lt. Compton would return soon, and I must go.

"But you may come tomorrow, my lady," he said brightly. I could almost see the visions of more shiny, new coins gleaming in his eyes.

"I will come every day until my husband is freed," I said firmly.

I tried to appear to be of good cheer, although my heart ached with pity for my husband. I was sure that, after I had gone, he would turn back to staring unseeing out the dark window, trying not to anticipate his fate. My first mission must be to make him believe that a most dreadful death was not inevitable.

All the way back to the gate, I expounded to Brickle everything he must do to see to the health of my husband—the hearty food he must allow my lord to buy, and the fresh water heated on the hearth my lord would require for regular washing, and at least a brief moment with his companions to keep their spirits up, if that was possible.

Brickle said he would do what he could and, of course, held out his hand to be crossed again with silver, as if he were a gypsy woman preparing to tell my fortune.

"I will do my part," I said, "by bringing in the occasional treat that all may enjoy. I'm going right now to see what good things can be purchased, though it be dead winter."

I hastened to the waiting sedan chair and wept silently all the way back to Smith Square, and then became very angry with myself. Tears and wailing would not solace my husband and only brought me lower in my own heart. What was needed was good, hard thought.

Three days later, my own Lucy arrived about the same time as Mr. Thrupp, who had had some business to do along the way. She was still a little pale and moving slowly, but otherwise she was her neat, well-ordered self, ready to be my sage advisor and companion once more.

When I was finally able to speak to Lucy alone after dinner in the blue bedchamber, which we were to share, I tried out on her the first part of the secret plan I had been cogitating. We were sitting up against bolsters in the blue-draped featherbed under the blue canopy with the coverlets drawn up to our chins, though the fire had not yet died on the hearth. When Lucy heard what I was considering, she looked at me as if I had been taken in fits and was babbling nonsense.

"I want to be entirely sure that I understand you," she said with heavy sarcasm. "You have not seen your apostate sister Aelwen in more than twenty-five years since you and your parents fled to France with the Stuarts? You have not written to each other, not so much as a single letter. Let me see...what else? The two of you have disliked each other ever since you were children."

"I was the youngest," I said, "and I believe she thought too much fuss was made over me, when all attention and all pampering should, by rights, have been lavished on her. She used to pinch me when she thought no one was watching."

"Shall I continue?" said Lucy, shaking her head till the lace on her cap quivered.

"If you must," I said.

Lucy counted off on her fingers all the reasons why I should have no hope of help from Aelwen.

"Please do correct me if I mistake any of the details," she said. "When your family was at the court of King James II, you discovered that your sister Aelwen, already betrothed to Baron Bronley, was engaging in a dalliance with John Churchill, judged by all to be the most beautiful man at court...and, of course, already married. You exposed this affair to your mother, thereby forcing Aelwen to end it?"

"Yes, and Aelwen slapped me for it and swore that I would be sorry," I said. "Her betrothal ring left a mark on my cheek for some time." I touched my cheek and almost thought I could still feel the sting of that slap.

"And afterwards," continued Lucy, "to avenge herself, she convinced one Viscount Markham, thrice widowed, that you, not yet fifteen, would be delighted to become his fourth bride, thus bringing him a sizable dowry and a close link to one of the most powerful families at the court of James II...Your sister even daintily suggested to this viscount that the quickest way to bring the nuptials about would be for him to visit you at Lincoln's Inn Fields when none of the other family members were home and force an immediate consummation of the union."

Oh yes, I thought, recalling the glitter in the black eyes of the viscount, the wiry, gray hair on his arm, and the curl of saliva in the corner of his mouth as he reached for my breast. I had only managed to escape him by abruptly feigning sickness, engaging in such a fit of violent coughing that I sprayed his face and wig with spit.

"I believe he thought I was infecting him with plague, or something equally loathsome," I said and could not help but laugh. "It was delightful to watch how quickly he made his exit after he had mauled me."

But the thought of the viscount still made me shiver in disgust and little flames of my old fury at Aelwen sprang up within my heart at the thought of the fate I might have suffered had I not been a quick-witted girl. Hush! I said to myself. That is years gone. Anger at Aelwen now is a luxury I cannot afford.

"And, as if these misdeeds were not enough," said Lucy, "your mother discovered before you all left London that Aelwen was drifting away from the Church of Rome. Her elderly husband Baron Bronley was dying, and your sister was already casting about for a powerful, Anglican husband to protect her during the reign of William of Orange."

"Yes," I said. "This is all true. When we last saw Aelwen before we left England, my mother, who, you may remember, was always calm and kind, all but disowned her. I never saw my mother so angry—first, because Aelwen had endangered me, and second, because she was endangering her own soul after all my parents had suffered for their faith."

"Well then," rejoined Lucy, "why should you *not* apply to your loving sister for assistance in your time of need? Why should she *not* hasten to provide you with whatever funds you require?"

Her sharp response reassured me more than anything else that she was indeed almost back to being my old, dearly beloved Lucy.

"Never mind," she added. "I see by that familiar expression on your face that you are determined. I have long known that, once you have fixed your sights on a goal, I might as well try to convince a full tide rolling in to turn and ebb away, as change your mind."

I set my candle down on the table beside the bed and seized her small, cool hands in mine.

"I am not mad, Lucy," I said. "I am desperate. I need more money to provide for Gavin in the Tower and to bribe his guards to treat him well and to allow me extended visits with him. Gavin will go on trial and we will need lawyers.

"If he is convicted, I must go to the palace and beg the king for mercy. That requires a suitable court costume, or I will not be admitted."

I had asked Amelia if she knew anything of Aelwen, but all that she had heard was that, since the death of her third husband, Aelwen, now the Dowager Marchioness of Marvelstone, had become something of a recluse. I noted that Aelwen's trajectory had moved upwards in the world through her marriages, first to a baron, then to an earl and finally to a marquess. I did not think that this steady rise in rank and wealth was the result of chance.

But, despite her status as dowager marchioness, Aelwen did not attend the court of the Hanoverian and did not visit her former friends...though I guessed there were not so many of those. Aelwen had always sought admiration rather than friendship. When there were no more admirers crowding around her, I would have hazarded she found that "friends" who had been no more than acquaintances did not seek her out.

I vowed to Lucy that I would attempt to call upon my estranged sister the very next day and blew the candle out. I knew Lucy so well though, that I could feel her disapproval even in the dark.

"I must make the effort, Lucy," I whispered meekly and thought I could sense her tight hold on her distaste for my plan finally relax a little before I fell asleep.

The next day there was more news. Phineas had gone out to his coffeehouse and come rushing back with word that the Chevalier, young King James III himself, had landed at Peterhead in Scotland on New Year's Day.

"Oh, but so late!" I cried when I heard the story. His followers had been defeated and his armies were melting away in the depths of winter. How much difference it might have made had he but come early in the autumn! But Mr. Thrupp reported that the young king, who was said to be thin and pasty, though of a noble bearing, had been delayed by a recurrent illness, evil weather in the Channel and a fruitless wait for support that had not materialized.

A ship carrying gold ingots from Spain to buy him arms and soldiers had foundered at Dundee and shattered off the coast. Fair-weather promises made to the prince by powerful lords had been forgotten, and some who had sworn they would join him found many excuses to stay at home. When he finally arrived in Scotland, James learned of the defeat of the Jacobites at Preston and the numbers of his followers imprisoned and likely to suffer ugly deaths, which dampened his spirits further.

Rumors of the progress of the Chevalier swirled around us like smoke while we were in London. There was a story that the rough Highlanders who first greeted him with joy had been put off by his sickliness, his stiff formality and his reticence.

If James was disappointed in the small numbers of those who remained to fight for him, it was said, the men were also mightily disappointed in James. They had, no doubt, hoped for a brash, young Henry VIII-like prince with a loud laugh and a bold spirit.

It was said that our dejected King James had ended a speech before the Highlanders with the rousing sentiment that, "for him it was no new thing to be unfortunate." The Highlanders even made fun of his fussy habit of rolling his bread into tiny pellets at table, and of his modesty in refusing to take advantage of the women who offered to bed him.

Poor James. He was his mother's son in his devotion to his religion and his chastity, and, though I admired his goodness, these traits did not serve him well in a crowd of rough clan lairds and their liege men.

But I had not much time, then or later, to think about him. My thoughts were entirely bent on saving my husband. I was determined to call upon Aelwen.

Chapter Eleven
The Wayward Sister

"I know you what you are;
And, like a sister, am most loath to call
Your faults as they are nam'd."

King Lear, William Shakespeare

I decided I would go to St. James's Square alone the following morning, close-wrapped against the cold, and would not take a sedan chair since the walk was a short one and much of it passed through St. James's Park, which Amelia said was lovely even in winter and less dangerous than in the greener seasons. The bare-branched trees provided little cover for unsavory assignations or the pickpockets who roamed throughout the city, and the broad lanes through the park were kept free of snow and other roadside muck. Amelia loaned me her wooden pattens to lift me off the ground and protect my shoes. I teetered a little at first, but soon found the proper balance.

I had made up my mind that I would send no note. I would give Aelwen no advance notice that I was coming so she would have no chance to prepare, whether to turn me away or leave me sitting alone in a deserted front parlor until I wearied of waiting for her to appear and left. To speak the truth, I was quite tumbled in my nerves about this visit. I had always been a little afraid of Aelwen's capacity for spite and could not come to any settled idea in my mind as to how she might react when she saw me.

As I was planning this visit, I would tilt first one way and then the other in my mind. I would tell myself Aelwen would not want a close relation, a brother-in-law, to be publicly executed and the family so shamed.

But then again, I would think that her hatred of me might have festered to such a degree that it would give her some kind of dark pleasure to see me cast down by the death of my husband. At last I sternly told myself to banish these absurd conjectures. I would discover how she would react soon enough. I set off to walk to St. James's Square through the pale gold light of the morning streets, empty of the usual bustle because it was Sunday.

The weather had warmed a little more, but snow still lay in heaps along the streets and across the sleeping grass of St. James's Park, and ice glinted on the surface of the canal that ran through the park. I passed a little teahouse on an island in the canal. Amelia had told me the island was designed to attract picturesque water-fowl and harbor ducks for the king's table. But I saw no birds about in the cold.

The park was an all too brief distraction. Soon enough I arrived at a large and imposing square, obviously intended to house the great of the nation who desired to live near the king at St. James's Palace. I found Aelwen's home tucked away in a corner—a three-story structure of brick and stone, all of an ivory color that put me in mind of Aelwen's ivory locks. A finely wrought iron fence lined the front of the property on either side of the front door and led to steps going down to a basement level for servants and deliveries.

I approached the broad front steps, paused, backed up, considered, slowly approached again and stared at the brass knocker on the golden oak door. Each of the large sash windows on the second story above was divided into small panes and was graced by its own shallow, curved, wrought-iron balcony. Within I could see heavy, dark curtains completely covering each window. How could anyone bear to shut out the light on such a bright day? Perhaps light poured in from back windows that opened on a garden.

Enough, I told myself sternly. I walked up the few steps, lifted the knocker and banged it several times with more force than I had intended. The resounding thwocks seemed to echo through an empty house, startling me to the point that I almost jumped back. After a short while the door opened a crack and a small, wizened face, overwhelmed by an oversized cap, peered around the edge. I waited for the woman to speak but she did not. She just fixed her black eyes on me and stood silently.

At last I said, "Please inform Lady Marvelstone that her sister Lady Clarencefield is here to see her." A long pause ensued. The staring continued. Then all at once the woman seemed to come to life, having decided that I was not an importunate tradeswoman and should not be left standing in the street.

In a high-pitched, rasping voice—seldom used, I imagined—she invited me to come in. I discarded the pattens at the doorstep and entered a front hall so dim that I could hardly make out my surroundings. The woman paused to lift a candle she had placed on a table by the front door, ushered me into a front parlor, gestured for me to sit down on a small sofa and placed the candle on a side table. Then, without another word, she glided out of the room.

I could only endure a few moments in the dark before I rose and opened a narrow aperture in the heavy, red velvet curtains covering the nearest window. A shaft of sunlight revealed a suite of dark furniture, heavily carved, a low fire on the hearth and a mirror shrouded in black hangings. I sat again. Time passed until I became a little sleepy in the warmth of the room.

I only became aware that someone had entered when the curtain was abruptly closed and my little sunbeam shut off. I looked up and a figure stood there, all swathed in black and heavily veiled.

"Bethan," Aelwen said, her low voice muffled by the veils but unmistakable. "So many years."

She came forward and lifted my hand. Her own was very cold. I wanted to cover it with both my hands and see if I could rub some warmth into it, but she withdrew it immediately and settled herself with a heavy rustling of stiff fabrics onto another sofa across the room.

"Our parents are gone," I said.

"I know," she said.

"Gwilym is yet at Castle Banwy. I believe your husband (I could not remember which one. The second, perhaps?) helped him recover the Carlisle estates?"

She nodded. Silence.

"Marged is in Ireland."

"Yes," she said.

"I suppose you write to Glynis?"

"Yes," she said, "and she replies to me, but not often."

"To me also," I said. "Sometimes I think I can feel her praying for us."

"Yes," said Aelwen. A long silence.

"I am very sorry," I said, "for the death of your husband. Was it recent?"

I felt that, if I did not keep talking, we would lapse into a silence that would never be broken. How could I possibly awaken her? Had her mourning for this third widowing so overwhelmed her, or was there some other reason why she kept to heavy widow's weeds in a dark house?

"A year ago," she said. "He died in the country. He seldom came to town."

"But you mourn him still?"

"I mourn my life," she said.

"You are alone then?" I asked. Long pause.

"Not precisely," she said.

"You have a companion?" I inquired.

"Not precisely that, either," she said.

I could not see her sneer but I could almost hear it in her dry tone. Aelwen had never been fond of female companions or female companionship. I thought how bereft I would be without Lucy.

"Do you take the air? Do you ride? The park is lovely."

"I never leave the house," she said.

And so we continued, almost in monosyllables. I did not see how I could possibly arrive at the purpose of my visit, struggling through such high grass as this, the thicket of resentments and grievances that had accumulated over time and distance between two who, though sisters, were never friends.

I was casting about in my mind for a way to break through, some subject I could introduce that might arouse her interest. She had not asked about my husband or my children. I hesitated to ask about hers, not knowing what children she might have had after the first boy, who was born before we left England but whom none of us had seen. My mother had sent Aelwen a silver teething cup with the child's initials engraved on it along with the Carlisle crest. She had been too angry to visit. She might have softened in time—the boy being her first grandchild—but we left England almost immediately afterwards and my mother and father never returned. I did not even know if the boy was still living.

This painful, stuttering reunion seemed about to stagger to an awkward close when someone strode briskly into the room and threw open the curtains over the front windows, which caused Aelwen to wince and hold her hand up to cover her eyes.

"Must you?" she complained querulously.

"Yes," said the firm voice of a young man. "You cannot hide from the light forever, Madam," in a tone that seemed both imperious and disdainful.

Then he turned to me, but his back was against the light and all I saw at first, my own eyes blinded, was a shadow, tall, long-legged, with narrow waist and broad shoulders. He crossed the room and when the full light of day caught him, I gasped. I could not restrain myself.

My first thought was that Aelwen must be living in seclusion with a young lover, but then I saw his face. It was if I had instantly been transported back to the long-ago days of the court of James II.

I was so startled and disoriented that I stood up. I felt as if I were a young girl again and had stepped into the privy garden of Whitehall Palace and spied the most radiant man at court framed in a window above me—the same languorous, dark eyes, full lower lip and fine complexion, a little more golden and less ivory than I remembered. In my memory the young man held in his arms my sister here present, and she was laughing and touching his face. The man who stood before me was John Churchill, restored to all his manly glory and beauty.

Was my sister's house peopled by the ghosts of her past? But this youth appeared to be quite solid and unlikely to dissolve into smoke and fly up the chimney.

"I beg your pardon, Madam," he said to me, and did not look

well-pleased at my unguarded reaction to him. "I did not know that my lady had a visitor. I am Oswald Nisingham, Baron Bronley. My father died three husbands ago." Here he nodded towards Aelwen and bowed towards me.

As I was already standing, I curtsied.

"I am Lady Clarencefield." I said hesitantly.

His angry frown faded.

"You are that brave lady of whom I have heard so much?" he said, face suddenly glowing with excitement. "Who fled with the Stuart king to France, danced once at Versailles, and then married and retired to Scotland...and whose husband at this very moment resides in the Tower for fighting on behalf of the Chevalier? I knew of you but never imagined we would meet." Once again, I was taken aback that my story, which did not seem remarkable to me, was widely known.

"Yes, I have the honor of being that unfortunate lady," I said. "And," I repeated, "if this lady is your mother, I am your aunt!" On an impulse I came forward, seized both his hands and kissed him very gently on the cheek. "I am so glad to make your acquaintance," I said.

His cheeks flushed a darker red. "Even though..." he said. "As you can see, my face has not been my fortune." He cast an icy glance at Aelwen. Beneath her heavy veils, I could only discern the pale oval of a face and darkened circles for eyes. I had no idea how she was reacting to this little drama of recognition playing out before her.

"My dear nephew," I said, "I would be pleased to know you if you resembled one of the gargoyles on the cathedral of Notre Dame de Paris. I'm sure you are a fine young man. Your very bearing suggests a noble heart."

"You are kind to say so," he replied. "I am told I resemble His Grace, John Churchill, Duke of Marlborough, much more closely than any of his legitimate children. His Grace is a great military hero and a chief advisor at court and does not wish to see me. Perhaps if I were not so striking a copy of His Grace as he was in his youth, it would be less embarrassing for him.

"As a result, there are no opportunities for advancement for me here. I have already fought in military campaigns on the continent and will soon return to France to continue my service to James FitzJames, Duke of Berwick, my cousin and illegitimate son of James II. Befitting, don't you think? One bye-blow serving another? In France, I find, no one starts at the sight of me and begins at once to whisper to his neighbor."

"You will fight for the French against the English?" I asked in alarm.

"France and England are at peace now," he said, "and I hope they will remain so. But I will serve Berwick in whatever he does. Our fortunes are aligned. He is as I am, a man of noble birth but without the blessing of legitimacy. There is no place for either of us here."

Tiring, no doubt, of this little tête-a-tête of mutual admiration, Aelwen broke in at last.

"So that is why you have come," she said to me, with a little color of triumph in her voice that seemed to make any notion of a warm reconciliation less likely. "Your husband has taken part in this foolish Jacobite uprising and is, as a result, a prisoner in the Tower of London. You are here because you are in need of my help."

I turned to her.

"Will you not allow for the possibility that I also simply wanted to see you again after so many years?" I pleaded. "I know we did not part on good terms and I have known very little of your life since then. But perhaps we could try to be truer sisters to each other now."

"Now that you have need of me," she replied coolly.

"You have acted before on behalf of the family," I reminded her. "You helped our brother regain Castle Banwy for the honor of the family, did you not? Now my dear husband languishes in the Tower and may be executed for treason, and, yes, I am frantic with worry for him."

I went to her and knelt—a posture I could never have imagined I would assume before my heartless, faithless sister.

"In all honesty, Aelwen, our immediate need is gold. That is true. Almost everything I had was spent getting to London through this terrible winter. Now I must supply Gavin's needs in the Tower, hire lawyers, and, if worse comes to worse, prepare to go to court to throw myself on the mercy of the king." I bowed my head against her knee, but she lifted her skirts and pulled away.

The young man, my newfound nephew, broke in.

"You must help her, Mother," he demanded. "Her husband has been taken in a noble cause. If you will not, I will. I know my duty."

I observed his shift from "Madam" to "Mother" in addressing her. I wondered if he only called her "Mother" when he wanted something from her and had learned long ago that the tender mode of address, to which he was obviously not inclined, struck some faint chord in her.

"Oh," she said, "you would have me give her the money I had reserved to pay for your equipage and continued service in France?"

To me she said, "Do get up, Bethan. You look absurd in that position. Making yourself ridiculous will not help your cause."

I stood and sat again on the opposite sofa and tried another gambit, though I was aware of the risk.

"May I not see your face, Aelwen?" I said. "It is difficult to address a specter. Those veils of yours are a barrier between us."

"She will not remove those," said young Oswald bitterly. "Why do you think she hides from the light like some nocturnal creature? Vanity must be served."

I saw Aelwen turn towards her son and then turn to me again, and, perhaps simply to spite him, she began to lift her veils, very slowly, one by one. I have to admit that I felt a rush of fear in my breast at this point. How might my sister, who had been universally acclaimed for her beauty, have ruined herself attempting to preserve her power over men?

I thought of all the terrible stories I had heard about the white face paint used by courtiers that caused inflamed blotches, scales and scabs, thinning hair, swollen eyes, loose, blackened teeth and headaches, rheumatism, even death. I held my breath, trying to prepare for what I might see, determined not to betray myself with a gasp or groan as I had when I first saw her son.

As she peeled away the layers that had concealed her, I was put in mind of snakes that shed their skins. I could not help but wonder if Aelwen's face now reflected her soured soul, and was surprised to find that I felt the stirrings of an emotion I had never associated with my detested sister. I felt pity for her, though I'm sure she had never had any for me.

At last she removed the last veil and even pulled off the lacy black cap that had further shaded her features. All the veils lay in a heap, overflowing the couch on which she sat, some trailing down onto the carpet.

What I saw was not some haggard, red-eyed hobgoblin, but merely a woman who looked her age, which I guessed to be about forty-seven, as I knew she had been a child of four when I was born. Her face was lightly lined around the cheeks and mouth and along her forehead, but there were none of the usual fan-shaped indentations at the corners of her eyes that mark the passage of laughter.

She had laughed when she was a girl. I was sure of it. But she had apparently lost the habit long ago.

Her lips were thinner and more compressed than I remembered. Her ice-blonde hair was heavily streaked with silver. Her pale blue eyes rimmed in long, pale lashes were still large and lovely, but the whites were not as clear as they had once been. I could not guess at the state of her neck or her bosom because her gloomy gown covered her right up to the chin, though that was no longer the fashion, even in mourning dress.

In a word, from what I could see, she was a handsome woman yet, but clearly no longer the splendid creature she had once been.

"You are surprised," she said, "that I have not utterly ruined myself with paints and powders of arsenic and mercury, baths of asses' milk and urine, and daily draughts of liquid gold?

"I observed the effects of these vanities on other women when I was still young and vowed that I would not destroy myself in the same way. But, as you see, age has come upon me nonetheless. So I do not go out. I would prefer that society remember me as I was."

Oswald said, "Society does not remember you at all, Madam. If you are spoken of, it is only when someone remarks that you must have died long ago."

Then he seemed to have a kindlier impulse. He gestured toward me, and I observed the gracefulness of the gesture and the fine form of his long arm.

"You see in your sister here," he said, "an image of yourself, and plainly she is lovely still. She does not hesitate to go about in the world and is intent on her cause and not overly concerned with her appearance."

"She was never a beauty to begin with, and thus never had a reputation to maintain," remarked Aelwen flatly. "She was not lifted up to a great height and had no distance to fall."

My nephew laughed, a full-throated, young man's laugh, but there was no mirth in it.

"And what was your reputation precisely, Madam?" he said. "That of a beauty who attracted too many suitors and did not keep them all at a distance—that of a woman who managed to marry three elderly noblemen in succession who no longer had the wit to see what you were."

I shrank in anticipation of the violent outburst I expected. The old Aelwen would never have tolerated such a frontal assault. I expected that this rash young man would find himself disinherited on the spot. In her fury, Aelwen would send me away with no hope of a future meeting.

To my utter surprise, Aelwen burst into tears and began groping for a black handkerchief which she pulled from her sleeve. For a moment or two, she wept into the little square of linen without restraint. Oswald and I exchanged glances. Clearly he was also taken aback by her reaction.

Then she lifted her wet face and abruptly stood, staring at me.

"Follow me," she commanded. She took the one candle and left the room. Some of the veils on the floor caught on her skirts and pulled others with them in a twisted tangle like a long train. I followed her through the darkened house and up the stairs, finally catching up and detaching the long stream of veils from her petticoats so that she might walk unhampered. She left them where they fell.

On we went, up a second staircase to the top floor of the house, every hall almost too dim to navigate and all the doors firmly closed. She reached a room lined with bookcases, though the shelves held few books. Instead there was a collection of porcelain figurines. Aelwen put the candle down on a small table and felt in the darkness along one of the shelves until her fingers reached a hidden switch. When she pushed it, one of the bookcases swung wide.

The room had only one window, heavily curtained like all the others. The candle cast such a small circle of light that I could not see what she was doing...until she used her candle to light an array of tall white tapers, and the little niche she had uncovered came to life.

It was a hidden chapel, like the one Amelia had shown me, but much more elaborate with red velvet hangings and an enormous portrait of a bleeding Christ on the cross. A rosary of gold beads with a heavy silver and gold crucifix—the cross in silver, the figure of Christ in gold—was draped across the shelf where the candles stood.

Before I could absorb this evidence of Aelwen's reversion to the Church of Rome, my sister threw herself down on the floor, fully prostrate before the improvised altar, and began to murmur the prayers of our childhood, punctuated with an occasional sob.

I could not think of anything to do but to kneel beside her and join very quietly in her prayers. After a long time she lifted herself into a kneeling position and said softly, "I only wish our Lady Mother could know that I returned to the true faith long ago. I wish she could know that priests from the Continent come to me and hide here and are fed and cared for.

"My many sins yet lie heavily on me. My life at William's court and the beginning of Queen Anne's reign was nothing but vanity and fear. As a known member of a rebellious Catholic family, I sought safety through my very public conversion to the Church of England and marriage to two lifelong Anglicans after the baron died.

"Apart from that I pursued pleasure, the pleasure of wearing magnificent gowns and jewels and being admired by all. Do you know even our cold little King William tried to seduce me while Queen Mary was still living, and more persistently after she died?

I would as soon have bedded with an adder. Besides, I knew a no-torious affair with the king would ruin me for good. My second husband was not quite such a fool as the other two."

She swiped at the tears on her face with the back of one hand and went on.

"I did not resist them all—my lofty suitors. They sent me vases overflowing with bouquets of flowers and love letters. They lavished jewels upon me. I was cautious, I was discriminating, but I was not entirely out of reach. One must do *something* with one's time."

She kept her gaze lowered as she continued her story.

"There were balls and rides in St. James's Park," she said, "and card parties and receptions where the highest lords in the land shoved each other aside to seize a stolen moment of conversation or a dance or an exchange of little notes with the most beautiful woman in England. There were afternoon rendezvous in my boudoir while my husband—whichever one—snored and dozed over his cups, and my son was safely tucked away in the nursery.

"But pleasure eventually tires one, body and soul." She sighed. "Whoever would have thought it? When the ball ended or the lover departed, I would sometimes stay in bed the next day. I could not re-member why I needed to get up. Another ball, another lover would be much the same."

She continued to dab at her nose and eyes with her black handkerchief and sniff. I was afraid to speak and, in truth, would not have known what to say to this astonishing confession. The deeds she recounted did not surprise me, knowing what I knew of her doings at the court of James II. But I never could have predicted her return to the Church or the intensity of her repentance.

So we both continued to kneel, though I was beginning to feel the cold even through the thick carpet. The room had a small fire-place but it was unlit. Aelwen rushed on, summarizing her sordid history, and it occurred to me that, having no women friends, she had not been able to tell her story to anyone, other than in the con-fessional, for many long years. Even an estranged sister was unlikely to repeat her tale, as her scandals would taint me and my family as well.

"As Oswald grew older," she said, "he became more aware of the exquisitely dressed gentlemen who would come and go, and the gold and silver coaches that waited outside.

"By then, in truth, I was already beginning to fade a little," Aelwen said. "I knew it was time to introduce my son at court, but I kept postponing the day. It never helps a woman's reputation when it is known that her children are no longer children.

"What finally happened was much worse. I watched Oswald grow into manhood very slowly and had not fully realized that his close resemblance to Churchill was inescapable. I was a fool.

"All my sins confronted me at once on that day. John Churchill, Duke of Marlborough, has become one of the great men of England and there were older courtiers who knew him quite well when he was younger. When I entered the royal reception room with my son—when we were announced—it was as if a spasm of shocked recognition, followed by whispers, flew across the hall as old gossip was recalled, revived and proven true. Illegitimate children are tolerated among the nobility and often given titles and positions, as you know, but Oswald looks like a very copy of the duke as a young man, and the duke has never appreciated humor at his own expense.

"My son has never forgiven me and has never returned to court since. My flock of would-be lovers fell away from me, repelled, not by moral considerations, but by titters and giggles. I became a figure of fun. Who wants to make love to a jest?"

At this she put her face in her hands.

All at once I saw her with stunning clarity. Aelwen had not become an entirely different being, free of her old vanity, abounding in repentance and compassion. She had simply focused her fondness for self-dramatization in a new direction. The former pinnacle of fashion and beauty had become the most penitent of sinners. I was indeed the audience she had longed for, clapped up as she was in her mausoleum of a mansion with a son disinclined to offer her his sympathy.

I thought also that Aelwen was afraid. She had abandoned the Church she had always been taught was the one true conduit to salvation and she was getting older.

I could make use of this new role of hers, I thought. Maybe she would like to see herself as the benefactor who had once saved her brother from losing his inheritance and now would save a noble brother-in-law from the gravest of perils. Maybe she would like to store up some good works in Heaven to balance against her many ill deeds.

Was this a wicked calculation on my part? Quite honestly, I would have done far more wicked things to save my husband than take advantage of my sister's extravagant penitence.

I still felt honest pity for a sister who had led such a wayward life and was now trying to repair her soul—though, having acquired the wealth of three deceased husbands, she was clearly repenting in comfort. She exhibited no inclination to cleanse herself more rigorously by retiring to Glynis' convent.

When I left Aelwen that morning, I was laden with bags of gold and wrapped with one of my sister's heaviest cloaks to hide the treasure from curious and possibly larceny-minded passers-by. Aelwen promised there would be more when I needed it—for the sake of her own soul, I knew, but I was grateful, nonetheless.

"What need have I of gold?" she said, daintily dabbing the remnants of her tears with her black handkerchief. "I have acres of it. Yet I do not spend it. I no longer dress or ride or gamble at cards or go to the theater. I used to waste enormous sums on dressmakers, shoemakers, milliners, jewelers...but no more. This is a better use for my money than accumulating vain trifles."

Oswald also promised to delay his departure to France until Gavin was safe. Though my sister could not yet be induced to leave her house, Oswald promised to give me whatever assistance he could. He vowed he would come to visit Gavin in the Tower and to Smith Square to meet the Thrupps and my Lucy, and would conspire with us to free my husband.

With my new funds in hand, I sent Lucy to secure fresh apples, small game birds that could be roasted over a hearth, good ale, meat pies, and other similar edibles that I could take to my husband. And so I continued to go to Gavin every day, sometimes with young Oswald or with Lucy in tow—bringing warm clothes and tasty delicacies, though Gavin remained drawn and gaunt. He did not speak his thoughts aloud, but I suspected it was hard for him to choke down food when he could already sense the rough rope of the hangman's noose or the swipe of the axe across his throat.

We did our best to cheer him. Oswald played the lute, and we would sometimes sing old songs and new—nothing too bawdy or too heedlessly gay, but no sorrowful laments, either, unless they concerned those who had died of love. No ballads of lost soldiers or hanged highwaymen.

Sometimes Lieutenant Compton, that solemn, humorless man of duty, even joined us and sang a few verses with us in his heavy baritone. Studying Compton closely, I eventually decided that he was very earnest about his position but neither a particularly intelligent man nor a particularly observant one, and this too could be used to our advantage.

I tried to see to it that Compton was very comfortable with me and with Lucy. We never challenged or accused him. We made no untoward demands. We never wept or begged. I wanted him to be convinced that we would cause him no trouble.

I always brought something to the Tower guards, as well, though I made no grand display of fortune. I tried to look a little reluctant when I carefully crossed their eager palms with silver, as if it hurt me a bit to reduce my small store of monies, but I wanted to be considerate of their burdens as well as my own.

For the moment all my thoughts were focused on the trials, which would soon be upon us. I prayed for mercy for my husband, although I agreed with him that mercy was unlikely. He was the highest-ranking nobleman in our part of the Lowlands and a rebel born of rebel stock. I did not think he would be pardoned, although I pretended to hope for Gavin's sake.

Chapter Twelve

Rebels at the Bar

"I feel as if I were thrown into a corner like a dead carcass. I am gnawed upon and torn by the basest and vilest creatures upon earth."

Letter from the Earl of Essex to Queen Elizabeth, May 20, 1600.

Rather than reanimating the Cause, the arrival of James III only made things worse for my husband and all the other prisoners. His landing in Scotland increased the fury of the king and Parliament.

In no time charges of high treason were drawn up against Gavin and the others—to be answered by the defendants in a mere six days. Phineas Thrupp and I scrambled to find lawyers. Many were afraid to advise such reviled rebels as these, even for gold. They were terrified of being accused of harboring a secret allegiance to the Mother Church and Rome.

Both Houses of Parliament had vowed to so utterly destroy the rebels that a like rebellion would never happen again. Every new blow that fell upon us resounded like a bell clanging in my head—a funeral bell that seemed to be ringing already for my husband, weakening my resolve to save him by instructing me that his fate was already sealed.

Would Father Jerome, if he were with me, advise me that Gavin would rise again with Christ among the Blessed by dying a martyr to the sacred cause of the Most Holy Roman Catholic Church? In being so determined to save Gavin, was I working against God's will?

That unworthy thought brought me to my senses and banished the bells from my mind for good. I prayed to the Blessed Virgin daily and I was certain in my inmost soul that *she* did not want me to abandon my fight for my husband's life.

The world is full of martyrs, some willing, more unwilling. So many had already died for the Chevalier that my husband's sacrifice was not needed. I *required* him to live. His children demanded that he live. I became quite stubbornly set on my mission to save him and no longer harbored contrary notions, even for an instant.

Before my husband and the others were sentenced, our true king, the Chevalier, had already left England. He had only been in his kingdom for a month. He sailed away from a little cove near Montrose, Scotland, on the fourth of February, taking the Earl of Mar and other lofty Jacobite gentlemen with him, and leaving all the rest to their fate.

It appeared that Mar, who had proven himself an utter failure as a military leader, was at least skilled at arranging escapes, especially his own. At the time of their departure, though, I had little thought to spare for them. My whole heart was for my husband.

One afternoon Lucy and Gavin and Oswald and I sat in the Lieutenant's Lodgings with the two lawyers Phineas had finally procured for us. Neither was very prepossessing, though we had been assured they were perfectly sound in their craft. Matthew Chipping was a nervous, neat little man with a well-trimmed dark beard and a few sparse hairs neatly spread over a high-domed bald head that gleamed as if he had been polishing it nightly. When he came to visit us at the Tower, he hired a public coach and so enshrouded himself in his cloaks within his carriage that passers-by might have thought he was a ghost haunting the docks.

Jeremy Wimborne was broad and tall and had rather too much hair, very thick and unruly. I'm sure he must have given up any effort to comb it long before we knew him. In fact, there were probably pieces of broken combs embedded deep in those wild, tangled locks. His face was blocky and blunt-featured, but somewhat redeemed by warm, observant brown eyes. He, at least, conveyed an aura of interest and concern for his client. Both Chipping and Wimborne seemed to heartily enjoy the good ale that Aelwen's gold had provided.

Oddly, Chipping had a deep voice and Wimborne's was high-pitched, just the opposite of what one would have expected. But, as different as they were, they were united in their opinions of Gavin's case.

"You have no choice, my lord," rumbled Chipping, "much as it pains me to say it. You must declare yourself guilty and throw yourself on the mercy of the court. That is your only possible hope of saving your life." Here he took an enormous handkerchief from his coat pocket and blew so furiously that his well-regulated little features turned scarlet for a moment.

"You cannot deny, sir," piped Wimborne, "that you committed the acts of which you are accused. You took up arms against your duly anointed sovereign. You even rounded up others and prevailed on them to fight with you."

"Not 'duly anointed,'" growled Gavin. "I can never allow that."

"You may not accept the fact, my lord," said Wimborne, "but according to the law, George of Hanover is the king."

Wimborne looked around as if he expected to find Lt. Compton leaning over his shoulder, lowered his voice and added, "And he had better be your king when you face your judges in Westminster Hall, sir. Quibbling over his right to the throne in that company will convince the court that you are not only a rebel, but a very hardened and stubborn one. You must not in any way attempt to plead the cause of the Stuarts to explain your rebellious actions. You may say..." Wimborne put his meaty elbow on his knee, leaned his long chin into his palm and appeared to give some thought to what Gavin should say.

"How can I tell lies?" Gavin interrupted. He could still be very obstinate when it came to what he would do and say in public before all the lords and the rabble as well.

"How can I maintain that I was duped into fighting?" he asked. "They know the history of my family these three generations past—and her family, as well," nodding at me.

"You must suit yourself," said Chipping, "but it will not serve you if you declaim the rights of Catholics to liberty in religion and the right of the Stuarts to rule, and review the reasons why a foreign prince should never reign over us...and *then* beg for mercy. Your argument will be shouted down."

"I must think," said Gavin, and dismissed them. Chipping seemed unwilling to leave the good ale behind, but I believe Wimborne was unwilling to leave both the ale and his client.

"Do not despair, my lord," Wimborne said, as he wrapped himself in his voluminous cloak. "We will speak of this again tomorrow."

When they were gone, Gavin said, "Nothing will change tomorrow. I am going to die."

His voice was weak and guttural from a recent chest ailment. I did not like the look of him. He was thinner than ever, despite all the good food we had brought him. His skin was sallow and loose as his face became leaner. Even when we built up the fire and wrapped him in the thickest blankets, he trembled from the cold. His beautiful dark eyes glittered with fever in his thin face. I sometimes feared he would not live long enough for me to save him.

Thus, I felt I must be ever cheerier and stifle my weeping when I was with him. I must give all my thought to doing him good. When I was there to beg him to keep his strength up, he ate a little. If it was just the two of us, he sometimes even allowed me to spoon porridge or bits of meat into his mouth.

It hurt me to watch him. My proud hawk of a Scottish lord did not seem to mind that he had been reduced to such a state. He clung to me so tightly and seemed so reluctant to see me leave—that I feared when I was gone, he would forget to eat at all. But I could not allow myself to sink with him into despair. I asked Lucy and Oswald to wait outside for a few moments so I could speak privately with my husband.

As soon as their footsteps had ceased to echo on the stairs, I showed Gavin my anger for the first time. I seized his bony hand and forced him to look at me.

"We are all working so hard for you, Husband," I said. "You must allow yourself a particle of faith! Lucy and Phineas and Amelia and Oswald and I are plotting every day to develop new plans to supersede any that fail. I have *absolute* faith that we can save you, but if you have already given up, we can do nothing for you. All I ask is that you fight for yourself! You must eat even when you have no appetite. You must pray. You must charm your gaolers. Help us, Husband. Add your might to ours."

I told him I would feed him no more. He had to make the effort to stay in this world with me, or everything we did would come to naught. He bowed his head and said nothing, but the next day he did look a bit brighter and from there, he began to add flesh to his body and color to his face.

The happenings of February 9 at Westminster Hall, however, would have discouraged a stronger band than we few. Lucy did not want me to attend, but I told her I could not leave Gavin to face the judges and the crowds alone, no matter how the condemnation we knew he would face would lacerate my heart.

We arrived early to get a seat because we knew all of London would seek entry to see the Jacobite lords condemned. I had not given any thought to how much being in Westminster Hall again would remind me of the glorious Coronation Day of April 23, 1685, when King James II came to the throne. I remembered the yards and yards of blue carpeting that stretched from Westminster Hall to Westminster Abbey for that resplendent procession of royalty and the nobility, celebrating what we thought would be a new era of religious tolerance in England. How miserably our hopes had been brought low, destroyed by the grasping ambitions of the high who wanted to keep power in the hands of the Anglicans, and the ignorance and wayward passions of the low, who had been so cleverly taught to hate and fear all Catholics.

Lucy and I entered Westminster Hall through an entrance designated exclusively for the quality, and yet were jostled and stepped on as we squeezed into our seats in the front row of the pews set up for us. The commoners came in through another, meaner entrance and had to stand behind the pews.

I could hear the squeaks and cries and cackles and grumbles of the mob throughout the trial. Their language was barely intelligible to my ears, accustomed as I was now to the Scots' burr. That was

147

something of a relief because I did not want to understand what they might be saying about my husband.

The London mob was even worse-behaved than I remembered from my childhood, gabbling, guffawing, quarreling—all at a volume loud enough to raise the souls buried in Westminster Abbey. Not one in a hundred, I thought, had any understanding that German Geordie was a false king and James, the true one, nor that Catholics were as devoted to their country as any Church of Englander or Dissenter.

Members of the House of Lords and the House of Commons proceeded into the hall and were seated. The Lords were arrayed in their red robes with white collars, trimmed with white ermine bars, and gold oak leaf lace. The Commons were mostly dressed in black frock coats and powdered wigs. Even the Prince of Wales, another George, was present, sitting in a large box by himself, a tall, red-faced man past his first youth with the infamous, bulging blue Hanoverian eyes.

All was done with great pomp and ceremony. These puffed-up members of Parliament were enormously satisfied with themselves, though they were but debased servitors to a fraudulent king.

I was told by an eager little woman on my left that it was the Lord High Steward, William Cowper himself, who sat down on the fabled woolsack, a large, stuffed cushion covered in scarlet. Cowper was a spindly, ungainly man with an enormous silver wig and a very long face. I noted with satisfaction that he seemed to be having some difficulty balancing on his woolsack. Under other circumstances it might have been difficult not to titter as I watched him lean to one side and then the other, trying to avoid an ignominious spill.

The rituals that ensued were tedious flummery. The king's commission was read, authorizing the trial of the rebels while all the Peers stood, uncovering their heads. The Sergeant-at-Arms bawled out, "God save the king!" The Herald and the Gentleman Usher of the Black Rod made three bows, knelt and presented the White Staff of office to the Steward, who—gratefully, I have no doubt—removed himself from the woolsack to a broad chair with arms.

At last the prisoners were brought in—my husband,

Derwentwater and Kenmure, along with others, William Lord Widdrington, Robert Earl of Carnwath and William Lord Nairn. Winton was supposed to be among them but, for some reason, was not.

I knew my husband had clothed himself in layers of his warmest clothes and had thrown on his heaviest cloak, a handsome dark blue, over all, so that, as he told me, he would not be thought to be shivering in fear when he was merely shivering with cold. I had brought him a simple, pigtailed wig to cover his head, now closely shorn, so he would not so much resemble a common prisoner.

Lord Kenmure, standing next to him, was a stalwart, older man with a long gray beard and very plain dress, who showed no emotion during the proceedings. Poor Derwentwater and Carnwath, almost as young as Derwentwater, touched my heart. They seemed barely beyond the age of children to me. They were far too young to be forced to play the role of men who were resigned to their fate and were prepared to die for the Chevalier.

I did not think Derwentwater shamed himself when he had to scrub at his face from time to time to brush away the tears that rolled over his full, rosy cheeks. His voice did not break when he spoke, but how hard it must be to face death when all of life yet stands before you!

When it was Gavin's turn to plead on his own behalf, I could not breathe but pride ran through me like a fire. His voice was clear and carried well, even in the great hall, though he did not seem to be shouting.

He began by assuring the Lords that he had never at any time intended any harm to the person of King George. This was true. Then he went on to imply that he had joined the Rebellion almost by accident and did not fully comprehend what was going on until they "were actually in arms."

This was a lie. But I could not fault him for this. Whatever ploy he thought might save him was more than acceptable to me. I had no desire for him to spit at the judges and be forcibly dragged from the hall.

Gavin spent most of the time given to him explaining that he had only surrendered at Preston because he had been assured many times most honorably by the king's men that the king would be merciful to him. This was entirely true. They had indeed assured him of Little Geordie's mercy.

He finished by declaring that he was entirely dependent on His Majesty's goodness and promised that if he were spared, he "would pay the utmost duty and gratitude to His Most Gracious Majesty, and the highest veneration and respect to Your Lordships and the Honorable House of Commons." I knew that uttering these words pained him greatly, but I could not begrudge him his effort to put his case in the best light.

As soon as all the prisoners had spoken, the Lord High Steward began to intone upon their sins and, despite Gavin's express denial of any desire to kill George, accused them all of waging war in order to "depose and murder" King George. He commented, oddly, that their religion alone was some sort of partial mitigation for the Catholics among the rebels, because it was natural that they should wish to engage in treason in order to restore the Roman Catholic faith throughout the land—which, of course, was not at all their intention. Catholics and Protestants alike who had joined the rebellion simply wanted a real English king and freedom for everyone to worship as they pleased.

Soon enough, we saw that my husband had humbled himself to no purpose. The Lord High Steward was finally done lecturing the prisoners and had now come to the part that he no doubt enjoyed most, though he claimed he took no pleasure in it. I had nourished very little hope that my husband might be spared execution, but Cowper's pronouncement was even worse than I had expected.

Cowper declaimed that all the men before him would be executed for high treason and further, that, although it was customary for "persons of your quality" to avoid the most shameful and excruciating portions of the penalty for treason, this time they would be forced to suffer the same punishment meted out to commoners. He then described it in detail: They would each be hanged by the neck, cut down while still living and disemboweled with the bowels and other body parts to be burned before their eyes. Finally they would be decapitated and quartered, the quarters to be sent to various parts of the kingdom and displayed as the king commanded.

I heard those words as if from a great distance, or as if my ears were covered and stoppered. I did not faint or scream. The world tilted. I was no longer seeing the judges and the prisoners and the crowd of Londoners, though I could hear them now, unleashed, screaming their unintelligible insults and oaths at the condemned as they were taken out.

I found I was lying on my back, cushioned by my thick cloak, though I could not remember falling. I lay, in a state of quiet detachment, observing the heavy oak hammerbeams, curved braces and multipaneled windows of the ceiling of Westminster Hall high above me. The sunlight of the winter day shattered against every windowpane.

At that moment I was not exactly thinking of my beloved husband. That pain would strike soon enough. I was puzzled because nowhere, in all this expanse of space, did I feel the presence of the sacred benefactress of my life, the Blessed Virgin.

I have said before that faith did not come as easily to me as it did to Glynis and my mother. But my love for the Blessed Virgin was different. I did often feel her presence when I reached out to her in need. I could put my heart in her hand. I could lay my head down on her knee. There was solace where she was.

But at this moment I felt her absence like the void of space between where I had fallen and the pinnacle of the vault far above me. All the air around me was empty and white. The blankness hurt my eyes and filled me with fear.

Had My Lady abandoned me just when I most desperately needed her? I wondered if perhaps she had just, at long last, taken off my leading strings and left me to walk on my own?

Whether she was testing my ability to survive without her, or had abandoned me for good, I knew with complete certainty whom I could rely upon instead. She had left me with all the supporters I needed, bless them. Lucy helped me to my feet, guided me out of the Hall and led me the short distance back to Smith Square.

Chapter Thirteen

Painting the Lily

To gild refined gold, to paint the lily,
To throw a perfume on the violet,
To smooth the ice, or add another hue
Unto the rainbow, or with taper-light
To seek the beauteous eye of heaven to garnish,
Is wasteful and ridiculous excess.

King John, William Shakespeare

I knew that, once Gavin was condemned, I was not supposed to be allowed to visit him again until the night before his execution. I also knew that my modest bribes would gain entry for me, as usual. My heart had been sickened by the trial and the terrible sentence, and I feared what I would find when I visited Gavin again, but there was no time for me to mourn. I must continue to visit and hide my fear to keep Gavin from total collapse.

Occasionally prisoners became so despondent that they found ways to accomplish their own end long before their execution. I remembered that Sir Walter Raleigh had tried to kill himself with a table knife, and afterwards was released from his imprisonment for a time. What if he had succeeded and never known that time of freedom?

There were also practical reasons for me to continue to culti-vate the goodwill of the warders. I had as yet vague notions in my head as to what I might do to save my husband if my plea for mercy was rejected, but any plan would necessitate a close knowledge of the Tower guards and an open and friendly manner with them.

My readmission to the Tower was also eased because Lt.

Compton had gone home to visit his family on the outskirts of London for a few days. His apartments below Gavin's were empty. Perhaps the Queen of Heaven was keeping an eye on us, after all.

Thomas Brickle was as eager as ever to accept whatever I wanted to give him and to take me to my lord—as was old Godfrey Hatton, who bobbed and swayed from side to side when he led me to the Lieutenant's Lodgings, like a sailor who had just come off ship after a six months' journey. He was a small man with a small head on which the warder's hat slid down over his sparse, gray eyebrows. With few teeth left, he gummed his food and was grateful for the soft pastries I brought.

Hatton had told me the entire story of how he had fought the French for William of Orange in the Nine Years' War and had been grievously wounded in 1695 when William's forces seized the town of Namur. Hatton described at great length how his leg had been opened up to the bone by a sword slice just as the city was surrendering and the battle was ending.

The surgeons told him he was the last Englishman injured in the battle. They also threatened to take his leg off, but he wept bitterly, moaning that he would rather die than be a one-legged cripple, so they left him to it. The wound healed on its own, and he recovered. But, in healing, the wound drew the one leg up shorter than the other, and he would always afterwards totter unbalanced like a drunk when he walked. He had been given the position of Tower warder as a reward for his service.

I had listened to his story with much show of interest and concern, and old Hatton had grown fond of me. He had no wife or children and the men around him had tired of his longwinded tale of how he had fallen doing battle for his country. In all his life it was the only event of note. I had no concern at the time that Hatton would hinder my plans.

I gradually grew to know some of the other yeomen warders as well. There was Horace Bigelow who was so fat that, when he stood up, he hoisted his enormous belly with both hands to maneuver it into an upright position. His bristly black beard spread like a fan of ferns over his upper chest so that it was difficult to ascertain what manner of man lay beneath beard and belly. He was quicker to grab at the little meat pasties I brought than at my handfuls of coins.

Merton Tewkins was, by contrast, a lean spindle of a boy, too young to grow a beard, who was constantly teased by the other men because he almost never spoke except when required to respond to an order or report on the prisoners. When he accepted a small gift from me, he would sheepishly doff his hat. Once he murmured his thanks softly, hoping the others wouldn't hear. But they did hear and teased him until his face was redder than his uniform. He never spoke word more to me after that.

Sergeant Matthew Putnam, on the other hand, was a man with a carefully tended moustache, who might have been handsome, had it not been for a deep scar that pulled down one corner of his mouth. Hatton whispered to me that Putnam had a tendency to drink to excess but kept it generally under control when he was on duty. Putnam, like Hatton, had fought in France, where he suffered his wound, but he had been an aide to an officer and had returned with a smattering of the manners and speech of his betters.

Whenever he saw me, Putnam pulled off his hat, made a low bow, and, whether it was a fine day or foul, said, "How are you, this lovely day, my lady?" I knew he was married and a father, but the other men, fairly or not, regarded him as a lady's man, mistaking courtesy, I thought, for flirtation. Putnam's courtesy would give me a bad moment before long, though he intended no harm.

I always spent a little time with the warders after I left Gavin, feeling sure that my affability would be rewarded in their care for my husband. They loved to regale me with legends of the Tower and tried to convince me that the grounds were haunted by Anne Boleyn or Katherine Howard or the Little Princes who were murdered in the Tower. But after my lord's sentencing, the warders told me no more of these little histories of woe and premature death, which was a mercy. They bowed when I arrived and bowed again when I left, and I thought I saw traces of sympathy on their bluff faces.

There was a new warder come to the Tower though who did concern me, one Aldrich Harrow. Young Harrow was long and angular with an outward manner that seemed almost sleepy. He had a slight, pointed, dark beard and even slighter wisp of a moustache, as if, though not as callow as Tewkins, he was not yet fully grown. I would see him folded up upon himself, knees almost to chin, half sitting, half lying against the stone wall when he had finished his rounds of the prisoners' cells, eyes at half-mast so that the other warders teased him about trying to steal a nap when he was on duty.

But I thought that, under his lowered lids, this Aldrich Harrow was always watching me with his little black eyes. When others thought he was dozing, I would catch him staring, and I did not like the look of him. I tried to draw him into conversation, but he had very little to say to me, though, like the others, he took the coins and treats I handed out. He would always be the last to accept a bun or a muffin with a laconic laying out of his open palm as if he were doing me a favor. There were never any thanks from him. I thought he was more observant than the others and was suspicious of my comings and goings.

"Never mind him," said Thomas Brickle to me one day. "He's a Dissenter and hates all Catholics. I caught him once keeping money that had been given to buy food for a Catholic prisoner. And he says to me, 'What care you if he eats? He's a *papist*.'"

"And I say, 'And what says you to the king if yon prisoner dies of starvation before they can carve him up?'"

This, of course, was meant, in Brickle's crude way, to curry favor with me and earn more coins. But it was a warning, I thought, that I should take seriously.

I had anticipated with dread that Gavin would be prostrate in agonies of fear after what he had heard that day. Much to my surprise, when I came to him that evening after the day in court, I found him a changed man. He was alone, calmly going through papers from the lawyers, drafts of a general petition to be presented to Parliament begging mercy for all those condemned that day.

He looked up at me, and I saw the old bright alertness and warm coloring in his face overlaid with a new serenity I had not seen before. He told me at once one reason for his composure. The lawyers had come to visit and informed him that, despite the display of severity for the public in court that afternoon, Gavin and his fellows would *not* be partially hanged and then ritually butchered as if they were commoners. They were, after all, to be accorded the nobleman's right to the executioner's axe.

This would seem to be little reason for increased composure, but my husband had been relieved of his worst fears—not only of the terrible pain of prolonged torture, but the dreadful humiliation. Strong, brave men subjected to a traitor's death had been known to snivel and weep and scream and beg during their last minutes on earth, bereft of all dignity and taunted by the avid crowds.

Once freed of his worst fear, Gavin's immediate concern was not for himself. Wimborne had told him of the sufferings of the commoners who had surrendered to the English at Preston and elsewhere. Twenty-six of the minor leaders had been summarily executed. Many of the rest, most of them Roman Catholic gentlemen of Cumberland and Northumberland, and their servants, were closely confined at Preston, Chester and Liverpool. As they were kept in close quarters with little food or shelter, disease overcame them and a large number had died. Hundreds of those who remained among the living had been transported to the West Indies where they were sold for forty shillings a head to work the plantations.

"Free men made slaves to slake the thirst for revenge of this implacable tyrant!" exclaimed Gavin, his face dark with fury. "All because they dared to give their allegiance to their rightful king."

I seized his hand, which had been so fragile a week before, his long fingers almost reduced to bone. Now it felt solid again. I raised it to my lips. With all our years together and all my admiration for him, I don't think I had ever loved my husband so much as I did at this moment. Death's shadow stalked him, and yet he had turned his thoughts to the sufferings of others.

I did not speak my own dreary thoughts, sensing that it was better to allow him to put his troubles aside and think on other men for a little while. Instead I asked him what he had heard of Winton, who had not been in court.

To my immense surprise, my husband burst out in a hearty laugh, the likes of which I had not heard from him since before he left for the war. It caused my heart to smile a little, even while I'm sure my face merely expressed shock.

"Wimborne learned that Winton came before the Judges last week," Gavin said. "They separated his case from the rest of us because they think he is mad. He acted as though he could not comprehend any of their questions. He steadfastly denied everything and refused to plead guilty! He declared that his estate had been attacked by the East Lothian militia and that he had been forced to flee, had ended up taking refuge with Jacobite rebels, and had been swept up in the rebellion by accident.

"This nonsense was apparently delivered with that intense stare of his and his strange laugh that bursts forth at the most unlikely moments. Wimborne says the Lords are much caught up in talk of his lunacy and whether or not it is just to condemn a madman to a traitor's death."

Glad to see that Gavin continued to focus on the fate of others, I responded that I thought Winton might be no madman but indeed the shrewdest of them all. Gavin laughed again.

"Thus it appears," he said. "But I'm not sure his ploy will succeed. There are witnesses who can report that he left his castle on his own with a force of men behind him. Wimborne predicts that he will be condemned in time, but no sentence has been imposed on him yet."

We came to the main business at hand.

"I intend to plead for you to the king," I said. "The lawyers are preparing a petition for mercy which I will present to the king myself. I am going to challenge his supposed reputation for 'mercy' in full view of his entire court."

Gavin turned solemn again and took both my hands in his. He started to speak, but then I saw that his eyes were brimming over and he could not.

Finally he said, "I would not see you humble yourself before that vile creature posing as king."

"The people of Britain have always had the right to petition their king for redress," I said. "He cannot deny me my right. As for humbling myself, there is no shame in seeking a pardon for my husband."

"But from such a one as he..." said Gavin, shaking his head.

"What if he refuses to see you?"

"He cannot," I said grimly. "I have discussed this with Aelwen and with Amelia, who goes to court sometimes. Geordie attends open assemblies each night at St. James's. Anyone properly attired in court costume is admitted. I will accost him, and he will not be able to avoid me."

"By all accounts he is an uncouth man with none of the bearing of a true king," said Gavin. "He may refuse to accept your plea or may throw it down and trample on it. What if he orders his guards to arrest you for importuning him?"

"For following the time-honored custom of petitioning the king? No. If he is cruel, if he violates all custom, he will shame himself before his entire court. Who will not pity a wife pleading for her husband's life?"

Gavin released my hands, sat back and muttered, "If you shame him before all, my prospects may become even worse."

"Perhaps I will give him an excuse to be merciful," I said. "In any case, all the wives are also presenting a petition to Parliament. I believe you hold a draft of it in your hands."

As he regarded the papers he held thoughtfully, I added with some hesitancy, "I have the barest beginnings of another plan in mind. But we must try my plea for mercy first. It will be dramatic. I will be appropriately gowned and will make an impression, I promise you. That is the advantage of lodging with a silk merchant." I smiled, as if I eagerly anticipated confronting the king.

That evening Amelia, Lucy and I began to plan my court costume.

"We must create something that will give you entry to St. James's," said Amelia, "but will not make you the object of everyone's eyes. Although, truth be told, the costumes at the Court of St. James's today are all so fantastical that it would be difficult to draw unusual attention to oneself by means of dress alone."

When Amelia began to show me sketches of court costumes she had designed for other members of the aristocracy to wear during appearances at St. James's, I was astounded. The *habit de cour* in England, called a "mantua" from the French word for *cloak*, was even more outlandish than the regalia I had worn when I visited Versailles with King James and Queen Mary Beatrice. I would not have thought that was possible.

The sheer spread of the mantua's massive hoop skirts was at least six times the width of a woman of normal size. Amelia explained that women dressed in this fashion had to fold their hoops up like wings to enter a carriage or sedan chair or to pass through an ordinary doorway. Jonathan Swift had remarked that a woman could hide "a moderate gallant" under one of those skirts to keep her company.

"And then there is the wig and the headdress," Amelia said. "When you are sitting in a sedan chair, you must lean back so that the headdress may protrude through the opening in the top of the chair and you must not move your head!"

"May we not," I begged, "concoct some modification of this masquerade? Some more modest width of skirt and height of headdress?"

"Not if you wish to gain entrance," said Amelia. She took Lucy and me upstairs to see her own court costumes. Each was housed in a separate wardrobe, complete with the accompanying precious-stone encrusted high-heeled slippers, the fans, the wig and the ribbons, lace, feathers and ropes of pearls used to dress the wig.

Amelia picked up one of my loose locks and looked at it thoughtfully.

"I see that your own hair is plentiful, and you could, as I have done, pomade and pile your hair up over some padding, and then add the bits of jewels and other frills that will complete your ensemble. But, honestly my dear, you will so mangle and dirty your own hair in the preparation that it is easier to simply wear a wig to carry off the costume."

I put a hand to my head as if to see if my own hair was still there. I knew my sandy brown tresses were now laced with silver, but they still felt silky and full. I decided it would be an absurd and destructive vanity to insist on using my own hair, although I knew wearing the wig instead would only be a different kind of misery.

It would take at least two weeks, Amelia said, to create the costume, even if the seamstresses worked night and day. I did not know exactly how much time we had, but I was sure the date for Gavin's execution could be announced any day.

I still had plenty of Aelwen's gold and she had promised more. I asked Amelia if additional money would pay for more seamstresses to work faster. Amelia said that was possible. We would inquire.

The very next morning, not long after cockcrow, Amelia conducted Lucy and me in sedan chairs to Spitalfields, the neighborhood where the silk weavers lived, to visit with James Leman, a renowned weaver and creator of fabric designs. Amelia had praised him as a very genius of the silk master's art, whom she had befriended when he was a young apprentice. I found him to be a tall, soft-spoken, self-effacing gentleman in a full, black peruke, wearing a subdued, dark-brown frock coat. When we were introduced, he was standing in his shop with lengths of satin and silk spread over both his extended arms, that were so bright with rich colors and shapes, both geometric and botanical, that my eyes were bedazzled.

In the midst of all my troubles, visiting James Leman's shop during London's early-morning bustle and industry, was like finding a hidden plot of early daffodils sparkling with dew under sloping willow branches after a heavy fall of winter snow. I was so astonished by this sudden display of an excess of beauty that tears stung my eyes.

The exquisite fabrics shimmered with a rich luster. I hesitated to touch them for fear of profaning their splendor. And such a profusion of patterns! Wrought into the silk were many-petaled flowers in every possible gorgeous hue, images of deep-watered ponds fringed with ferns, lush pears and apples, golden-domed cupolas, arches, columns and fountains. My eyes kept returning to one length of satin that displayed a pattern of leaves and flowers in shades of emerald, celadon, myrtle, cerulean, indigo, heliotrope, crimson, periwinkle and chestnut, splashed and curled across a lattice of gold squares.

Mr. Leman, alert to the unspoken inclinations of his clients, immediately saw that this was the fabric that most attracted me. He lifted that length of satin away from all the others and asked if he might drape it over my shoulders. As soon as he did, Amelia and

Lucy broke out in smiles and agreed at once that my mantua must be made of this material.

There followed an endless morning of dozens of measurements, interspersed with debates over the best length for the train and whether silver or ivory-gold lace should be used to trim the sleeves and the neckline. Mr. Leman was permitted no scope for his genius in the overall shape of the gown. All mantuas were essentially the same—a long train in back falling straight from the shoulders, a pinched-in whalebone bodice, the same square neckline front and back, elbow-length sleeves with precisely three rows of stiff ruffles, and, of course, the enormous skirts, like immense humps on each side of the body.

I simply could not imagine how female courtiers navigated the halls or the Grand Reception Room of St. James's encased in this absurdity. St. James's was not a palace of grand dimensions. Weren't the women's petticoats and trains constantly tangling with or blocking each other? I was told that, when one wore the mantua, one was forced to walk with tiny steps. One learned to glide soundlessly across the floor.

When we were finally done with Mr. Leman, we were far from finished with the expedition. We had yet to visit the shoemaker and the master of wigs.

I refused to visit a jeweler. I was loath to spend Aelwen's gold on jewels that I would only wear for one night. Most of my own jewels were buried under the snow at Heath Hall, but I had sewed a few of the most valuable into the lining of one of my dresses and could cut free my mother's ruby ring set in gold for this occasion. Amelia insisted that I wear her own pearl eardrops and wind her own strands of pearls into my wig.

I was so exhausted by the time we reached the wigmaker that my mood had changed entirely from the elation of the morning. Before he was done trying various creations on my head, as I argued strenuously for the simplest structure that would be adequate, I found myself suddenly weeping for no reason. Lucy dabbed at my eyes with her handkerchief and asked the wigmaker and Amelia to leave the two of us alone sitting before the array of mirrors in the fitting room.

"What is it, my dear?" she asked with unaccustomed gentleness.

"My husband is condemned to death and I am wasting treasure we may need on this frippery...satin, lace, silver and gold metallic thread, a vast expanse of hoops and petticoats, shoes that would not last a day in the streets, a needless wig of ridiculous proportions...in short, an outrageously preposterous costume that I will never wear again," I wailed, and then almost began laughing and crying at the same time at my own folly.

Lucy patted my shoulder and whispered in my ear.

"No, my dear," she said. "You are simply doing what you must. Amelia is proposing to buy everything from you after your evening at court. She will have the gown remade and resold to another woman who will never even know it has been worn before."

The plan, of course, was to slip into St. James's Palace and perform my mission according to longstanding ritual, and then slip out again. I would barely be noticed. No one would remember what I had been wearing. My purpose was to blend in with the rest of the monkeys on display, not to stand out among them.

When we returned to Smith Square, we learned that, with the help of connections, and the charm and beauty of the young Countess of Derwentwater, Parliament had indeed passed a petition for clemency that day, but it only asked the king to "reprieve such of the condemned lords as deserve his mercy."

The next day an order was given out to spare Widdrington, Carnwath and Nairn. But Kenmure and Derwentwater were not to be pardoned.

Nor would Lord Clarencefield be reprieved. The Glentaggarts had always been for the Stuarts. That was their fate. Now that allegiance would be the cause of Gavin's death if I could not find a way to save him.

While we waited with increasing fear for the mantua to be finished, Amelia dressed me in one of her own court costumes so that I could practice the difficulties of moving in the wretched apparatus. The first time I took a single step across the carpet, my shoe caught and I tumbled over, petticoats and hoops flying over my head. The help of two maids was required to help me right myself.

"You see the problem now," said Amelia, watching me thoughtfully. She put her chin on her palm, as if she were thinking, but I think it was to cover her smile.

"This is precisely why you must practice every day until the time comes," she said. "After you've learned to walk on a flat surface, you must learn to manage a staircase—upstairs and down. Then we will take you outside and attempt to bundle you into a sedan chair. Finally we will add the wig. Remember, I said you must take tiny, tiny steps. If you attempt to stride, the mantua will surely send you head over heels and foil your purpose."

Every day Amelia had her maids lace me more tightly and warned me that, although the Great Drawing Room would be lined with tables of sweetmeats, the ladies never attempted to consume anything other than champagne while wearing the mantua.

"Once you are laced into the mantua," said Amelia, "there is no place for food to go. If you try to eat something, you will make yourself miserable and possibly ill."

"No fear of that," I said. "I am not going to court to try Geordie's table."

"We will have little to do but stand around and fan ourselves," Amelia said, "perhaps for an hour or two...or even longer. I have observed that the king does not enjoy these receptions and tends to arrive as late as possible. They say he is awkward in company and embarrassed by his lack of knowledge of the English language.

"But I think he is also bad-tempered by nature and sorry that he ever abandoned his little provincial capital for the maelstrom of England. Plucking him from Hanover and installing him as king of England was like putting a small child in an oversized suit of armor on a big horse and forcing him to joust in a tournament. He is unfit by nature and ill-prepared by any sort of study or training."

"He is certainly welcome to crawl back inside the undistinguished burrow from whence he came," I said. "We have no desire to keep him here." We smiled wryly at each other.

We knew there was precious little chance that Geordie would leave the English throne willingly, no matter how uncomfortable he found his new position. Being jumped up to a position of much more grandeur than he had ever known, appealed, no doubt, to his pride and his avarice. He might not relish the experience, but there had been no sign that he was going to loosen his grasp on the great prize he had won in the royal lottery. Nor would his entourage of German courtiers willingly return to playing whist in a barnyard when they could play for much larger stakes in gold and property on the world's stage.

To my amazement, my mantua was completed in only one week. I suspected Amelia had paid even more than I had for additional seamstresses to work on the gown so that it could be finished with remarkable speed. But I did not ask her. I was already so deeply in her debt, morally and financially. We were well aware that the order of execution could be handed down any day. What good would my trip to court do for my husband if it came too late?

While I waited, I had little to do but think, and I began in earnest to map out in my mind various schemes for saving Gavin if my petition to the king was unsuccessful. I had noticed that, despite the rules, as the time of execution drew inevitably closer, there were more and more visitors to the condemned men in the Tower. It was only natural, was it not, that those who loved a man who was doomed to die—family, longtime friends—would want to spend time with him before he left them for good? I presume that most of these visitors bribed the warders, as I did, to gain entry despite the rule that condemned men could receive no visitors until the night before their executions. But I believe the Derwentwater women were exceptions.

Anna Maria, the young Countess of Derwentwater, came to see her husband every day, accompanied by his mother, Mary, Dowager Countess of Derwentwater, a grand old dame with a regal bearing. The woman was still handsome at her great age, with a long nose, high cheekbones and large eyes sunk deep in their sockets. Her face bore the marks of both sorrow and a fierce will to command that suggested she had long been used to being obeyed.

But she was not able to command German George. She and gentle, downcast Anna Maria had both already presented petitions for mercy to Geordie at court, but their petitions were not granted.

They now came daily to the Tower, hunched over with fear and horror to sit and weep with the young Earl.

Even the warders pitied them and let them through without asking for gifts. I could imagine the look the Dowager Countess would have given Brickle had he put out his hand and demanded that his palm be crossed with silver. Such a look, from a woman about to have her beloved son taken from her, was a visible curse that could wither and destroy a man as surely as an arrow to the heart.

The young countess did often tell the warders she would pray for them as well as for her lord and that seemed to touch even Brickle. She was a simply dressed, pale, fragile, little thing with limp, flaxen hair and light green eyes, but, despite her obvious dislike of being stared at, she had done her best for her husband. She had dared to plead for him in Parliament. She had gone to beg the Hanoverian to commute his sentence. Nothing had availed her.

I lay awake at night wondering if I should embrace her and bring her into my circle, if it might be possible to save *two* condemned men. But my courage failed me. What I was thinking of attempting would be immensely difficult and could well lead to my execution as well as Gavin's. I did not dare complicate the task further. Still my heart sank every time I saw her and witnessed her despair.

In the end the Countess of Derwentwater proved more audacious than she looked. There was a persistent rumor after her lord was executed that she had disguised herself as a fishwife and driven a cart under Temple Bar, having bribed some people to remove her husband's head from the spike on which it was placed and throw it down to her so it could be properly buried and not left to rot and be picked apart by birds. And, truly, after his execution, Lord Derwentwater's head did not appear among those that decorated the iron spikes atop Temple Bar.

I have heard ballads written about the poor lad, some in the name of Lord Derwentwater and some in the name of Lord "Allenwater," which does have a more lilting rhythm. It was said that young John Radclyffe was the most generous lord in northern

England and had given bread to hundreds of the poor folk without regard to their faith.

The speech young Derwentwater gave on the scaffold has survived to this day. It concludes:

> I die a Roman Catholic: I am in perfect clarity with all
> the world (I thank God for it), even with those of the
> present Government, who are most instrumental in my
> death. I freely forgive all such as ungenerously reported
> false things of me; and hope to be forgiven the trespasses
> of my youth by the Father of Mercies, into whose hands
> I commend my soul. If that Prince who now governs
> had given me my life, I should have thought myself
> obliged never more to have taken up arms against him.

This young man's death was a loss to the world.

As for Kenmure, his sickly wife was housebound at Kenmure Castle on Loch Ken in Kirkcudbright and had not been able to come to him in this harsh winter. But Kenmure was a philosophical man of unusual learning and, from what we were told by his friends who had visited him, he had accepted his fate with a rare composure, like a stoic Roman of old. God forgive me, I gave less thought to him. It was said afterward that he refused to speak when he stood on the scaffold.

At any rate, it was the flow of visitors to the condemned men that had given me an idea. I thought it was time for us to add more visitors and create more confusion at the Lieutenant's Lodgings. I often brought Lucy and Oswald and Amelia with me to the Tower, keeping the women heavily veiled so that their faces could not be seen. In the bitter cold, this seemed perfectly appropriate.

But the thought nagged at me that we four were not enough. One more was needed—a figure who was as tall as Gavin and even more thoroughly veiled than my friends. I began to devote much of my time to visiting Aelwen, urging her to come out into the world, to take the fresh air and escape her morbid fantasies and fears for a little while. But she seemed entrenched in her martyr's pose: she played unworthy sinner as dramatically as I am sure she had played the role of uncrowned queen of William of Orange's court. I began to form the notion of creating a new role for Aelwen that would capture her imagination as much as that of penitent.

But before my plot—which might not be needed—was fully developed, the time had come to confront the Usurper. My costume was complete, as was my training in guiding the massive petticoats and train along a walkway and around a reception room. I had the petition for mercy itself in hand, a single page of thick, creamy paper exquisitely inscribed and rolled into a narrow scroll tied with a silk band. I had tried on the gown and shoes and wig, and all necessary adjustments had been made. Amelia determined that we would go to court the very next night. It was time to do battle at the Court of St. James's.

At this point my fears almost overcame me. I am not even sure what frightened me most—the idea of making a surely unwelcome visit to St. James's Palace, the fear of carrying off my performance before a debased and false monarch, the fear of being humiliated in a room full of spiteful courtiers, or the fear of failing and having to try to put my alternative plan in play.

Chapter Fourteen
Plea to a False King

"*All you sage counselors, hence.
And to the English court assemble now,
From every region, apes of idleness.
Now, neighbor confines, purge you of your scum.
Have you a ruffian that will swear, drink, dance,
Revel the night, rob, murder and commit
The oldest sins the newest kind of ways?
Be happy, he will trouble you no more.*"

Henry IV, Part 2, William Shakespeare

After a sleepless night, I found myself trying to convince Amelia at breakfast that perhaps this night would not be the best time to go to St. James's.

"It's the dark of the moon," I argued, "never an auspicious time to embark on a new venture. The weather has warmed a bit but not yet enough to turn all the icy roads to slush, which means more courtiers will brave the cold and the reception room will be more crowded than usual. I may not even be able to reach the king to present my petition."

Amelia merely looked at me across the teapots and toast. Phineas was off on another trip to see to his merchant ships, so it was just the three of us—Amelia, Lucy and myself. Amelia was, as usual, a perfect picture, even early in the morning. Her cap was snow white, exquisitely starched and ironed, with an edging of delicate lace that had probably been purchased in Flanders at great expense. Her dressing gown was a pellucid sea-green that matched her brilliant eyes.

I sometimes felt that Amelia's authority, while clearly derived from her personal strength, was enhanced by the daily perfection of her appearance. Who could oppose a woman who put herself together each day with such consummate self-possession?

"Of course, we can postpone the visit," said Amelia at last. "And perhaps we should kill some poultry so we can read their entrails, as the Romans did, in order to identify the most auspicious occasion for daring deeds. I will ring for the scullery maid to bring us a chicken to sacrifice... Or we could go to St. James's Park and chart the flight of waterfowl overhead and thus determine our course of action."

I eyed her steadily and then dropped my gaze.

She reached across the table and took my hand.

"I understand that you are afraid," she said. "But you know as well as I that time is growing short. Now that everything is ready, you cannot afford to wait. Delay could cost you everything."

"Forgive me," I whispered, staring into my teacup.

"There is to be no talk of *forgiveness*," she insisted. "You didn't ride to London through the worst snowstorm in decades to lose your nerve now. It is understandable that you will quail at the task before you from time to time, but you will take a deep breath and summon your fortitude. I've never met a more intrepid woman."

Then she began to give me a series of instructions. I must eat during the day, she said. "Fear feeds on an empty stomach," she told me sagely.

"And just before we leave for the palace," she added, "I will give you a half coupe of champagne, which you will drink very slowly after the bubbles have dispersed. No more than that. Just a little taste of courage."

She reviewed the procedure for presenting a petition to the Hanoverian again. We were to wait with the massed courtiers until he entered the room. She would point him out to me.

She smiled. "He is short," she confided. "If he is surrounded by taller gentlemen-in-waiting, you will not even see him."

I began to protest. How would I complete my mission if I could not even locate my target?

She laughed softly. "But he is vain and so aware of his lack of stature that he will seldom permit tall men to stand close to him for more than a minute or two. Why do you think all of his ministers have taken to wearing shoes with only the slightest elevation of heel? It has become a new style!"

She entertained me with court gossip while she near handfed me white soup (veal, cream and almonds) and bits of toast to keep my stomach calm. My heart overflowed with gratitude. I could tell from the way Lucy beamed upon Amelia that she was equally appreciative.

But whenever I tried to bemoan the fact that I would never be able to repay Amelia for her generosity, she put a long, cool finger against my lips and assured me she was in reality a very selfish woman and was merely making use of me to pile up credits for herself in Heaven.

"Because of you," she said, with another of her broad smiles, "I have already skipped Purgatory and am well on my way to Beatification. You will attest to my performance of miracles and by the time of my death, I will already be Saint Amelia, patroness of all worthy women in need."

I could not help but laugh.

Inevitably night fell. Making ourselves ready to attend the king's reception required at least two hours of placing layers of petticoats and hoops, lacing the bodice and arranging the fine satin gown over all the underpinnings. Then came the elaborate ritual of painting face and bosom while sheets were draped to protect our costumes from stains.

Amelia did not think that either she or I would need to apply the full mask of cosmetics—the stark white forehead and décolletage, startlingly jet-black eyebrows, brilliantly rosy cheeks and deeply crimson lips.

"Let us retain some semblance of who we are in our appearance," she said. But after I was done up with a "light touch" by Amelia's chambermaid, I hardly knew myself. It was hard to see the woman beneath the paint.

Then the maids brought the heavy wig, which had to be firmly fixed in place, dressed with tiny bows and bits of lace, and heavily powdered while I held a mask over my face to protect my eyes, nose and mouth. The last portion of the process was the laying on of the jewels—the pearl eardrops, my mother's ruby ring and the draping of Amelia's pearls around my wig.

I found myself envying with a sigh Charles Perrault's heroine Cendrillon, who was transformed from a servant comfortably resting in warm ashes on the hearth, to a princess fit to go to the prince's ball with nothing more than the wave of a magic wand.

At last we were ready. Amelia was resplendent in a sunlit yellow gown with a more subdued pattern than mine, composed of golden apples and pears against a background of umber stems and pale green leaves.

The maids threw fine woolen cloaks over our shoulders. Lucy blew us each a kiss, since an attempt at embracing us would have rumpled our skirts. Amelia's steward sent a boy to bring us two sedan chairs from among the chairmen who congregated in Smith Square.

Just as Amelia had warned me, it was nearly impossible to squeeze the mantua hoops into a sedan chair. The skirts had to be folded and compressed while the wig was precariously positioned through the opening in the top of the chair. Because of the volume of the skirts, I could not fully sit down on the sedan seat and had to maintain an awkward half-squatting position while tilting my head back. Fortunately, we had not far to go.

I was able to draw the curtain slightly aside as we approached the red-brick gatehouse of St. James's Palace with its two octagonal towers on either side of the central arch. Much to my amazement, in addition to the crush of sedan chairs trying to get through the arch, there were hundreds of Londoners gathered by torchlight to watch the court beauties and gallants arriving.

Never comfortable, as I have said, amidst a nighttime crowd lit by flickering flames, I pulled the curtain closed, my heart beating faster. It was a relief to pass under the arch and emerge in the Great Court, even though we were still caught in a boiling sea of sedan chairs and carriages, bustling servants, and imperious courtiers attempting to dismount.

Once we had breached the curtains and disentangled ourselves from our chairs, Amelia and I had to rearrange each other's garments as best we could. The hoops snapped back into shape instantly, but the skirts over them still required pulling and straightening.

As soon as we were presentable, we went through the columned portico and glided up the grand staircase past the scarlet-uniformed Yeomen of the Guard, who reminded me uncomfortably of the Yeomen Warders at the Tower. Amelia had warned me to adopt an air of complete confidence, as if I had visited the Court of St. James's many times before.

I did not remind her that, in fact, I *had* been to St. James's Palace many times before and had been present when the Chevalier, young James Stuart, was born in the queen's bedchamber in that very palace. But my memories of the joys of the court of James II and the birth of the young prince seemed like tales I had heard in the nursery. It was all so long ago and far away and had possibly happened to some ancestress of mine, in a previous era.

Still, my knowledge that I had once been a young lady-in-waiting to a *real* queen in this very palace inspired me to straighten my shoulders, hold my head erect and roll forward down the long halls with tiny steps as I had been taught. We went on through the guardroom, the presence chamber and the privy chamber till we came to the new Great Drawing Room.

Through the floor-to-ceiling windows, we caught glimpses of the torchlit park outside. A heavy gold chandelier hung above our heads and the tapestries, which looked to be from the time of Henry VIII, were interspersed among large portraits in ornate gold frames.

My primary impression of the room was that there was a stultifying excess of both heat and light. The myriad of candles in the chandelier and in sconces around the room sent rays of light bouncing off so many jewels and bright silver and gold designs on the gowns of the women and waistcoats of the men, that the overall effect was dizzying. I found myself staring down at the carpet from time to time just to rest my eyes.

The night was cold but there were soon so many courtiers pressing into the room that there was hardly a breath of air to be had. There were no chairs, of course, so that no one could possibly commit the unpardonable faux pas of being seated at the moment the monarch entered the room.

I fanned myself vigorously but soon saw I was in danger of elbowing a neighbor or accidentally slamming the fan into my own nose. Fortunately, as the crowd became too large for the room, it overflowed into other nearby rooms so that waves of glittering lovelies and would-be lovelies and their attendant suitors washed back and forth, in and out of the Great Drawing Room where we remained.

I spotted the blue sashes of the Knights of the Garter and the red sashes of the Knights of the Bath, and noted that the younger men seemed to be indulging this season in a fashion of pale blue silk coats. The mantua gowns I saw were undoubtedly all fearfully expensive, but few were as tasteful and beautiful as the one Amelia had arranged for me. Some of the flowers on the gowns around me were so large they reminded me of silver soup plates.

I noticed that the largest crush seemed to eddy, with much pushing and shoving, around two particular figures. Amelia indicated with gestures, since she could not be heard above the cacophony of shrill voices, that one of these magnets was Prince George Augustus, Prince of Wales and heir to the throne, and the other was his wife, the excessively rotund Princess Caroline arrayed in bright pink. Set among her ladies-in-waiting who were garbed in paler pink, Caroline resembled, as one observer later commented, "a lobster among attendant shrimps." I realized that I had already seen the prince at my husband's trial and quickly looked away, fixing my eyes on rosy Caroline.

Occasionally a female courtier would drop a nod in Amelia's direction with a slight curtsy. Amelia had already told me that many of these women came to her to advise them on their mantuas, since she was noted for her intimate knowledge of fine silks. She recommended dressmakers and fabric designers like James Leman. Amelia visited the Court of St. James's occasionally, partly to amuse herself, partly to display the sophistication of her taste and partly to remind the gilded ones that her husband was a renowned silk merchant without saying a word. As Amelia had explained to me before, anyone who was properly attired was admitted.

I saw that the most experienced women at court seemed to spin gracefully from place to place, somehow never colliding with their neighbors. I thought they were like women who, as a consequence of some curse, were buried to the waist in huge, misshapen cakes mounted on wheels and had learned to twirl their cakes around and about in a strange dance of confections.

I was so intent on watching for any sign that the Hanoverian was coming that I did not notice for some time that I myself had attracted some interest. I'm sure that newcomers generally stimulated speculation—especially if the newcomer could not be readily identified. Amelia would gaze at me sweetly until she had my attention and then drop a subtle nod in the direction of a courtier, male or female, who was unabashedly staring at me.

At one point she managed to whisper, "Don't you see? The women are envious of you, and the men are intrigued." I rolled my eyes. How could an unknown woman at my advanced age of forty-three arouse any emotion other than disdain in these radiant creatures?

At any rate it was immaterial. I was not there, as they were, to flirt or to seek advancement. This place of idle revelry and vain display was only the necessary backdrop to my plea for mercy for my husband. I did not care if I was admired except as it might help my cause.

Amelia and I waited...and waited, as the hours passed. Candles slowly burned down and were replaced. The crowd dwindled. Some of the courtiers, a little the worse for champagne, abandoned their hope of seeing the king that evening and tottered off to their waiting sedan chairs while they could still maintain a vertical position. At least we could then move about a bit and fan ourselves more freely.

I was beginning to think that all our effort had been wasted. I would have to come again the following night and perhaps the night after, and was it even permissible to wear the same mantua to court two nights in a row?

All at once a frisson passed through the remaining aspirants to royal favor. Amelia gave me a meaningful glance, and I realized that George was nearly at hand. Moving as swiftly as I could, heart pounding so hard I thought it might bend my whalebone stays, I managed to position myself near the entrance to the Great Drawing Room so that I would be one of the first to confront him.

A small group of courtiers entered the room together, gabbling in German. I missed my first chance to reach my target because I was not sure which one he was. When I had identified him, I was so shocked by the appearance of the man who was styling himself king of England that I could not act. I have never seen a man who less resembled a king.

He was indeed the Toad that I had heard tell of—only worse than I had imagined. He looked like the kind of troll who lived under a bridge.

He was startlingly short and bandy-legged with a sizable paunch, an over-large cranium and a blunt, square face. His large, blue eyes protruded from his head, his long nose broadened into the shape of a flower bulb at the end, his mouth was disproportionately wide and his short, plump chin was supported by three or four additional chins.

I gasped but quickly got over my shock and glided after him, almost tripping him as I managed to drop to my knees, holding out my petition, and cried out in French (which I had been told he understood) that I was the most unhappy Countess of Clarencefield who had come to court to beg mercy for my husband. To my horror, he made as if to ignore me completely and began to move around me and pass me by.

This I would not allow.

In all likelihood, he would not grant my plea for mercy. But he could not be permitted to behave as if I, a most pitiable petitioner, did not exist.

I was overcome with fury that this grotesque creature, given such immense power, might flout all the traditions of English kingship by refusing to even *accept* my petition. In my extremity I reached out with both hands and grabbed the lip of his pocket, attempting to thrust my scroll inside it.

He still refused to look at me and kept walking—as if I were a troublesome young terrier that had not yet been taught to sit. Or not even so much as that. As if I were no more than a ball of lint that had caught on his coat.

But I would *not* loosen my hold on him. He dragged me along the carpet as my hoops flew up behind me, and first one shoe, and then the other, dropped off my feet and were left behind.

I became aware of the strong odor of snuff about him, snuff mingled with too much scent of bitter almonds. The heavy wool scratched my skin and the capacious pocket was beginning to tear loose just an inch or so from the coat. I thought it might rip entirely, and I would be left sitting on the floor with a royal pocket in my hand.

I heard the exclamations of the courtiers around us. I heard audible gulps, small cries and even one suppressed giggle, but I did not care. I had come to court to get the Usurper's attention and to beg for a life worth a thousand of his, and I would not let go until my purpose was achieved.

The brute pulled me the full length of the Great Drawing Room, but still I hung on to him. The layers of petticoats under me kept the rug from burning my legs, but the awkward position and rapid forward motion threatened to dislocate my shoulders or wrench my arms from my body. The initial squeaks and mumbles of the crowd were succeeded by an echoing silence in the room that had been so full of noise, as shock at such a display of cruelty caused even this raucous assembly to lose its voice.

At last the German's attendants seemed to come to their senses. One grabbed me around the waist and lifted me away from the king while the other opened my fingers, one by one, almost gently, removing them from the lip of the coat pocket. I lay in a collapsed heap, my wig awry, my petition still clutched in my damp fist.

The king moved rapidly through a door into the next room, never looking back, as the startled courtiers slowly recovered themselves and followed after him. If they turned to stare as they passed me, I did not see them. Abandoned, crumpled on the great carpet, I was lost in my own circle of despair.

Amelia and I were left almost alone, save for the ushers who remained still and impassive around the perimeter of the room. Amelia gathered me up and lifted me to a sitting and then slowly to a standing position, deftly straightening my wig. She had even managed to collect my shoes and put them down on the carpet in front of me. I was able to lift my front petticoats and step back into them.

"We had better go," she said quietly, equal to every circumstance. "That was a rather dramatic moment and not to his credit. The king may decide to send guards to seize you, once he knows that there is no longer an audience to witness his revenge."

I was still stunned and her words puzzled, rather than frightened, me.

"His revenge?" I said. "For what? He got the better of me."

"Oh no, my dear," she said, guiding me towards the door so we could return the long way we had come. "All he had to do was accept your petition and move on, as any true English king—as any gentleman—would have done. Taking the petition from a petitioner is not a commitment to grant what the petitioner asks, but merely a traditional gesture of kingliness. But you took him by surprise, and he behaved precisely as the untutored boor that he is. The entire court witnessed his shame. He will never forgive you."

I could not absorb her words. I was still too intent on getting my petition to the king somehow. Just then one of the beardless young men in a pale blue silk coat, probably not yet twenty, returned to the Great Drawing Room. He walked boldly up to us and held out his hand for my petition. At first I would not hand it over. In my dazed state, I imagined he might be planning to rip it to shreds to please the king.

Amelia took it from me and gave it to him. He bowed deeply.

"His Royal Highness the Prince of Wales will make a point of delivering this document personally to the king," he said, with a slight German accent. "His Highness regrets that you were discommoded this evening." He bowed again, turned and left.

"Lord Dorset," said Amelia. "He is one of the close attendants of the Prince of Wales. The prince will certainly make sure that his father receives your petition, if only to embarrass him further."

"Oh!" I wailed. "None of this will save my husband." I would have stood there longer, tears cascading shamelessly down my cheeks, if Amelia had not insisted that we leave at once.

I said nothing more until we had returned to Smith Square.

The maids were able to help me shuck the entire absurd costume much faster than they had caged me in it. They washed the sticky cosmetics off my face. My cheeks were already pink and tender to the touch from the vile stuff, but lavender water soothed them.

They wrapped me in one of Amelia's dressing gowns, carefully removed the wig, and Lucy brushed out my curls with a damp silver-handled brush till my hair lay long and loose and unencumbered on my shoulders.

Through the entire process of the hair brushing, having already cried until I could cry no more, I sat still and stony, and remained so as Lucy plied me with tea in the parlor. I was fighting the darkness that was attempting to drown me. I was trying to pull threads of hope from the web of despair that bore in on me.

At last Lucy said, "You always knew the petition was unlikely to win His Lordship a pardon. You have another plan."

"Yes," I said. "I do, but we will need the devil's own luck." Then I put my hand over my own mouth. If I sought the renewed blessing and presence of the Blessed Virgin, I would do well not to lapse into blasphemous language.

Lucy was unperturbed. "*Audentis Fortuna iuvat*; Fortune favors the brave," she said smugly, enjoying the opportunity to trot out one of her store of Latin phrases. "You've always known that. I believe the Blessed Virgin also favors the brave in a righteous cause."

She put her hand on mine and said, "Tell me of your plan."

Chapter Fifteen
A Plot with Many Parts

*"By the Lord, our plot is a good plot as
ever was laid;
Our friends true and constant: a good plot,
good friends
And full of expectation."*

Henry IV, Part I, William Shakespeare

For so many of my years, I and those I love have been victims of the times, blown from pillar to post without any volition of our own. We have been able to find some happiness for a while, only to see it taken from us, simply because we are loyal to a disfavored faith, and because we subscribe to the belief that the English should be ruled by an Englishman.

We have won large and small personal victories. My family and I escaped from England. We withstood our exile in France. Gavin and I met and were well matched. I survived childbirth and most of our children lived.

But what was coming now and could not be avoided would be the trial of my lifetime. If I succeeded, Gavin would be spared. If I failed, Gavin would die, and I and my dearest friends might all be imprisoned or even lose our lives.

There was no time to settle into my miseries, to sink into the cruel injustice of our circumstances and allow myself a few days or even a few hours of paralysis.

In truth, the plan I devised was not entirely original. We used to spend long winter nights sitting by the great hearth at Heath Hall after the children had been put to bed, while Gavin regaled us with tales of Scotland. Of course, most of these stories involved bloodshed and gore as the Scots—especially the ferocious Highlanders, as far as I could tell—preferred fighting to any other activity. If they did not war upon the English, they warred upon each other to the point that I was amazed that Scotland ever had enough populace left to produce the next generation.

Amid all the brave deeds of derring-do, there were also humorous episodes and audacious deceptions. The one I remembered now was the story of Lord James Ogilvy, second Earl of Airlie. During the time when Royalists were battling Covenanters in Scotland, not long before Charles I was executed and Oliver Cromwell took over the rule of England, this Lord Ogilvy was captured at the battle of Philiphaugh.

Lord Ogilvy was condemned to death with the other officers, but his clever sister Isabel swore to save him and did so by visiting him in the dungeon at St. Andrew's Castle and swapping clothes with him. Ogilvy went out, disguised in female garb and his sister remained behind in his cell wearing his clothing.

Maybe it was a good omen, that, just before he left to join the rebellion, Gavin and I had talked of the Spartan wives who exchanged clothes with their husbands, so the husbands could sneak out of gaol and go back to the fight.

I never heard what happened to Lord Ogilvy's sister. Did the gaolers release her or was she executed in her brother's stead? It seemed wrong to me to leave her behind.

I thought I might be able to improve on the primitive design of the Ogilvy deception.

I knew I had to begin to test my plan at once. First I had to visit Aelwen and try to enlist her in my little squadron of women (of which her son Oswald was now an honorary member).

I could not say that Aelwen's house had been radically transformed, that all the curtains had been thrown open and the darkness banished, but there were some changes. The windows that opened onto the square were still closed with the curtains drawn, but on the rear side of the house, some curtains were open and windows raised partway, and Aelwen was even giving some attention to organizing the garden in back, which she had long neglected, in preparation for spring.

She received me wearing pale lilac instead of black and, though she was still veiled, the layers were not as thick as before and were so diaphanous that I could see her face clearly through the lavender mist. We sat in the front parlor, in the same places as before across from each other, but I now felt as if I was conversing with a human being rather than a spirit from another world.

I noticed that the heavy red velvet curtains, which had appeared black in the darkened house, had been replaced with lighter silk ones, though they were still a deep shade of maroon. Some of the brightness of sunlight on snow sifted through these curtains and lightened the room.

"Are you here because you are in need of more of my gold?" she asked without preamble. "Or do you seek my son to help you with your intrigues?"

Tact had never been Aelwen's strong suit.

I bit my tongue and did not answer her in kind.

"Neither gold nor your son," I said. "Though I am deeply appreciative of both. I've come today, Sister, because I am in need of *you.*"

"As you know full well," she said, "I do not leave the house. I devote myself to prayer and repentance. I honor all the offices of the hours as Glynis used to do, from Lauds to Compline."

"I would like to pray with you," I said. I thought I might feel closer to Glynis' strength if I followed a prescribed prayer at close to the same time that Glynis might be performing the same prayer in Bruges.

"But first," I said, "I would like to suggest that you undertake a great good deed beyond giving alms to the unfortunate or hiding itinerant priests. But this deed will require you to re-enter the world outside—at least briefly."

I hesitated.

"Oh, Aelwen, Sister," I said with all the earnestness I could muster, "I need you to help me save my husband from the axe—not with gold alone, but with your own presence. I need your knowledge of men and your talent for deception—that is, I mean, your *cleverness*—to be used in a righteous cause, the best of causes," I added hastily. "My few friends here are not enough. Oswald cannot help us with this. My plan relies entirely on a community of courageous women. It relies upon you and your widow's weeds."

"You expect me to go with you to the Tower, don't you?" she asked in a low voice. She shuddered, causing the gossamer folds of her veils to quiver.

I appealed shamelessly to the way she had always lived her life before she retired from society—as the heroine of her own drama, the magnificent center of all attention.

"Only you can do this," I said. "Lucy Dunstable and Amelia Thrupp will support me, but they cannot carry it off with your style. I must have your help."

A pause and then there was a kind of cracked sound like ice splitting, and I slowly realized she was actually laughing. On an impulse she leaped up and reached out a hand to beckon me, as she moved quickly towards the stairs.

She had forgotten to maintain her previous lugubrious and regal, almost weightless, drift up the stairs. She tripped over the treads as nimbly as a young girl.

"Come," she said, "let us pray on it."

We prayed for an hour in the cold upstairs room. Aelwen was well-versed in the services for the different times of the day; I stumbled along. She was silent for a long time afterwards, still on her knees, looking heavenward at the crucifix with her hands clasped and raised to chin level. Her pose was so exaggerated that I thought I might giggle.

There is nothing at all amusing about this, I admonished myself, and my renegade desire to laugh curdled and shrank away.

Then I thought of the Blessed Virgin, trying to sense whether I could feel her touch again in this holy place. I could not be sure. Perhaps there was a moment when her sweet breath seemed to linger on my cheek, my hair. But I sought her presence in my heart with such longing that I might have only imagined she was there because I needed it to be so.

"Yes," said Aelwen at last. "When you are ready, I will go with you as you desire, clad in my heaviest and blackest widow's weeds."

Then she added with a flash of her old mischief, "It would please me to help you cheat the Hanoverian of his prey. These Tower warders—they are only men, are they not? How difficult can it be?"

That night I explained to Lucy and Amelia the plan that had come to me in bits and pieces, in hints and glimpses, and, over time, had taken on a near-finished form in my mind. They were to play the part of visitors to the Tower to bid Gavin farewell, visitors overcome by sorrow. When I had finished, both women became very quiet and pale. Which was as it should be, I thought. They must fully realize the danger they are facing so they do not panic at the last minute when they are in the midst of the play I have devised.

"As a token of the love I hold for both of you," I said, "I must say that, if you feel you cannot do this, I will accept your decision and love you nonetheless."

"But you *must* have us," said Amelia slowly, as solemn as I had ever seen her. "If you do not have your full complement of actresses, your play cannot go forward."

"Aelwen has promised to join our little theatrical," I said, "and Aelwen is tall, almost as tall as Gavin."

Both of them looked at me as if I had said that the Prince of Wales had promised to carry Gavin out of the Tower on his shoulders.

"But," said Lucy, "Aelwen has not left her house for—how many?—years. What if, at the last minute, she cannot bring herself to do it?"

I smiled and said, "You do not know Aelwen as I do. I think she has spent these last years waiting for her moment to act a heroine's turn upon the stage once more. She must have thought her time had passed. Now that she knows it has not, I don't believe she will fail us. Not for a minute. She will not miss this."

In the end they both insisted they would not fail me, either. But Lucy looked so stern that I thought she might have something more to say. When we were alone under the covers in the bed in my room, she did speak up. But what she divulged had nothing to do with my scheme to save Gavin.

"There is something I must tell you," she said, barely above a whisper, head bowed. "I can no longer postpone my confession."

Then she said nothing for so long that I, seeing her eyelids were closed, thought she had gone to sleep. But I noticed by the light of the candle we had not yet blown out, that her cheeks had turned pink.

She was blushing. I had never known her to hesitate when she had something to say, and I had almost never known her to blush.

"I am..." she said. Another pause.

I was frightened. Was she going to leave us? Was she weary of our travails? But where would she go? I thought of her collapse at Stilton. Was she dying of some ailment she had hidden from me?

At last she said, "...I am *married*."

I gasped aloud—almost a shriek. It came to me at once. The glances I had observed, the smiles over whisky, the conspiratorial flavor of their quiet conversations that I had attributed to their united effort to protect us from the dangers all around us.

"Alistair of Wamphray!" I cried.

"Yes," she said, and turned a yet brighter shade of pink.

"But..." I protested.

"As you know, of course, we do not live together at Wamphray," she said, anticipating my questions.

She opened her eyes and looked at me as if pleading for my forgiveness, but she uttered no apology, no single word of regret for her deception.

"I told him," she said, "I would marry him only if I could remain at Heath Hall. Why would I want to live in isolation at Wamphray while he rides about the countryside on his many duties and errands? My primary obligation in this world has been to you and your family."

"But you are telling me your secret now because..."

"If you manage to save His Lordship's life," she said, so softly she was barely audible, "you will both have to leave the country. I will not go with you. But I swear to you I will cleave to you and give you what assistance I can until you are out of danger."

At that her head bobbed and she fell fast asleep.

I sat still, shocked, trying to grasp what I had just heard. I wondered why a man would marry a woman who would neither live with him nor reveal their union? I wondered how long they had been married and what other secrets my longtime companion might be keeping from me. But these would all have to be thoughts to puzzle over much later.

I knew the loss of Lucy would cause me much pain. No doubt of that. She had been my dearest companion and had helped me rejoice in our fine days and overcome our hardships. But other dangers and losses loomed before me now. I envisioned running and hiding and trying to get safely to France once more. My life had turned and turned in one large circular revolution that I had not recognized and had finally brought me back to where I had begun almost thirty years earlier, when I ran headlong into exile with my parents, the queen and the infant prince.

Lucy would be only part of what I would lose. Everything would be different. I might never see Heath Hall again. I might not see my beloved children for years—though, in time, they might be able to visit us. At least we had made arrangements to keep them safe without forcing them to share our exile. This time, when Gavin and I left England, we would almost certainly be fugitives and refugees for the rest of our lives.

But I could not dwell on those anxieties. If we lived to experience the difficulties of exile, we would be fortunate indeed. I swore I would remind myself how fortunate we were if my plan succeeded, no matter what tribulations we had to face afterwards. I am ashamed to admit that it was only much later that I found a moment to be glad that Lucy had found some happiness with a kindly man, whose nature suited her own.

The next day we received the news that Gavin's execution, along with that of Derwentwater and Kenmure, had been set for February 24. Of Winton, we had heard nothing except that he was still imprisoned in the Tower. He was under sentence of death, but he was not to die with the others.

I thought I was prepared for the news, but I was not. For two days I could keep nothing in my stomach. Lucy and Amelia took turns sitting with me until I could rouse myself from my despair. We all knew full well that, if my strength failed me, my husband would surely die.

Gavin was moved from the second floor to the top floor of the Lieutenant's Lodgings, to a garret with one grilled window facing over Tower Green and another facing in the opposite direction towards the Thames. Under the pretext of maintaining a closer watch on the prisoner, some of the warders had taken over Gavin's previous lodgings in what was called the Council Chamber, which, with its broad fireplace and handsome paneling, was large enough and warm enough for their wives to visit them, and sometimes even their children. I had been told that Guy Fawkes, the Catholic who tried to blow up king and Parliament during the days of James I, had once been interrogated in this room, possibly by the King's Council, after he was tortured. That is why the room was called the Council Chamber—not a pleasant omen for our own plans.

The relocation of Gavin meant I now had to climb *two* wobbly, steep staircases to reach him instead of one. Not only that, but all the women—all of them—who would carry out my plan would have to navigate the two staircases as well. I thought, however, that, taken all in all, it might be for the best that Gavin had been moved upstairs because the room below was now always full of hubbub and noise, warders and their families coming and going. The noise might serve to cover some of our doings above.

I began to supply the warders with more ale—for themselves and their wives, I said. I thought it would be helpful to keep them a little less steady than usual. I was still uneasy about Aldrich Harrow. While the other warders took off their flat caps, loosened their belts, and grew ruddy and jovial, teasing and laughing with their wives in all good geniality, Harrow drank very little and looked upon me with what appeared to be bitter suspicion.

One evening I arrived long after dark. Harrow was at the gate and volunteered to escort me to the Lieutenant's Lodgings, which the other warders at the gate readily accepted. The night was intensely cold with many little stars above, glittering like ice crystals in a black sky. Ice patches lay everywhere in the yard. Once I almost slipped and Harrow put his hand under my elbow, which seemed a kindly gesture until he spoke.

"I know what you're up to," he hissed. "Papists are traitors, every one." He uttered the insult in perfectly even tones. It seemed my heart turned over and skipped several beats.

But I could not allow myself to react as I naturally would have to his insult.

"What do you mean?" I said evenly. "I am 'up to' visiting my lord who is soon to die." Had he guessed my plan somehow? Was the game already lost?

"These other fools," he whispered, "all think you're a great lady. They sigh and swoon for your misfortune. But I know you better."

I glanced at his dark face and saw such a hatred in his eyes that I thought it might verge on madness. I looked away quickly and said nothing but wrenched my arm from his grasp.

"You're fattening these clods up so's you can blind 'em to some plot of yours. But I will catch you out."

I chose my words very carefully.

"I fear," I said, "that your hatred of Catholics has made you daft. You imagine that the wife of a prisoner can fashion wings so that her husband can fly away over these walls?"

I gestured to the great stone towers and walls around us.

"Would that I could," I said in all heartfelt sincerity. "But I cannot. I cannot defeat the Tower of London."

"Nonetheless," he said, "you're planning something. I see you. You're clever but I'll catch you."

We walked the rest of the way in silence. I made sure not to slip again. The touch of his hand would have made me shiver openly. But I determined then and there that I must do something to eliminate Aldrich Harrow. He seemed the greatest danger to the success of my plan.

Gavin's new room contained only a small hearth and a straw mattress laid on knotted thongs tied across a bed frame. There was a table and a candle, and I had paid for decent food and ale, but I saw that Gavin was beginning to look too lean again with a haunted, abstracted quality to his eyes. Once his initial relief that he would not be tortured to death before a crowd had passed, he had begun to confront again the fact that he would still die.

His gaze and his mind roamed when I spoke to him, and I would have to call him back with some severity to whatever we needed to discuss. I also saw that he needed new breeches. The knees were becoming threadbare in the pair he had been wearing, I supposed, from much kneeling in prayer.

I saw that I must enlist him in my plan at once to keep his wits from wandering away for good in his attempt to escape what must have been a fear that strangled him.

"You have so little room to hide things here," I said, pondering my first problem aloud.

He sighed and slowly turned to look at me.

"What would I wish to hide?"

I began to explain that I needed to bring him over several days bits of women's clothing hidden under my own—a petticoat or two and women's stockings.

Now I had his attention indeed. He looked so completely dumbfounded at the idea that I might need to bring him women's clothing to hide in his little chamber that I saw I had better explain. But, once I outlined my plan, he caught on quickly and appeared to be more animated than I had seen him in days. He could not talk openly about his dread, but he could help me unravel small knots in the web I was beginning to weave.

"I believe I could insert a few items into my mattress," he said. "But we cannot leave them there for long. They shake out the mattresses every week or so, looking for vermin and hidden weapons. Sometimes they even bring new straw to add to the old."

I saw at once that this routine would push the time to carry out my plan right up against the eve of Gavin's execution. We could not count on putting things into motion gradually. We would have to implement almost the entire plan—the first stages in the few days after the last turning of his mattress before his execution—and the rest during one fast-moving, extremely dangerous day right before he was doomed to die. The date set for his execution was less than ten days away.

"You must tell me the next time they turn your mattress, and I will bring the petticoats the following day," I said.

Amelia and I racked our brains trying to settle on a petticoat material that could be crushed and stuffed inside a straw mattress. Most petticoats were designed to be stiff—that was their very purpose. But Amelia obtained some of soft cotton, which could be mashed into a small enough mass to insert in the mattress.

Gavin and I nearly had a misadventure at this very first, preliminary step in my plan. I had just released the ties on the under-petticoat that I planned to hand over for hiding and, as it settled to the floor in a white foam around my feet, Thomas Brickle—of all people—knocked briefly and then burst into the garret room.

I do not know why he came into the room. He seldom interrupted our visits. I had plied him with sweets and good ale and small coinage to the point that he had come to be quite pleasant and cheery towards both of us and made sure that *most* of the food I brought for Gavin actually came to him.

But on this occasion there was a sharp, quick knock and then the door slammed open, and my stout friend bounced into the room and stopped stark still. Gavin and I both froze, my mind scrabbling for something to say that would explain the petticoat on the floor. I felt my face drain of blood and then flush intensely red and hot as I slowly realized that the only way to remedy this unanticipated hazard was to embarrass my husband and myself. I forced out an uncomfortable gurgle of laughter and threw my arms around myself as if to conceal a loosened bodice.

"Thomas Brickle!" I cried, in my best imitation of a lady accosted in an awkward moment of undress.

Brickle began a stuttering apology, turned fairly crimson himself, and slowly backed out of the door. But, as soon as the door closed, I heard his loud guffaw as he took the stairs down two and three at a time.

I neatly stepped free of the petticoat, lifted it from the floor and began to fold it up into the smallest square I could manage. But as I folded, I made the mistake of looking at Gavin and we began to laugh, though we could not allow ourselves to laugh aloud.

We were, after all, a long-married couple, were we not, who had been caught—according to the tale Brickle would tell—as we were about to engage in conjugal relations in a Tower of London prison cell no bigger than a wardrobe. This might have resulted in an embarrassed giggle or two between us, but what could possibly excuse gales of hilarity? And so, for several long moments, we shook with silent laughter, until the tears came and we sank down together in a heap on the spiky straw mattress.

When I descended the stairs later, it seemed that the warders and their rosy wives were staring at me with expressions that ranged from ribald, to arch and knowing, to sympathetic pity—and not a one noticed that my skirts were a little flatter than they had been when I arrived.

Even Harrow leered a bit with the same nastiness in his expression as when he was cursing me. I was still cogitating as to how I would deal with Aldrich Harrow.

Brickle was full of winks and chortles as he bowed me out. I was sure he had told them all that my lord and I were coupling like rabbits above. I carried it off with a little smile, knowing what I knew, that they were more fooled than before as to what was really going on.

The two problems that most vexed my devoted coterie of women and myself during the next few days were *shoes* and *poisons*. Shoes, because wherever would we find women's shoes that would fit Gavin, with his exceptionally long foot, high arch, and slim, elegant toes, the second toe longer than the first on each foot?

Should we buy a pair of large women's shoes and slash the sides to accommodate him? I was intensely mindful that such a small thing as men's boots peeping out from under even the most convincing expanse of petticoats could expose our plot.

I absorbed myself completely in the myriad details—bricks as it were—of my plan that would lock together to create a ramp to convey Gavin out of the Tower of London. The alternative was to spend my days and nights transfixed by visions of my husband's handsome head rolling across Tower Green, which would have left me too petrified to function.

"The shoes must be sober," said Amelia, "in keeping with Aelwen's mourning costume, but nevertheless, they must be women's shoes. I think we will have to have a special pair made." I was tasked to measure my husband's feet as best I could with a notched piece of string. Amelia and I took the measurements to a cobbler and told him the shoes were intended as a gift to an exceptionally tall cousin who was too ashamed of the size of her feet to attend on him herself.

"All of her life," I explained, "our dear cousin has suffered pain and shame because of her height and her large feet. She has never owned a pair of shoes that fit her well and, as a consequence of being squeezed into elegant shoes that are too small, her feet are now rather gnarled. We would like to give her the first comfortable pair of shoes she has ever owned."

The cobbler was a young man who had once been tall but was already bent from his endless labors over his bench. He peered at us sideways, brushed a long, damp lock of hair out of his eyes, and appeared skeptical when he looked at my scrawled list of measurements.

"My lady," he said with a weary shake of his head, "are you quite certain of these figures? The size of these feet seems extraordinary for a woman, no matter how tall she be!"

"I assure you absolutely," I responded, "that these measurements are correct, though our cousin is so accustomed to hiding her feet that it was difficult for me to persuade her to let me measure them. I told her it was for a gift of stockings."

Amelia and I did not look at each other during this exchange. Nevertheless, I could feel the corners of my mouth twitching. When we finally escaped into the street and walked far enough away from the shoemaker's shop that we would not be heard, we laughed a little and then harder, as we elaborated on the story of our monstrously tall cousin.

"Your cousin is so large that she eats with a shovel and

pitchfork," Amelia said. "When she stands on a hill, her red hair is used as a signal fire to draw the clans to war."

"Her dresses are made from tablecloths and bedsheets," I gasped out between bursts of giggles. "She walks across the Thames at its widest in five strides."

At last we began speculating on what my giant cousin might use for a chamber pot—an empty wine barrel? A laundry basket? An old butter churn?

The joke tailed off at that point as we ran out of absurdities and tried to catch our breaths.

Laughter cleanses the spirit. I felt cheerier and more hopeful during the entire chair ride back to Smith Square. But by the time I was inside the Thrupp home, the Black Wolf of my terrors was sniffing me out again. It was hard to keep outrunning him. Much of my energy during those days went to simply holding him back, keeping him from overtaking me and chewing me to pieces.

The shoes for my "cousin" were ready two days later—modest black ones with moderate heels and silver lacings—ideally suited to the task at hand. I would take them to Gavin hidden under my cloak the day before our plot was put into motion.

The matter of how I could put Aldrich Harrow out of commission for an evening required much more discussion. We were considering such measures as a dilute infusion of arsenic, hemlock, monkshood, henbane or deadly nightshade, which provoked a lively debate, until Lucy asked me the essential question.

"What is your purpose?" she said. "Do you want to put this man to sleep? Are you meaning to sicken him? Or do you intend to risk killing him?"

That sobered us all at once.

"I am no Lady Macbeth," I said. "I do not wish to assassinate this man, though I confess I would not weep at his death. My purpose is to disable him, to veil his sharp eyes for one evening so that my strategy may succeed. I am convinced that, if I do not, he will somehow thwart even the most carefully prepared plan."

"I am not known in London as Amelia is," said Lucy. "I will go to a different part of the city and ask an apothecary for a fast-acting medicament that merely induces sleep. I will say that my husband is troubled by sleeplessness and is worn out with his struggles to find peaceful rest at night."

"Go to Apothecaries Hall," said Amelia at once. "Black Friars Lane. It's just around the big curve of the Thames on the site of the former Dominican priory of Blackfriars. A fine old building with a handsome courtyard. Don't be dismayed by the size of it. Most of the structure is what they call an 'elaboratory' where the medicines are made. But, if you walk around to the Water Street side, you will see a small shop where elixirs and compounds are sold to the public.

"It's always very crowded. No one will notice or remember you." She laughed. "Apothecaries are quite full of themselves these days. They have been given permission by the courts to treat illnesses, not just sell medicines. I've already observed a marked improvement in their dress."

As I was not known in London either, I decided it was safe for me to accompany Lucy to Apothecaries Hall. If one of the nobles who had seen me dragged across the floor by the king at St. James's Palace had need of a medicine, I was certain that a servant would be sent to fetch it.

We found several chairmen nearby and in no time were carried to Black Friars Lane. Amelia's account had been accurate in every respect. The headquarters of the Worshipful Society of Apothecaries of London was a very large building, but most of what was done there was hidden from the sight of mere mortals.

We had the chairmen release us on the Water Street side and immediately saw a throng of men and women, mostly of the merchant and burgher class, entering and emerging from a small shop door set in a corner of the building.

We entered the shop, pushing our way through the masses of folk who were congregating there. We meant to attract no special attention, so we waited our turn patiently at the counter where the apothecaries stood, enveloped in full, white aprons that almost completely covered their clothing.

When at last we had burrowed our way to the front of the line, Lucy, who was wrapped in a brown cloak of good wool, as became the wife of a respectable burgher, began to tell her tale of a husband whose brain was so crowded with worries that he could not sleep at night.

"I am sorely troubled about him," she said earnestly. "I fear, if he cannot get a good night's rest, he will be unable to conduct his business. Have you something that will help him sleep without doing him any harm? His wits must not be clouded during the day. I fear some sleeping potions leave the patient in a state of lethargy for hours after awakening."

The apothecary we spoke to was not a tall man, but he seemed to pull himself up to his full height and expand his chest slightly with pride in his new responsibilities. I noticed that he kept patting and smoothing his handsome periwig tied back with a black satin ribbon. As he conferred with us, his extraordinarily mobile eyebrows, as black as two crow's feathers, rode up and down on his forehead, expressing the degree of his enthusiasm for each drug he described.

He looked thoughtful for a moment, massaging his chin with one hand while the other supported his elbow. A well-practiced pose. Then abruptly he turned and, opening several small drawers in the cabinet behind him, pulled forth with a flourish a little bottle of elixir, a leather bag and a large glass jar containing some sort of plant—leaves, stem and roots.

The apothecary opened the jar first and gently removed a plant with broad green leaves, small greenish-white blooms with yellow centers, and a thick root.

"Some," he said, "believe this noble mandrake root resembles a human body and has human properties."

It looked like a thick, furry, curled brown root to me—no more, no less—but perhaps I lacked the second sight to see the mythic beneath the outward appearance. The root had a slight odor, not unpleasant, like the tang of an apple.

Our apothecary now fell into the sonorous rhythms of the tutor directing his students to focus their attentions on the lesson of the day.

"You see before you," he intoned, as he displayed the mandrake, "a root whose special properties have been known since the days of the ancients. Uncommon courage is required to harvest this plant. When pulled from the earth, it emits a piercing scream of agony that causes the gardener to immediately expire, if he has not armed himself in advance by stuffing cotton wadding in his ears.

"The root is to be grated, and gratings and juice are then to be administered to the patient in a liquid or food. Given in the proper dosage, it will induce unconsciousness. But, be warned"—here his forefinger waggled at us—"a large dose may cause delirium and madness followed by a sleep from which the sleeper does not wake."

"What is the precise dosage then?" asked Lucy, not unreasonably.

"It depends on the strength of the particular root," replied the apothecary unhelpfully.

"What if a small amount is administered from a rather weak root?" asked Lucy.

"Then nothing at all will happen," said the apothecary with a smooth, reassuring smile. His eyebrows came to a resting position in straight lines over his small, blue eyes.

"That will not do," said Lucy emphatically. "I will not trouble my husband with a remedy that may either be entirely useless or cause his untimely death. What I require is a physic that will speedily and reliably waft him gently into slumber."

The apothecary closed the jar, put it aside and opened the leather pouch.

"Let us consider the deadly nightshade then," he said. "Some have called nightshades 'primroses with a curse on them.' Rather poetic, don't you think?"

From the pouch he shook out several shiny black berries, some green leaves and a handful of small purple flowers. The mandrake had not disturbed me, but these elements of the deadly nightshade plant seemed to emit a subtle miasma of evil. The aroma of the plant was slight and not unpleasant, but the berries, in their glossy black coats, suggested an enticement to commit wicked deeds. Our faith tells us that we humans cannot resist fruit that is both luscious and depraved. I took a couple of steps back. I had an instinctive horror of this plant.

I suddenly remembered hearing, when I was at Saint Germain, a different name for this plant with the bright black berries, a beautiful Italian name, *belladonna*. Women in Italy, it was said, placed drops of the juice of the nightshade in their eyes to enlarge their pupils, thus enhancing their beauty. Hence the plant was given a name that means "beautiful woman." Overuse, however, could impair one's vision or even cause the "bella donna" to go blind.

I tapped Lucy's arm gently. She turned to me, and I shook my head. This nightshade frightened me. I wanted nothing to do with it.

Lucy looked at the apothecary and shook her head. He immediately put the pieces of the plant back in the leather bag and moved on to the slender bottle.

Holding it up between his thumb and forefinger he said, eyebrows wiggling upward once more, "I believe this elixir will resolve your husband's sleeplessness with much less risk than the other two remedies."

"What is it?" asked Lucy.

"Ah," he said, relishing his superior knowledge, "It is called *lau-da-num*. It is a carefully balanced tincture of opium in alcohol. The great English physician Thomas Sydenham invented it, he who was called, 'the light of England, the skill of Apollo, the true face of Hippocrates,' by the great Herman Boerhaave of Leyden."

"Never mind all that," Lucy broke in. "What does this wondrous drug do? How is it used? What does it accomplish?"

"A few drops will send your husband sweetly to sleep," he promised, "but the taste is excessively bitter. You will need to disguise it in tea or porridge, or indeed any drink or food with a strong taste."

"And is it always effective? Is the effect swift?" asked Lucy.

The apothecary's eyebrows knitted themselves together anxiously. Might he yet lose this sale?

"My dear madam," he said, with a disparaging sniff, "there may be shops where the laudanum is unduly diluted and therefore does not achieve the desired result. But our remedies are prepared under the supervision of the most skilled apothecaries in England and our word is inviolate. You may absolutely depend on the quality of the drug. Within minutes of the consumption of the laudanum, you will hear the happy sound of a gentle snore."

"Oh!" he added, "and it is also very effective in the treatment of pain, cough and the flux, should there be a need. You may even rub a small amount on a baby's gums to relieve soreness when the child is teething." This remark was followed by a large, reassuring smile displaying his broad, yellow teeth.

The price for the laudanum, we learned, was exorbitant. This was no surprise. I suspected our friend quoted his price according to what he sensed to be the client's level of desperation and ability to pay. But we had come to the very capital of the apothecary profession, where only the most reputable and modern of remedies were sold, I told myself. If this drug put Aldrich Harrow out of my way on the night of our great enterprise, it would be well worth the cost.

Chapter Sixteen

The Uses of Chocolate

"Oh, divine chocolate!
They grind thee kneeling,
Beat thee with hands praying,
And drink thee with eyes to heaven."

Marcos Antonio Orellana, quoted in
Manual de fabricacion industrial de chocolate, Valencia,
by Gregorio Mayans, a booklet with verses dedicated to chocolate.

Lucy and I soon realized that, though we had the drug, we needed to devise a way to administer it to Harrow without arousing his suspicion. Our debates about poison were superseded by endless arguments on the subject of what beverage or food would be the best repository for the dose I intended to give to Harrow, and how I would tempt him to consume it at the propitious moment.

Any sort of food seemed unreliable to me. What if he rejected the food or took only one bite and discarded it? What if the texture of the food prevented the potion from being absorbed quickly and doing its work?

"I do know," I said, "that he has a weakness for sweets, for anything made with sugar or honey. He always wants to refuse my offerings, whatever they are, but when I bring tarts, I see him take one with seeming reluctance and then later sneak away with two or even three more."

"So," said Amelia thoughtfully, her long fingers running through the honey-colored curls that dangled from her cap, "perhaps then it should be something liquid and sweet. Liquid because it will be easier to put the sedative in a portion of liquid than in a portion of solid food. Sweet because a sweet taste is what appeals to him. Ale? Coffee? Tea? None of these fit that formula."

201

"There are sweet wines, of course, and champagne," said Lucy.

"I am not sure that he partakes of spirits to any degree," I said. "I have never seen him drinking more than a few swallows of ale. In any case, I don't believe wine would disguise the taste adequately."

Amelia rose and went to the kitchen to consult with her cook, a French Huguenot immigrant, surprisingly skilled for one so young, who had no idea she was preparing her delectable dishes in the bosom of a Catholic family. Phineas had not wanted to take her on. He thought it was too great a risk. Her reaction, if she discovered the family's secret allegiance to the Roman Catholic Church, would be unpredictable. But Amelia was prepared to take a small risk in return for the woman's superior competence in cookery.

When Amelia returned from the kitchen, she was smiling.

"I believe our Madeleine Leblanc has come up with the perfect solution. I told her I wanted to prepare a special treat for my husband when next he returns, a superior and warming drink, but without the overheating of spirits or the excessive liveliness produced by coffee. I am in need of a pleasant beverage to be enjoyed before bedtime, if such a thing can be found."

Lucy and I could not imagine what that could be. We plied her with questions until she finally satisfied our curiosity. Her solution was indeed ingenious. Madeleine had heard tell of an exceedingly delicious beverage from a friend who worked in the kitchen at St. James's Palace. It was specially prepared every morning to be served with the Hanoverian's breakfast. Though the Spanish had first brought cacao beans from the New World to Europe, the French had made *xocolatl* into a fashionable beverage, as they are the first to devise all fashionable things.

Madeleine had heard from her friend that coffeehouses in London were already giving way here and there to new "chocolate houses" that sold the beverage and called it "hot chocolate." The drink was expensive, but, nevertheless, had a following beyond the upper classes.

"But why would I bring something so exotic and costly to the Tower warders?" I asked.

"Because," said Amelia, "you are going to tell them you are

celebrating with them. You believe your husband is to be pardoned and you are grateful for their honest care of him. Later, we will all hasten away in tears because no pardon has arrived."

"Oh," I said, trying to take in this new idea and look at it from all possible angles. "And somehow, as I pour, I must slip the laudanum into the cup that I give to Aldrich Harrow and make sure that he, and only he, receives that cup."

"No, no," said Amelia, "you will be too busy conducting your friends upstairs to see your husband. Lucy must take over the duty of handing about the chocolate."

Lucy never failed me.

"I know which one is Aldrich Harrow," she said, "the overly tall, very young man with the attempt at a moustache, who glares at everyone."

I nodded.

"It will be a delicate task," Amelia warned. "You don't want to put the wrong man to sleep. Yet you must not openly reveal that a certain cup is just for Harrow. It must all be done in a completely natural way."

"I believe I can manage this task," said Lucy dryly. "I have managed harder ones."

Amelia, ignoring Lucy's tone, merely nodded and smiled.

"Of course, you have," she said placidly. "And you, my dear," she said to me, "you must leave Lucy to do it. You cannot be hovering over her or fussing or watching too closely."

"I will send you to the Tower with my best porcelain pot and cups," she added. "I doubt we will have time to collect them. They will be lost."

After a moment she mused aloud, "Perhaps my second-best cups will do."

"Send the chocolate in a plain pewter pot with plain pewter cups," I said. "A fine porcelain tea set may raise suspicions among others besides Aldrich Harrow."

I learned the next day that Lt. Compton had returned to the Lieutenant's Lodgings, but, annoyed by all the noise the warders were making on the floor above him, he had moved himself temporarily to the Bell Tower. He did not often leave his quarters in the bitter winter weather. He seemed to have faith that his prisoners were secure without taking any extra steps to assure it. He knew he would soon be done with the most important ones, who were about to be executed.

The lieutenant's complacency was understandable. The Tower had kept many another wily nobleman safely incarcerated for years. Compton was well aware that his prisoners were lodged in the most forbidding prison in England, from which very few had ever escaped—and those generally by getting the warders drunk and smuggling in rope which enabled them to climb down from an open casement to a waiting boat rocking on the Thames.

Gavin's windows were nailed shut, and the warders kept a close watch on the moat and the Thames. How could they know that my plan did not involve ropes or dangling from windows over a small boat bobbing on a turbulent river? It did not, in fact, involve anything that had ever been attempted before at the Tower.

Madeleine Leblanc was sent on a special errand—to find the slim slivers of pure chocolate made from roasted beans that were called "lozenges," in the marketplace. Failing that, she was to locate the best cacao beans.

It took Madeleine three days to find the chocolate lozenges. She took them to the palace kitchen and asked her friend to inspect and approve them before she returned to the market, bought several bags and brought them back to Smith Square. Then the experiments began.

Madeleine heated the lozenges and tried whipping them with water, with port wine and with milk, adding a generous amount of sugar and a variety of spices, from chile and black pepper to anise and cardamom. We women were helplessly drawn to the kitchen where little dark-haired Madeleine, as slight as a child, glossy black hair drawn up into an oversized cap, bent over, stirring her chocolate pot, alternating spoon and foaming whisk. The blends of fragrances filled the entire house, bringing such sweetness to indoor air as I had never breathed before.

As soon as a batch was finished, Madeleine would give us each a dainty wee spoon to dip into the chocolate, taste and offer our opinions. We had a tendency at first to simply ooh and ah after each exquisite sip, failing to note any useful comparisons. Lucy quickly found paper, quill and inkstand and we began to record our ratings of each new batch. We soon agreed the chocolate was best mixed with milk. The ranking of seasonings was more difficult.

Madeleine would ask in her small, piping voice, "*C'est bon? Lequel est meilleur?*" Then we would launch into cross questioning among ourselves as to which combination of spices was the tastiest. Throughout this culinary trial and error, I was always aware that, at the end of the short span of days that remained until February 24, a large man waited, still obscured by shadows. I could see this much of him: he was wearing a mask and brandishing a gleaming axe.

But I would shake myself and turn from this nightmare vision, to vigorously debate the virtues of cardamom versus vanilla, or cinnamon versus black pepper, with Lucy and Amelia. Once I even dreamed that, instead of the axe, Gavin was offered poisoned hot chocolate to drink, as Socrates had been given a cup of hemlock. But mostly my dreams at this time were blanks that left no memories behind. The nightmare was waiting for me when I woke.

In the end I believe Madeleine settled on using very small amounts of each of the spices she had tested. The result, we all agreed, was sublime.

Lucy was to carry the chocolate in its pot, wrapped in thick cloths to keep it as warm as possible, and then set it on a large stone that rested on the hearth in the Council Chamber. There she would reheat and whisk the chocolate until it foamed and serve it up. Stooped as she would be, stirring by the fire with her back to the room, it should be a simple matter to bring forth the laudanum from an interior pocket, and pour it into the cup intended for Harrow as she handed the cups about.

My brave Lucy even insisted on testing the elixir on herself, just to be sure that the bitterness of the laudanum did not overwhelm the chocolate, and that the drug did quickly induce sleep. We had to save most of the costly liquid for Harrow, so Lucy could only imbibe a few drops.

When she tasted the rich, steaming brew infused with laudanum, she immediately went to the kitchen and ordered Madeleine to add more sugar to her concoction.

"There is room for more sweetening here without ruining the taste," she told us. "Harrow must not become suspicious of the taste, or he may not drink enough of it."

As soon as Lucy had bravely downed her cup, we noticed that her eyelids began to droop. Within minutes she had fallen asleep, curled up in a corner of the sofa, and had begun to snore softly with her small mouth hanging open, revealing a tip of pink tongue. She slept peacefully in the same position throughout the night but woke at dawn with stiff joints, a raging thirst and a sharp headache.

I held her sweet face in my hands and kissed her on the forehead for her courage.

"I thank you for suffering these after-effects," I said to her, "for I hope they will be visited upon Aldrich Harrow tenfold! You have given us the best possible illustration of how the drug will affect him."

"Yes," said Lucy grimly, thin lips pursed. "And he will itch as well." She rubbed her arms vigorously to dispel the sensation.

"But, most importantly, we know now that the drug performs as promised," said Amelia. "We need have no more worries on that score."

You would think our preparations would have been completed at that point, but I insisted that we must also conduct drills and that all of us must practice running up and down stairs and changing clothes in all possible speed. Amelia wore a tiny watch on a chain looped over her waistband, which she would consult, or loan to one of us to time her when it was her turn to race.

I did not practice because I alone would not be changing my clothes. I would remain Lady Clarencefield throughout, conductress of this mad exercise which the French might have called farce. We would be a parade of women upstairs and down, in and out of doors, skirts, bodices and petticoats flying off and on again behind the scenes, swapping out the parts we were to play—it was like farce indeed, but with a deeply serious purpose. If we failed to distract and confuse the warders sufficiently, the result would be imprisonment or worse, perhaps for more than one of us.

I was grateful that we had so many problems to resolve in refining my plot. If any of us had had time to sit and ponder our probable fate, our courage would have abandoned us entirely.

I visited Aelwen three times, begging her to come and join us in our exercises. Even Oswald, who seemed more solicitous of his mother than I had seen him when we first met, pleaded with her to improve our chances by practicing with us, but she—always Aelwen—disdained our efforts at persuasion.

"You have forgotten, Sister," she said to me, as she spread pale green skirts across the sofa in the front parlor, "that I once bewitched the gilded denizens of an entire court, who hung on every sweep of my fan and every lowering of my eyelashes. I believe I can manage to outwit a troop of loutish warders."

"This is a bit different," I argued. "Your purpose this time is not to draw the attention of all, but to slip in and out without attracting a closer look."

"I have played many parts in my time," she said with satisfaction. "I have also been the shadow behind the curtain who goes unnoticed. Lovers' trysts, you know, can only be managed with secrecy and discretion."

The curtains of Aelwen's home on St. James's Square were flung open now and sunlight sought every corner of the room. My sister no longer veiled her face, and I found her quite handsome still with the silvery veins threaded through her ivory-gold hair. It seemed that she had left the graveyard behind and was ready to step back into the living world. I urged once more that she and her son take her carriage into St. James's Park, just to accustom herself to the open spaces of the out-of-doors. But she continued to assure me that I need not bother myself about her ability to perform the part she was assigned.

I did worry, nonetheless. I knew that a last-minute panic on her part would destroy the vertical column of blocks that was my plan and bring it all crashing down. She was the essential block in the center of the column that would make all the other parts fit together. If she failed me, we were lost.

Later, on the evening following my last visit to Aelwen, I sud-denly realized that I had left one part of my plot, an essential part, entirely blank. If I did manage to free Gavin, where would we go? We could not take refuge in St. James's Square or Smith Square. It would be easily discovered that Aelwen was my sister, and that I had stayed in the home of the Thrupps.

Both Aelwen and Amelia could claim that they had known nothing of my plans and had only gone to the Tower to bid farewell to Gavin. Phineas Thrupp was a powerful merchant who played an important role in keeping the commerce of England afloat. And Aelwen was widely known to have married prominent Church of England Whigs and to have been a much-admired fixture at the court of William and Mary and even, for a time, at the court of Queen Anne.

Despite all this, I warned both Aelwen and Amelia that their homes would almost certainly be searched. They must temporarily dismantle their Catholic chapels, hide the instruments of worship and keep priests away.

But this did not solve the problem of where Gavin and I would hide when we fled the Tower. Amelia, who knew London so well, had heard of a small inn located on a quiet street in Bethnal Green. It was clean and discreet, but the landlady, it was whispered, was known to take on almost any dubious tenant for a price. Secret liai-sons of all kinds took place at her establishment.

We would need to stay in hiding at the inn for a week or longer, but Amelia did not think we would be the first outlaws to find refuge for a prolonged period under the sign of The King's Oak. The proprietress was not known to particularly favor Catholics or the return of the Stuarts, which Amelia insisted was a good thing.

"Can we trust her then?" I asked. "If she provides a haven for money, will she not hope to gain more by betraying us? There is bound to be a hue and cry throughout the city, and perhaps a reward offered, once it is known that Gavin has escaped."

"I will make more inquiries," said Amelia, "but I believe this woman, Mrs. Culpepper, steers clear of politics. She could make a great deal of money betraying the secrets of her customers, but what would happen to her business if it became known that she had sold out people who trusted her? The neighborhood is a refuge for many secret Catholics. I believe they would fall upon her and destroy her or burn down her inn if she were to commit such a black deed."

Besides, Amelia reminded me, the king's men would assume that Gavin and I would make for France right away and would look for us at Dover or Gravesend. If that initial search failed, they would suppose we had fled north to Scotland and would cross the Channel from there. Would it not seem absurdly foolhardy for us to remain in London? Amelia did not think they would search London as carefully as those other parts of the country.

When they did not find us, Amelia said, they would think they had missed us and we were already gone. Amelia thought that Phineas could support this assumption by making a well-timed trip to the continent where he could drop hints in certain inns English spies were known to frequent, that we had been seen in France or Italy.

I think the inn in Bethnal Green was only permitted to keep its name, The King's Oak, because it was a long-established place, out of the way, in an obscure corner of London. Perhaps the Hanoverian and his people did not even understand its significance.

It had been well-known in my younger days that Charles II had avoided capture by Cromwell's troops during the Civil War by hiding in an oak tree on the grounds of Boscobel House in Shropshire. When he returned from exile in 1660, he wore oak leaves in memory of that perilous time. For the rest of his life he delighted in telling the story of his hair-breadth's escape and would muse that only the heavy rain that day had kept Cromwell's soldiers from thoroughly searching the forested portion of the grounds of Boscobel.

The inn had thus been named The King's Oak by its original owner who was a Catholic. I thought the name was an auspicious sign and immediately agreed that we would go there if my plan succeeded.

Chapter Seventeen
The Curtain Rises

"The trumpet sounds: be mask'd; the maskers come."

Love's Labours Lost, William Shakespeare

At last Friday, February 23, arrived, the day when my plan must be set in motion. I would either succeed and Gavin would live...or I would fail and he would be executed on the morrow. Then I might be forced to take his place in the Tower with no loving spouse to bring me food and hope.

I was not at all hungry that morning, but Lucy insisted on making me drink a little beef broth and munch on a bit of toast for strength. Generally Lucy and I dressed each other, since we had no ladies' maids to hand. But this day my hands were trembling so badly that I had to call Amelia's maid to do up the hooks and lacings of Lucy's dress and could barely lift the cup to drink the little bit of broth I managed to get down.

"You must," said Lucy sternly, insisting that I not hasten to the Tower fasting, even though my innards threatened to reject whatever food I ate. "You will be as agitated today as you have ever been in your life and you must not let that sensation engulf you with no ballast in your stomach."

She was right, as always. The meal calmed me and we spent the morning laying out the necessary clothing and reviewing our entire operation, step by step, as if we were highwaymen planning to waylay a stagecoach full of London merchants carrying bags of gold. We determined to put our plan into motion in the afternoon with the last element to fall into place just as the early winter dusk arrived. Oswald was to take my few belongings to store at The King's

Oak before we had need of his coach and coachman to carry us to the Tower.

We took turns going out into the garden to observe the weather. It was cold but clear, well enough for now, but I thought it would be nice if a deluge of snow would begin later on to discourage any possible pursuers.

Sadly there was no sign that the weather would turn snowy later to suit us. The sky seemed very high and faraway, a crystalline blue. Only traces of the last snow remained in the parks and flowerbeds. The grass was stiff and frozen and crunched underfoot.

As Madeleine was whipping up the chocolate in the kitchen, Amelia gave us each, as before we went to St. James's, a half coupe of champagne for courage, not a drop more. Lucy and I looked at each other over the edges of our glasses, and I knew we were both thinking that we would have preferred our favorite Scottish whisky, but, like everything else in the Thrupp household, the champagne was of the best, shimmering and crisp. I would have welcomed another half coupe, but I pushed the half-formed desire out of my mind at once.

Oswald arrived with Aelwen's second-best carriage, which had seen better days, but had had new wheels installed for this occasion. Aelwen had neglected it because her best carriage was handsomer, trimmed in gilt and graced with her most recent husband's coat of arms.

The nondescript, black, secondary carriage was far superior for our purposes. It had been in Marvelstone's family for some years before the marquess married Aelwen. Oswald had taken care to rub dirty snow on the new wheels to disguise the fresh shine. The carriage resembled the hackney coaches that were available for hire and always showed much use.

I was not so anxious that I did not notice that my nephew looked younger than usual with a bright pink flush on his comely face. I believe his father John Churchill had given up the habit of flushing with innocent excitement long before I met him at the court of James II.

Oswald was dressed very soberly in dark coat and breeches,

but the buckles on his shoes had a bright sheen and his periwig was well-brushed. I had come to treasure this new young kinsman and hoped I would see him again when he came to take up his military career in France.

Oswald would not enter the Queen's House with us this time but would simply instruct his coachman in shuttling the women back and forth as needed. At the end of the day, Oswald would dismiss the coachman and take my husband to The King's Oak himself, if all went well. I could not dwell on that hope. Too many elements of my plot had to fall precisely into place before we would arrive at that moment.

Lucy emerged from the house very slowly, carrying the heavy pot of chocolate, wrapped in a thick quilt. Amelia followed with a basket full of pewter cups. For once, I was not eager to arrive at the Tower. As it was a frigid day in winter, the city was comparatively quiet. But other carriages and sedan chairs did pass us in the streets. Those who had to brave the cold on foot were wrapped in as many garments as they possessed. They walked quickly with their heads down and did not greet each other cheerily as much as they were wont to do.

All too soon we arrived at the Byward Arch, which I had inwardly titled the Gate of Gloom. I was so well-known that the Tower warders at the gate waved us through without a second glance.

We passed under the Bloody Tower where Sir Walter Raleigh had languished for thirteen years and Archbishop Cranmer was kept just before he was sent to Oxford to be burned by "Bloody Mary," the queen who tried to force England back to Catholicism by burning almost three-hundred stubborn Protestants as "heretics." How I despised all the cruelties on both sides of the religious conflicts!

This dark knowledge of vast and needless suffering felt like it would suffocate me, but I pushed it away and muttered to myself under my breath, reviewing one more time the steps I must take in the next few hours. Lucy and Amelia both glanced at me but said nothing.

We stopped in the courtyard by Tower Green. I took the basket of cups from Amelia and followed Lucy to the Lieutenant's Lodgings.

Even the Tower of London looked bright this day, I thought, its venerable keeps and turrets stalwart images of the strength of England to Englishmen who had never set foot on its grounds.

But to me the sunlight glinting off the walls of the original White Tower and the washed glass of old window casements were a deceptive, sinister facade, because I knew what lay behind those walls. I fervently wished that, after this day, no one I loved would ever lay eyes on the Tower of London again.

Only one guest at a time was allowed to accompany me to Gavin's room. In any case, there wasn't room for more than three people in his garret, and the back and forth of successive guests would help us to confuse the warders. This was all part of my plan.

We came to the Lieutenant's Lodgings, and Lucy and I climbed up to the second floor where, as usual, the guards and their wives—and three children on this day—were chatting and laughing before an enormous fire in the Council Chamber. Horace Bigelow sat with his arm around his red-headed wife, Annie, who looked very small next to him and very round. They were expecting the birth of their first child in the spring.

Young Merton Tewkins, as was his wont, blushed scarlet when I as much as glanced at him, so I smiled and nodded to him but did not speak. Sgt. Matthew Putnam's very pretty wife Deborah was visiting him, I saw. Embracing a small girl on either side of her, she sat on a long bench. All three stood up and curtsied shyly when they caught my eye. I did not think the littlest girl could have been much above two years.

Old Hatton reclined on a wooden chair pulled up as close as he could get to the fire without falling into the embers. He tipped his hat to me.

Thomas Brickle stood leaning on the fireplace mantel, regaling Bigelow with a loud, longwinded story about George Plantagenet, first Duke of Clarence. Clarence was a great drinker who, it was claimed, was drowned in a butt of his favorite Malmsey wine in the Bowyer Tower as punishment for treason against his brother Edward IV. Brickle's rather tipsy acting out of the drowning with loud gurgling, choking noises did not seem fit entertainment for the little Putnam girls, who stared at him. But this was no time for me to admonish him.

It occurred to me that all these men might be dismissed from service if my plan succeeded. I was sorry for it because none of them were bad men...except for Harrow.

I spotted Aldrich Harrow, by himself as usual, in a corner away from the fire, and felt his hard glare upon me as soon as I entered the room. But I was careful not to look at him directly. I did not want him to think I was paying him any mind.

"My friends," I said, trying to lift my eyes, the corners of my mouth, my cheeks, to feign a barely suppressed glow of happiness, "who have been so kind to my lord and myself. I believe we will have good news this day. I believe that my husband will be pardoned. I have brought a special refreshment to share with you on this loveliest of all of the days Our Lord has given us."

I nodded toward Lucy, who was carefully placing the pot on the large stone on the hearth, stooping down, lifting the lid and starting to stir with the whisk she had brought. The women crowded around her to see what she was stirring and erupted in exclamations of excitement. The fragrance of spiced chocolate began to fill the room, an aroma like no other.

"It's what I heard tell of," cried one woman whose dark braids fell out from under her starched cap, "the special drink the king takes of mornings!"

"It's called *chocolate*," I said, "and it is very sweet and spiced with all good flavorings. Please partake while I go up and visit my husband."

In the meantime, Lucy was urging the women to step back in case the hot liquid splashed out of the pot. I did not dare look directly at Harrow but sensed that he would be slow to stir himself and express interest in the beverage. Lucy might be able to serve him last.

I wanted to give Lucy a tap on the shoulder for courage but felt that I should leave her to complete the business her own way. I also feared that, if I drew closer to Harrow, I might be tempted to look at him and give the game away. The essential thing was to ignore him completely. I knew he would be angry at the very possibility that my husband, one of his reviled papists, might escape punishment. He might sneer at me. I might be inclined to respond harshly...that would not do.

I turned and almost ran upstairs to Gavin, as if I truly had good news to impart. Once within his room, I embraced him, ignoring his pallor, and brought out two essential parts of his disguise from the pocket under my skirt, an ivory-yellow woman's wig with falling ringlets in the way that Aelwen wore her hair, and the giant women's shoes. Petticoats were already hidden under and inside his mattress—all placed there within the last few days, after the last shaking up and remaking of the straw pallet.

Despite the difficulties of shaving in cold water with only the bottom of a pewter plate for a kind of mirror, Gavin had followed instructions and kept his face clean-shaven and the hair on his head very short. His guards thought he did it to keep away the lice that plagued prisoners. He had also done as I had asked in trimming his heavy, dark eyebrows.

Whenever any of the warders entered his room, Gavin reclined on the mattress so they would be loath to disturb him. Their searches for hidden contraband were cursory anyway. They were comfortable with him by now, and their oversight was half-hearted. He had never caused them any trouble—as "mad" Winton often did with his rants and lunatic demands. They knew Gavin could not squeeze himself through either of the small windows and fly away, even if he had managed somehow to remove the nails. They were convinced there was not the slightest possibility that he could flee his prison.

In a little while, Lucy came up and joined us.

"I've done it," she said quietly, but her pale blue eyes gleamed with satisfaction. "Sure enough, he was the last to accept a cup. I could see he wanted to reject the chocolate, but finally could not bring himself to do it." The tantalizing fragrance, the exclamations of pleasure from the others, were too much for him, Lucy explained.

"What do you mean?" demanded Gavin.

"It's better that you don't know everything, in case we are discovered," I said. "I promise to explain all in due time."

"He almost caught me putting the bottle away," Lucy said. "I did not hear him. He was suddenly there at my shoulder. Thanks be to Heaven the bottle is small. I was able to quickly encompass it in my hand and conceal it in my inside pocket. He said nothing at all to me—just stuck out his hand for the chocolate."

"That is his way," I said. "He thinks he advances his faith by being ever offensive and discourteous. He is an ass."

Gavin looked at me, startled. Then he laughed.

"You have more bite to you these days, Wife," he said, contemplating me with a smile.

"Cruelty angers me. Injustice angers me," I said, "and, since our times have been overfull of cruelty and injustice, I have been angry for a long time."

Gavin touched my cheek and smiled, the ghost of his old, familiar grin when he might pretend to question my occasional fits of temper, but all the while, I knew he was proud of a wife who was not too restrained by formalities to speak her mind.

"You are true in heart and mind," he once said, "and your anger, when it flares, is generally inspired by righteousness, not petty annoyances. A rare thing. A woman of noble breeding who is more than an image of elegance."

"Ah," I had replied, laughing. "I wish you had known my mother. I am only a flawed copy of her...and I can imagine nothing more tedious than being an image of elegance!"

Lucy continued her story.

"I made Harrow wait," she said, "while I employed the whisk to make sure his chocolate was well mixed. I would imagine he has drunk it all by now."

I embraced her.

"Oh, my Lucy," I said, thinking that she had always handled more than her share of my burdens, and how could I possibly do without her? But that unhappy thought had to be left for another day.

Gavin was instructed to turn his back while I helped Lucy remove her heavy cloak and unlace the butternut-colored bodice and skirt underneath, similar to the ones Amelia would wear. All of us were dressed in clothing of a similar amber or pale chestnut color except Aelwen, who would be swathed in her ebony widow's weeds once more. Beneath Lucy's bodice and skirt were others of the same color. I took the top pieces and tucked them under the mattress.

It was our great fortune that it was winter, when everyone was heavily wrapped and muffled to the ears against the cold. Had the same circumstances arisen in summer, I would have had to invent a different plan.

"I must guide Lucy down and bring Amelia up," I told Gavin. "Be patient. All goes well so far."

We emerged from the garret. Lucy hastened down the stairway and began gathering the pot and cups in her basket. We had decided that, after all, it was best to leave behind no evidence of what we had done. But as she was bent over her task, Aldrich Harrow rose from his corner, ambled slowly to the stair, stumbling a time or two over invisible obstacles, stationed himself with a foot on the bottom-most step and looked up at me with a stare so intent, so enraged, that I felt myself gasp and fall backwards and had to put my hand on the door of Gavin's room behind me to catch myself.

"What're you doing up there for such long time?" he managed to say, though his words were slurred and hard to decipher. I thought the laudanum must be beginning to work and, if I could just brazen this out, he would collapse.

But, before I could speak, he began to climb the stairs. If he were to burst into Gavin's room and rummage through it, we would be discovered.

"No!" I cried. "You will not disturb my lord at his prayers this day of all days."

"Prayer'll not help, not him," Harrow declared, spraying warm, chocolate-flecked spit towards me. "Hell waits for filthy papists. Fires are building up for him now…The devils are dancing with their pitchforks…But you're…I know you're contriving something. I know it. With all your women." His long arms opened and waved about as if to embrace an innumerable collection of malevolent women.

He took a few more steps up, weaving and wavering on his feet but still coming. I felt as if I were teetering on a seesaw, a plank balanced on a log such as I had seen where children played. I might fly up to the sky and win all I sought. Or this man might slam me down and I would lose everything.

I vowed that, before I would allow that to happen, I would leap upon him and knock him back down the stairs, even if I were to injure myself in the process.

"No!" I said again, holding my hands out, palms turned towards him, "You may not."

Lucy was trying to balance the large basket, but she heard this last near scream of mine and started towards the stair. At the same time Matthew Putnam rose, as did Bigelow and old Hatton, and even Brickle turned and fixed his bleary eyes on Harrow and me.

"Harrow," cried Putnam, in his strong baritone. "To me at once. It's your turn to make rounds."

But Harrow, obviously addled, was so fixed on me, the prey he had longed for, that he did not even seem to hear Putnam. Bigelow moved slowly, ponderously in our direction, so slowly that I did not think he would reach us before Harrow thrust me aside, perhaps even off the stairs to the floor below, and burst into Gavin's room.

"Women such as you..." uttered Harrow, now mumbling, eyelids drooping but still coming up, though more slowly. "Always leading men to their doom."

Then, "Papist whore!" he hollered, so abruptly that I almost lost my balance and fell off the stairs myself.

"Harrow. Now!" Putnam ordered. Harrow ignored him.

Over his shoulder I could see Putnam's wife and their two little girls standing in a row staring at me, their pink mouths all framing big O's.

I had nothing in my hands, nothing I could use to block him or fend him off. But I had forgotten about Lucy. I could see her place her basket on the floor but could not see what she did after that.

I was prepared to lunge with all my might when I saw Harrow's head jerk and heard him roar as the chocolate pot bounced off the back of his head and flew away, spraying the remaining drops of chocolate on poor Merton Tewkins before skidding, spinning and falling over on its side on the floor. Harrow whirled around and half ran, half fell down the stairs, but Lucy was ready for him.

The warders had laid their halberds in a heap against the wall, ready to be taken up when next they stood watch at the gates. Lucy had seized one and thrust it upwards towards Harrow. As he headed towards her, arms flailing, she stuck the halberd behind one leg, jerked it forward, and tripped him. He slid, more than fell, down the remaining stairs and lay there at the bottom dazed, as if he could not remember what he was doing or why he was there.

Putnam came, seized his collar, dragged him to the opposite wall and released him, whereupon Harrow collapsed in a heap. His eyes rolled up in his head, and he turned over and passed out of consciousness, face nuzzled into his elbow. The others stood and stared at him.

"D'you suppose he be all right?" asked old Hatton.

"He didn't hit his head that hard. He must be roaring drunk," said Putnam. Then, musing, he added, "The lieutenant should hear of this. Harrow is a poor match for this work. Why must we have him when so many good men need employment?"

Bigelow approached him and whispered something in his ear.

"Constable's wife's cousin-in-law?" said Putnam. "We have too many such already. Useless mawkins. Warders need not be the king's torturers as in olden day. We've no need of his kind."

Yes, I thought, you are right, Matthew Putnam. Harrow's viciousness is only matched by his stupidity.

I was still trembling, but Lucy—my Lucy—had already thrown the halberd aside and was retrieving the chocolate pot from where it lay. She stopped to look at Harrow, who was, to my amazement, already beginning to snore. Then she shot a glance at me, one corner of her mouth quirking upward.

At that I revived and tripped the rest of the way down the stairs. But I did not smile. I let them overhear me say to Lucy, "Why has the pardon not yet come?"

Lucy merely shook her head, balancing her basket, and we went down the next flight of stairs and out into the cold where Lucy would now take her turn sitting and waiting in the carriage and Amelia would come with me back into the Lodgings. Oswald had stepped down and was walking back and forth with the coachman in the frosty air, rubbing his hands together and stamping his feet, trying to warm himself.

Though it was only mid-afternoon, the sun was already waning. Blue shadows of the Lieutenant's Lodgings peaked roofs were extending their long fingers across Tower Green. Amelia and I hastened back inside. The first part of our plan had taken too long to execute. We must move faster.

Amelia was wrapped in two deeply hooded cloaks of an identical buff color, but the top one completely covered the one beneath so that it could not be seen. Now I was no longer affecting gaiety. As Amelia and I climbed the stairs to Gavin, we bent our heads together, faces buried in our handkerchiefs. I managed to emit a small sob. It was quiet around the fire. I sensed that the warders and their wives had never really believed my lord would be pardoned and had anticipated that my optimism would be short-lived.

I turned from the top of the stairs and said to them all, "Please call to me if a messenger comes." Then we entered Gavin's garret. In no time, Amelia had shed her top cloak and thrown it over Gavin's one chair for Aelwen's use. We could not risk getting bits of straw strewn over this outer cloak, which would cover all the rest.

Amelia lingered for a few moments. We spoke in low voices. I had been so caught up in carrying out my plan that I had not dwelt on the realization that, when Lucy and Amelia rode off into the night, I would more than likely never see either of them again, these two women who had become almost as dear to me as my husband and my children.

Lucy had been my companion for so many years. She had given me comfort in some of the most bitter episodes of my life and shared so many of my adventures. Amelia, by contrast, was a very new friend, but had played the decisive part in making this escape possible by contributing her wisdom, her courage, a portion of her fortune, even her intimate knowledge of fashion, to the cause. I told Amelia I would pray for her and for Phineas and for her son and daughter and their families, whom I had never met, every day for the remainder of my life.

Then it was time to take Amelia back down, weeping gently into her handkerchief. By now my eyes were red as well; I had no need to feign distress, as the warders could surely see.

At the carriage I embraced both my beloved friends and made them swear to write to me and think of me and pray for me, as I would pray for them. At the last, I held Lucy so tightly, I believe I knocked the breath out of her a bit. And she, even she, always the very model of reserve and dignity, allowed a stray tear or two to slide down her cheeks.

In my last moments with her, I did not think so much of how she had come to me in Paris when I was in such despair at the loss of Glynis, or how she had been my mainstay and comfort at Heath Hall, helping with the children and keeping me in spirits when Gavin was gone.

Instead I thought of the four of us sisters—Marged, Aelwen, Glynis and me—practicing the gavotte under Lucy's tutelage, tip tap, step, step, skip, so long ago in the ballroom of the house at Lincoln's Inn Fields. In my memory sunlight streamed in through the long windows illuminating the radiance of our youth, we four Carlisles and Lucy. Lucy, who had seemed so old to me at the time, was probably only in her twenties then.

I could still hear Lucy saying, "No, no, girls. The minuet *shuffles*; the gavotte *lifts!*"

I saw again in my mind the moment when she gave me the little volume of John Donne's poems, which I have kept with me through all my troubles. And with the book, the gift of reading for learning and for joy, which has eased my heart in many a hard time.

"Pray," I said to Lucy, "look after my children for me and tell that...gentleman of yours...that he is a man who has found a great treasure. He must always be worthy of it."

"Oh, of course," she said, smiling through her tears. "I will remind him daily and scold him with great severity if he ever lapses from perfection in his regard for me." With a gesture of uncharacteristic tenderness, she touched my cheek very softly, very briefly and smoothed away a tear with her thumb.

Then they were gone. They would be safely stashed far away

from the final stage of this escapade. Oswald would return as quickly as he could with Aelwen, who was the linchpin of the entire precarious structure of my plan.

That made me more than a little anxious. What if, after all, Aelwen could not bring herself to leave St. James's Square? I did say a prayer then, for what more could I do? I had stopped asking myself if the Blessed Virgin was near me. I had decided I would discover the answer to that question in the success or failure of my plan.

I went back upstairs to wait with Gavin, who had begun to put on his new ladies' shoes. The time between when I saw the black coach depart under the Bloody Tower and the time when it was due to return—though it was to be less than an hour—seemed the longest expanse of time in my life. Longer than childbirth, longer than my winter's journey to London, longer even than waiting for Gavin to come home from the war.

This time, bless him, it was Gavin who calmed *me*. I kept going out to the stairs and two flights down to the door to see if I could spot the carriage, knowing that the warders would think I was still watching for the imaginary messenger carrying a pardon.

Finally Gavin made me sit with him on the mattress and catch my breath.

"If you are caught," he said, "you must allow me to take all the blame. I will say this entire plot was my idea and I forced you to carry it out, although you always thought it was foolishness."

I said nothing. I uncorked a small jar I had brought with me and was busy brushing white powder over the remnants of his dark eyebrows and the stubble of his beard.

When I was done, I put the little jar and brush in my pocket, and Gavin put an arm around me and pulled me close to his side.

"If it happens that I must die tomorrow," he said, "I will know that I have enjoyed the love of a rare wife indeed, a woman of such wit and perseverance that no man has seen her likeness before." That made all my tears come. For once, I had no rejoinder but to lay my head on his shoulder. This great love had been given to us. For a brief moment, I thought I might find a way to be grateful for that, no matter what happened.

But soon enough, the room began to seem too quiet. I lifted my head. I strained so hard to hear the coach returning that it seemed something must have stopped up my ears.

We had no way to track the passage of the minutes, Gavin's pocket watch having been stolen from him on the road from Preston to London. But it seemed to me that it was taking much too long for the carriage to return. The shadows outside were longer, the air more chill. It would be dark before long and we must hasten away.

I began to contemplate all the disasters that could have befallen Oswald and Aelwen—Aelwen refusing in the end to leave the house, the carriage losing a wheel on the road, a horse throwing a shoe, an unexpected visitor to Aelwen's house (quite a fantastical notion since Aelwen had almost no visitors). My thoughts tumbled over each other in a long chain of dire imaginings.

The warders and families below had quieted too. The children had gone home. Only Bigelow's wife remained with the men. The Bigelows lived in a small apartment on the grounds of the Tower and could easily walk to their dwelling. As I clambered up and down the stairs, trapped in a full-blown nervous anxiety that was no longer just a performance, I observed that the group below were no longer teasing and buoyant, and no longer looked at me.

I had just begun to think I might have to dress Gavin in the women's attire we had cobbled together for Aelwen and try hiding his face under the hood of a cloak as we sneaked down the stairs. But without the veils I did not think the improvised disguise would be adequate.

At last I heard horses' hooves in the courtyard and ran downstairs and out the door once again to see the same black carriage pulling up in front of the Lieutenant's Lodgings with Aelwen alone inside and Oswald now on the coachman's seat. Aelwen's coachman had been dismissed for the night.

"You are much delayed," I charged with no preamble, but in such a quiet, hoarse tone that at first they could not hear me, and I had to repeat myself.

Oswald eased off the high seat and jumped lightly down onto the cobblestones. "Thanks to my lady," he told me with a roll of his eyes and an exaggerated sigh. "She spent so much time on her toilette that I thought we would be fortunate to arrive at midnight." In a lower tone that only I could hear, he added, "I think she may have become confused and imagined she was to attend a ball at St. James's, instead of playing a grief-stricken mourner visiting the nation's most fearsome prison."

Meantime, Aelwen was trying to alight from the carriage without falling over her multitudinous layers of black petticoats and skirts and full-length veils. She looked even more specterlike than she had the first time I had seen her. I could barely glimpse her silvered golden hair and saw only two black holes that were her eyes under the hood overhanging her face and shadowing it even further.

Her full suite of mourning attire included oversized black-glazed gloves, which she carried rather than wore, a large black handkerchief and a black paper fan. She was so thoroughly enshrouded that I thought it might take too many precious minutes to divest her of her garments and array Gavin in them.

I did not waste time scolding her but hustled her inside and up the stairs, putting her on the outside towards the wall, handkerchief to face, as we climbed so that I would partially hide her from the warders and prevent their getting a good look at her.

I have to admit that I had had some concerns about depending on my mercurial, self-centered sister to carry off this critical phase of my plan. During my long wait for her, all those doubts began to haunt me again. Was her heart truly changed?

Now that she was finally here, I wondered if she could, after all, resist drawing attention to herself, becoming the heroine of the little drama I had devised. Would she faint on the stairs or give forth exaggerated cries and sobs?

But, whatever her many faults, I had never thought Aelwen to be a witless creature. Whether her newfound piety was sincere or not, she must have known that if our scheme failed, she, and perhaps her son, would be caught in the net as well as Gavin and myself. It was difficult to imagine Aelwen eating stale bread and drinking befouled water in a Tower dungeon.

But Aelwen was true to her word and played her part superb-ly. Her tears of grief were authentic enough to dampen her veils, but her sobs were muted. She moved slowly as if burdened by grief but proceeded steadily up the stairs and did not pause for dramatic effect. She was so convincing that for a moment I thought she was genuinely weeping soft tears—perhaps out of anxiety at this abrupt emergence from her long seclusion. But then she turned to me between sniffles, and I thought I glimpsed a quick flash of white teeth in a smile. The smile vanished and was followed at once by another sob.

At last we were inside Gavin's room, and I saw him visibly suppress a startled cry when he saw my sister for the very first time in her elaborate black ensemble. He recovered himself and bowed, which I knew expressed gratitude for her assistance rather than def-erence to her higher rank.

Gavin and I began pulling off her many layers at once. When we got to the point of undoing the long row of small buttons down the back of her black silk dress, Gavin left that task to me and began to draw out the bodice and petticoats we had secreted in the mattress, which were almost an exact match in color to the tawny costume Amelia had worn that afternoon. As soon as I had removed the black dress, Gavin drew it over his own head, and Aelwen began to pull on the buff-colored bodice, petticoats and skirts we had ac-cumulated for her.

Nothing could be heard in the little room but the rustle of silks and our heavy breathing as we tried to perform in a matter of minutes two toilettes that would normally require an hour or more each.

It was fortunate indeed, I thought, that Gavin had grown so lean in prison since Aelwen remained slim. I had feared that Aelwen's gown might be too small for him, but I could see at once that the black silk gown would fit him, although it would be a bit short. Aelwen, tall as she was for a woman, was not as tall as Gavin. As I laced her into the butternut-colored bodice, she began to fasten the buttons in back on the black dress Gavin had assumed, which amazed me, though I said nothing, either to tease or praise her.

I saw that Aelwen had gotten entirely into the spirit of the moment. She who, for years, had stood perfectly still, arms outstretched, while a maid—or two maids—enrobed her, layer by layer, from head to toe, was actually carefully buttoning a dress on a man. Of course, neither Aelwen nor Gavin would be dressed as carefully or as thoroughly as they would have been under normal circumstances. We were confident that the veils and hooded cloaks would cover each enough that small details like skipped buttons would not be noticed.

I cast the buff-tinted, hooded cloak over Aelwen and was struck by how much she did resemble Amelia—at least she would appear so to a casual observer. We were depending on the hope that, with all the comings and goings all day, no one below was keeping track or making note. I was praying that no one would notice that only *three* friends altogether had gone up to see Gavin, but *four* friends would be coming back down, especially since the gowns of the women were similar and their faces would be hidden. If anyone was surprised to see that a woman who had already come and gone, had now returned, would any warder paying attention not assume that he simply had not seen her when she entered the second time?

Though the warders' wives had all been kind to me, I had had some fears that they might notice the differences in dress with their keener eyes for women's clothing. I had even imagined at times that one sharp-eyed woman among them might discern the entire scheme, but I thought that her woman's heart might tell her to say nothing and let us escape.

That was a vain wish, of course, that put too much weight on the camaraderie among women. Any wife of a warden who realized Gavin was escaping would also understand at once that her husband might be blamed, along with the others, and might lose his much-sought-after position at the Tower, or even be accused of helping us. That concern would surely supersede any sisterly feeling. Even a kindly soul, who was truly saddened by our plight, would decide that her husband's income, necessary to her family's survival, outweighed the loss of my husband's life.

Aelwen's outfit was complete, so I concentrated on pulling the blond wig down on Gavin's head as hard as I could and pinning it, and then throwing the hooded cloak and the many veils over all. Oh, but I had not thought how he would navigate those steep stairs in his skirts, being used neither to the skirts nor to the way the veils would hinder his vision.

I could see Aelwen was trying not to giggle at the sight of my husband transformed into a weepy widow, but I could find no amusement in any of this. It was full dark now, and we were still not away.

I conducted Aelwen back down the stairs as quickly as I could, the two of us leaning our heads together and weeping. I glanced very briefly at the warders. Harrow was still in the same spot on the floor. His snoring was louder and full of bubbles.

I would have so loved to kick him at least once while he was unconscious, but there was no time. Anyway, it would have been dreadfully out of character for me to do such a thing. I must maintain my pose as the charming noblewoman who would soon become a tragic widow—no pardon having arrived.

Old Hatton dozed in his chair by the fire, and Horace Bigelow and his little wife Annie murmured in low voices, their backs to me. Only Merton Tewkins glanced our way for a moment and quickly looked away again.

I ensconced Aelwen in the carriage. Poor Oswald had huddled in a corner of one of the benches inside with a fur robe wrapped around him and still looked terribly cold. His teeth were chattering. What a day it had been for him—waiting and shivering, shivering and waiting. I seized and pressed Aelwen's hand and then Oswald's, and turned once more to hurry inside. We did not speak. We all knew this next step would be the most delicate and difficult moment of the entire day.

Weary of climbing and weary of the squeezing of my innards with tension all day, I trudged once more up the two flights of stairs and entered the little garret. Gavin was so white that I could see his pallor even through the many black veils.

"We will go slowly," I said, "taking the steps very carefully. You will be weeping into your black handkerchief and will be partially leaning on me in your extreme grief. Whatever you do, don't try to descend at your normal pace. You will go pell mell, somersaulting, petticoats up and wig askew."

I also warned him not to raise his skirts too much in the effort to avoid falling. A genteel noblewoman would prefer to drag her petticoats in the mud and snow rather than lift them higher than would be considered acceptable in polite society.

He nodded, too overcome with fright to speak, I thought. My brave cavalier of just a few months ago had been reduced by imprisonment and the near threat of death to this fainthearted creature.

But I realized that was unjust. I was asking him to execute an intricate maneuver while encased in unfamiliar and cumbersome attire. Young women who are beginning to learn how to walk in long skirts usually don't have to worry about getting their heads chopped off if they trip. Another thought I must not think as we made our way down the stairs.

We opened the door and stepped out onto the landing. I carefully pulled the door closed behind me to conceal the disarray of the room. As I did so, I spoke into the empty room, "I will return in a moment," I said, my voice convincingly choked.

Now I was as frightened as Gavin. The decisive moment having arrived, I was not sure I could perform the task I had set for myself. I thought of millers' daughters told to spin straw into gold, and goose girls ordered to empty a river with a nutshell. But there was nothing for it but to make the attempt.

I turned and took Gavin's arm and we two forlorn, weeping women began to descend the stairs very slowly, step, pause, step, pause. At one point Gavin caught his heel on an edge of petticoat, tripped and began to fall. I caught his arm and was able to right his balance.

My husband, who had been such a powerful, though lithe, figure, a solid mass of sinew and bone, was now fragile and light, leaning heavily against my shoulder. All at once, I was furious at what the Hanoverian had done to him—and to me—and that overwhelmed and snuffed out my fear. I almost began to descend too fast, but restrained myself before I caused Gavin to teeter again. I vowed I would somehow, in time, restore Gavin to his old self.

The moments lengthened. We seemed to be moving so slowly that I felt as if we were wading through some glutenous mess up to our knees. I was afraid to look at the warders, for I did not want to attract anyone's attention. This made me feel like a blindered horse. I could not tell if anyone was watching, if anyone was suspicious.

Moment crept after interminable moment. We reached the bottom of the first flight of stairs, and I thought that at least the second staircase to the ground floor would be easier because the room below was dark and no one would be watching us. I was mistaken.

Halfway down this last set of stairs, Gavin caught a wide measure of hem with his foot and fell to his knees, bumping down two stairs with an oomph and then a cry that, to my ear, sounded rather too low in tone, not like a woman's high-pitched exclamation.

Matthew Putnam appeared at the top of the stairs.

"All's well, my lady?" he called to us.

I was trying to help Gavin stand up but it was difficult. All those petticoats. Putnam bounded down the stairs to help.

"Sh-h-h-h," I hissed softly in Gavin's ear.

Now we are truly lost, I thought.

Putnam soon gently lifted Gavin by an elbow and righted him. Sensibly, Gavin did not look at him and said nothing, not even a thank you.

"It's all been too much for my cousin," I managed to say, little above a scratchy whisper. "Her husband died only a week ago."

"I am sorry to hear it," he said. Putnam was always courteous.

"I must get her into the carriage," I said. At last we reached the bottom. But Putnam insisted on coming outside and assisting with that effort. Together we bundled all Gavin's stiff skirts and under-layers in after him. Once Gavin was inside the carriage, he plunged his face into the black silk handkerchief.

Thank God, I thought, for the black gloves. Otherwise, Putnam could not have helped but notice Gavin's large, long-fingered hands, unlike the hands of any noblewoman ever born.

At last I was able to slam the carriage door. Putnam, kindly soul that he was, stood awkwardly regarding us all for a very long moment, and then turned to go back inside, thinking, I am sure, to leave me alone to say goodbye to my dear friends in peace.

"Now you must go," I said softly, "and go quickly. I will play my little game again upstairs pretending you are still there until I am sure you are safely away and cannot be followed."

Aelwen, Gavin, Oswald—who was about to climb up on the coachman's box—all stared at me. They had assumed I would jump in and leave with them.

"But you will have no means of escape!" Gavin declared.

"As you came up the hill just now, did you see hackney coaches for hire at the bottom of the hill?" I asked Oswald. "There are nearly always two or three there."

"Yes," he said, "but the night grows late and cold. They may leave any time for want of a fare."

"I'll take that chance," I said. "I must be sure you are full away before I depart. If the coaches are gone from the Tower gates, I'll walk until I find one. It can't be too far, and I've my warmest cloak."

"Wife...," Gavin began. All at once, at the most inopportune moment possible, he came completely to life. He began to open the door of the carriage. "I cannot leave you here alone. I can't let you run the risk of suffering the punishment meant for me."

I pushed the door hard against him, admiring his chivalrous instincts but knowing there was no time to argue. Not now.

"You've trusted me so far," I said, as I squeezed his hand gently through the carriage window. "You must trust me a little longer."

He shot me a suspicious glance. I guessed that in his extreme fatigue after long days of despair, he was beginning to wonder if I had foolishly determined to be a martyr, to sacrifice myself to assure his safety by staying in his room until dawn.

"It would be a poor end," I said sternly, "to give up my life for yours. I intend to save us both. I give you my word I will follow you." I did not think he was entirely reassured but he said nothing more.

Oswald called to the horses and whipped them up, but little force was needed. They knew his voice. The carriage turned and, for the last time, passed under the Bloody Tower arch and vanished into the blackness. I looked around me and shuddered. How dark this place was at night, I thought, with only a candle in a high window here and there and the occasional lantern hung on a nail high up on the stone walls. I had not lingered outside here at night before.

When I turned to go in, I was alarmed to see Putnam standing, waiting for me, just inside the door. Had he heard me mention my "little game"?

But he did not seem to regard me with mistrust. He offered me his arm, and we climbed the first flight of stairs in silence. Then I gestured to him to signify that I would go on alone.

"I must go up and see my lord again before I leave," I said. "He is so distraught. We believed today would bring relief but..." I bowed my head.

I thought Putnam was about to say something to me once, then twice, as we climbed. But he could not say that German Geordie was unjust. He could not say that the Usurper was a tyrant and my husband should not have been condemned. So Putnam did not speak further, only expressing his sympathy with considerate gestures. I was grateful for his kindness and even more grateful for his failure to see what was going on right under his nose.

They all—with the exception of Harrow, who was motivated only by a generalized suspicion and hatred of all Catholics—thought they had my measure. I had drawn out their compassion with my warmth, my faithfulness to my husband, my little gifts, even my willingness to toast to the health of the Hanoverian with the ale I myself had purchased. I was performing the part they expected—the highborn lady who, after she had made every effort within reason to save her husband, would submit with no further outcry to the cruel whim of the Fates.

They did not know I had been dragged across the elegant carpet the full length of the Great Drawing Room at St. James's rather than let go of the Toad King. They could not gauge my determination.

I had done nothing, not so much as a single thing, to make them wary or dubious. I had asked for no favors other than that my husband be well fed and cared for.

I gave myself only a limited amount of credit for cleverness. If

I succeeded it would be because, when people see what they expect to see, they look no further.

But they would know me better soon enough.

Despite all this, I would have preferred to sit on a witch's dunking stool than to climb that last flight of stairs one more time and so went up very slowly. All day I had been frustrated by delays in the forward movement of my scheme. Now the more time I could waste, the better were Gavin's chances of getting well and truly away. But it was one of the hardest things I have ever done to discipline myself to take my time and not race down the stairs, out the door and down the hill to safety.

I entered Gavin's empty room and began to speak aloud, first in my own voice, then in a lower voice, hoping I would sound a bit like Gavin. As I spoke, I walked around the room, stepping lightly and then tromping more firmly as Gavin would have done.

I told "Gavin" I still expected the pardon to come. He must not give up hope. "He" responded that he was grateful for my fortitude but felt what he must do now was to write down his final thoughts and repent of his sins. Thus we continued for a few minutes, as I played both parts.

My plan was that the warders would hear two different voices, not necessarily understand any of the words I spoke. But I followed a little "script" I had devised that fit the moment anyway, just in case.

I even staged a little softly spoken disagreement between us, very affecting even to me. I was complaining that Gavin must maintain hope, and he was insisting that it was better for him to be resigned and prepare himself for the worst. I observed that tears were leaking from my eyes but did not try to wipe them away. I needed to be tearful.

I have already saved him, I thought. Now I will discover whether I can save myself as well.

Then a terrible notion occurred to me. The authorities would expect me to know where Gavin was hidden. If I were caught, they would try to force that knowledge from me. How long would Gavin wait for me at The King's Oak before he would realize I had been arrested and he must change houses?

At last I thought sufficient time had passed that Gavin must be out of reach and hidden. I had performed my touching, little solo scene long enough. I slipped once more back through the garret door, reassuring "Gavin" that I would return early in the morning, still hoping to have good news. This time, before I closed the door, I pushed the string that lifted the latch through to the other side so that it would be difficult to open the door from the outside.

I started down the stairs for the last time, breathless and hoping that the most precarious part of the ordeal was now over. But halfway down, I saw that, of all people, old Hatton stood rheumy-eyed at the bottom. He had roused himself, determined to express his condolences to me before I left, although he might well already be listed as one of the guards who was to march my husband to the executioner's block the very next morning.

I had perhaps been a little too attentive and patient with Hatton. Now would I pay for that misjudgment? With all good intentions, in his effort to repay my kindness to him, he was preventing my escape.

He stuttered and stumbled through his words, trying to convey his admiration for me and my lord and his great sorrow that the pardon had not come. I knew well how longwinded he could be.

"My lady," he said, "all the men are overcome with sorrow for you and your lord. And we want to say that we only do our duty as we must but take no pleasure in it, where your good husband is concerned...not that we ever take pleasure in the prisonings and... doings in of others...a' course..."

And on and on he went, going forward with one line of thought and then veering sideways through another and another, while I pictured the last coachman for hire drifting away from the Tower gates, abandoning his post for the night with no fares in sight.

I listened to Hatton for a bit, and finally I thought, mayhap I could make use of these kindly emotions. I could ask him for a final favor.

With the tears in my eyes that were born more of frustration than sorrow at that moment, I said, "There is one last boon you can give me and I trust you will do so. My husband has asked that he not be disturbed throughout this night, which, it appears, is to be his last on earth."

Here I did almost burst into tears. My whole body was shaking. The drawn-out day's performance had been too much. But I was a Carlisle and would retain my dignity before the warders, no matter what. I did not break into open sobs.

Hatton was plainly distressed, but he did not know what to do for me. He was afraid to touch me, for which I was deeply grateful. If he had tried to squeeze my hand or pat my shoulder, I think I would have screamed and might even have roused Harrow. Somehow I continued.

"Please attend to me. My lord wants no supper," I said. "He intends to pray, cleansing his soul for what lies beyond, until the cock crows. He also needs to give much thought to what he will say on the scaffold. May I trust you to see that no one disrupts his solemn preparations? May I ask this last favor of you?"

Hatton was so moved he could not speak. He just nodded his head and bowed, an awkward motion where he stood on the lowest step. In truth, I felt sorry for the old man and feared he most of all would be likely to lose his position and his pension. But there was nothing I could do for him.

I told him I would return very early in the morning, as I had promised my lord.

"Please," I said, "make sure that he is given the peace he requires. Thanks be to you and your fellows again for all your kindness to him and to me. I will see you in the morning."

Then at last he moved from my path, and I almost ran to the last flight of stairs, taking them two at a time.

I emerged from the Lieutenant's Lodgings into that chill, dark night, and admonished myself to walk slowly. A woman who knew she would be a widow the very next day would not romp. I walked under the Bloody Tower arch, and down the long hill, along the wall behind the Lieutenant's Lodgings, past the fat Bell Tower and the narrow rampart called Elizabeth's Walk that ran from the Bell Tower to the Beauchamp Tower, then through the Byward Arch and finally out into the black streets.

Not a single carriage awaited.

For the first time in this long day, I had absolutely no idea what to do. I knew vaguely the whereabouts of The King's Oak Inn in Bethnal Green, but had no notion in which direction it lay from the Tower. North perhaps? And which way might that be with no sun in the sky to guide me?

I wrapped my heavy cloak more tightly around me against the sharp gusts of raw wind, and knew that, whatever I did, I could not stay here where I might be found. If the warders had decided, after all, to violate my last orders and enter Gavin's cell, they might already be heading down the hill trying to catch up to me.

I had just made up my mind to follow the riverbank and search for another coach when I heard horses' hooves coming towards me. I pulled back from the street, but there was no place to hide where I stood.

And then I saw, oh bless his sweet, young soul, it was the black carriage with Oswald on his coachman's box, a torch by his side, looking for me. I ran at him waving and calling. When he stopped, I fell into the carriage and gave way to the tears that had accumulated all that long day.

As we gathered speed, I did not look back at the Tower, which had so dominated my life. My most fervent prayer was that neither I nor Gavin would ever see the City of London again. My relief so overwhelmed me that I forgot to listen for horses behind us, as Oswald drove through the streets which we seemed to have almost entirely to ourselves.

Just as I was beginning to snuffle instead of sob, we arrived at The King's Oak. I barely had time to embrace my nephew, now known and loved, or to thank him for coming back to find me.

I had some hope of seeing him again in time, and perhaps his mother also, now that she had so brilliantly overcome her fears—or perhaps had decided that she had worn out the limited charms of being the Mysterious Recluse of St. James's Square and needed a new role to play. But I was hardly done thanking Oswald when Mrs. Culpepper, a comely woman of middle age, dressed in dark colors and wrapped in a good wool cloak, came out of the inn and ordered me to go inside.

"There must be no noise in the street," she whispered.

Oswald promised me hastily that as soon as possible he would send a message or come himself with the details of the arrangements to transport Gavin out of the country. We knew the king's men would be searching for a man and a woman trying to get across the Channel and thought it more prudent that Gavin should leave first and alone.

From her many years at court, Aelwen had retained one friend, formerly a very good friend, who still worked at the Venetian embassy and could help us. Gavin would wear livery and leave England in the guise of a servant to the Venetian ambassador.

I had determined that, when I judged it to be safe, I must go back to Scotland before I could follow Gavin to France, though I had not yet told him. I felt I must see the children. And there were documents and valuables we could not do without in exile.

Gavin would surely disapprove. But, at that moment, overcoming Gavin's objections seemed no more than jettisoning a pebble from my shoe compared to what we had just managed. I was in less danger than he, for there was no sentence of death on my head, and I would promise to be prudent. I had already proven myself.

Oswald jumped back up on the coachman's box and with a silent wave, he was off and soon vanished into the shadows.

There were no other lodgers in the house, but Mrs. Culpepper hustled me upstairs at once where she knocked softly on a door at the end of a long hall, opened the door and ushered me within. The tiny room contained a narrow bed and a table where bread and cheese and wine had been placed. A fire had been made up in the little hearth.

"It is not the best room in the house," she said, "but it is the most secluded. Nonetheless, you must get in bed with your husband and stay there. I expect other lodgers later tonight, and tomorrow the inn will be full. There must be no noise coming from this room or, as unseen guests, you will cause talk."

She commanded us to stay in bed and not walk about. If we had to use the chamber pot, we must tiptoe in our bare feet and make no noise. She would bring more food the next day when she could. Having delivered her admonitions, she left us.

My husband had managed, no doubt with Aelwen's help, to divest himself of his disguise. He must have left some of the veils and underskirts in the carriage, as I saw that the pile of discarded black garments, thrown into a corner of the room, was not very large. On top of the bundle sat a pair of black oversized women's shoes with silver lacings.

Something about those shoes that had caused us so much trouble, and my husband's dear, shorn face with the powdered eyebrows, peeking over the top of a sheaf of quilts, seemed to me to be the most comical things I had ever seen. I began to laugh and could not stop. Of course, I was to make no noise, so I only shook violently and wept profusely, as if all the water in my body was flowing forth.

Gavin looked at me with enormous eyes, thinking, I'm sure, that this entire escapade had broken me, and that he had no idea how to bring me back to my senses. But then, because I could not talk, I gestured at the shoes, and he looked at them and caught my hysteria and began to laugh as well, as we writhed and wept and clutched at each other for some minutes, hands pressed tightly over our mouths.

When our wild mirth finally began to subside, I think we suddenly, both at the same time, understood what we had done. Without a word we realized that Gavin was free of the grasp of the false king and would live. He would live.

Our madness leaked away. He seized my shoulders, and I put my hands on his dear face, and we began to cry in earnest. Despite the tears, I have never known such joy.

Finally he whispered, "You have done what could not be done, what has never been done, Wife."

And I demurred. "I have not. Other men have escaped from the Tower."

"By giving the guards strong drink and money. By knotting sheets and dropping into boats. Not by a brilliant subterfuge such as this," he said. "Not by using a relay of women and spiriting a prisoner away under the very noses of his keepers. You have performed a miracle!"

Then I told him the whole story so he would see that this had not been the doing of one woman alone, but that all had contributed, and it could not have been done without all.

"But it was *your* plan," he said, knowing of my great love for the theater and for stories. "The others helped, but you wrote the play and directed the actors. I don't believe any man has ever had such a wife."

"I had to do it," I said simply, "or allow you to die. That was not possible."

So it was that for three days we could not leave the bed, and had nothing to do but drink the wine, and the bed was narrow, and we were overflowing with happiness, we clung to each other as husband and wife. By the time I joined my husband in France, I knew I was with child again. Her name, when she was born on French soil, was Liberté Lucy Amelia. We called her Libby.

When we reached France, I was surprised at the legend I had become. Women especially sought my advice, not just about helping imprisoned or endangered relations, but about sickness, family squabbles, even issues of inheritance. I tried to deal with all in kindness and help them find wise counsel.

In my later travels and travails, I gave credit for Gavin's escape to the Blessed Virgin. But in my heart, although I feel her with me again and believe she was testing me in those hard days, I always knew whose hands had delivered my husband from death. I knew their names and I knew that it was our joined wisdom, our long-schooled fortitude, our care for each other, that had accomplished the deed.

THE END

Author's Historical Note

**Spoiler alert! I'm suggesting that readers not read this histori-
cal note until after they have finished reading** *A Noble Cunning.*
**There are many spoilers in the following discussion of the rela-
tionship between the novel and the true story that inspired it.**

When my husband and I visited Traquair House in Scotland
in October 2014, we heard the story of the exploits of Winifred
Herbert Maxwell, Countess of Nithsdale. During the aftermath of
the 1715 Jacobite Rebellion, Winifred rescued her husband from
the Tower of London the day before his scheduled execution by
carrying out a complicated plan with the help of a group of devoted
women friends. Her feat was unique in the history of the Tower.

Despite my lifelong fascination with the history of the UK, I
had never heard this story before. I could not stop thinking about
it. I thought that Winifred Maxwell was a true, unsung, feminist
hero, and, what was even more remarkable, she had overcome all
the limitations placed on women in the 18th century to accomplish
this remarkable deed *with the help of other courageous women.*

The essential events of Winifred's dramatic life, as set forth in
this novel, are all based on fact. Her home in Scotland was raided
by Covenanters, she did travel to London alone in the midst of one
of the worst snowstorms in many years to try to save her husband,
and she did visit the Court of St. James's and was dragged across
the floor by King George I when she tried to present her petition
for mercy for her husband.

She also did, in fact, choreograph the visits of a series of
women friends to the Tower and the disguising of her husband in
women's clothes so that he could be smuggled out and away. To fool
the guards, Winifred even, like Bethan Glentaggart, the protagonist
of my novel, went back to her husband's cell after he was gone and
pretended to talk to him before she made her own escape.

Most of the villains in my version of the story are fictional,
other than King George I himself. Though the Covenanters who

raided Winifred Maxwell's home were certainly dangerous religious fanatics, there was no literal model for Minister MacGurk. The real Winifred had sisters, but none of them, as far as I know, resembled the troublemaker Aelwen. Sadly, Phineas and Amelia Thrupp are also fictional creations, though Winifred did have women friends living in London who took her in and helped her carry out her plot. Bethan's children are fictional and not to be identified with Winifred's actual children. On the other hand, the character of Lucy Dunstable in the novel is based very loosely on Winifred's longtime companion Cecilia Evans.

Catholics were indeed persecuted and treated as second or third-class citizens in England for over 200 years as depicted in *A Noble Cunning*. The laws against them were Draconian but were more vigorously enforced during some periods than others. It was true, for instance, as illustrated in the novel, that Catholics in England were not allowed to possess physical items of worship identified with Catholicism, such as rosaries. The Roman Catholic mass was forbidden. Everyone was required to attend Church of England services or pay a fine. Catholics were also forbidden to hold public office or own land. Priests from the Continent risked their lives to come to England and perform religious rites for Catholics.

Catholics were accused of utterly absurd crimes, especially during the reign of Charles II. Roy Hattersley in his history *The Catholics* comments that the "Popish Plot," dreamed up by Titus Oates, an anti-Catholic liar and all-round scoundrel, was "a concoction of such obvious nonsense that it could only have been believed by fools and accepted by rogues for whom truth was less important than power."

During my research I came to have a somewhat jaundiced view of the so-called "Glorious Revolution" in 1688 in which William of Orange forced James II off the throne. I had read that the 1688 "Revolution" was "glorious" because William of Orange freed the English from a tyrannical Catholic king and restored their rights and liberties.

But it was James II, far ahead of his time, who proposed a *Declaration for Liberty of Conscience* that would have extended religious liberty not just to Catholics but to all—nonconformists, Jews, even non-believers. Of course, James undertook this *Declaration* primarily to improve conditions for Catholics, but, nevertheless, had it been accepted as drafted, it would have benefitted everyone. Imagine if such a law could have established religious freedom in England as early as 1688!

The *Declaration*, instigated perhaps by James' friend, the famous Quaker William Penn, was generally rejected because the people did not trust a Catholic king and suspected that the *Declaration* was just one step towards restoring Catholics to dominance, and because Anglicans and the dominant political party, the Whigs, did not want to share power. The persecution of Catholics continued for more than sixty years beyond the time of this novel.

A law passed by Parliament in 1701 also forbade the accession of any future monarch who was Catholic or married to a Catholic. Thus, when Queen Anne, the last Stuart monarch, died in 1714, the lawmakers skipped over more than fifty closer claimants to the throne, bringing in as Britain's next king a German ruler of a small principality in Central Europe who spoke no English, just because he was a Protestant.

The Jacobites (*Jacobus* means "James" in Latin) who supported James II's son, James Francis Edward, the "Chevalier," wanted to get rid of the foreign interloper George and put the true Stuart heir on the throne, thereby ending persecution of Catholics. They were joined in that effort by many non-Catholics who couldn't stomach the notion of a greedy and uncouth foreigner on the British throne. Details of the feckless Jacobite campaign that ensued and its aftermath, as described in the novel, are historically accurate.

I also found a larger meaning in Winifred's story. It reflects the cruelty and horror of religious persecution in any age, including our own. But Winifred Maxwell also represents the courage and daring of those who refuse to submit, who fight back and sometimes succeed, even against the most fearsome odds.

Appendix A

Bethan's Family in *A Noble Cunning*

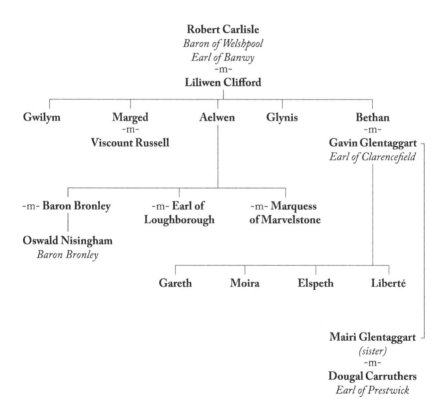

Robert Carlisle
Baron of Welshpool
Earl of Banwy
-m-
Liliwen Clifford

Gwilym   **Marged**   **Aelwen**   **Glynis**   **Bethan**
-m-   -m-
Viscount Russell   **Gavin Glentaggart**
                                   Earl of Clarencefield

-m- **Baron Bronley**   -m- **Earl of**   -m- **Marquess**
                          Loughborough   **of Marvelstone**

Oswald Nisingham
Baron Bronley

Gareth   **Moira**   **Elspeth**   **Liberté**

Mairi Glentaggart
(sister)
-m-
Dougal Carruthers
Earl of Prestwick

Appendix B

Chart of Stuarts and Possible Heirs

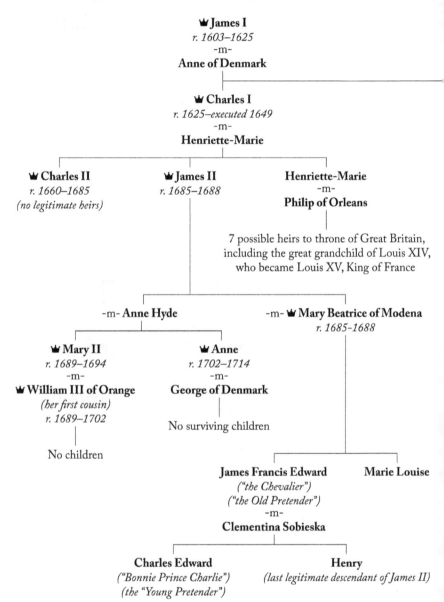

James I
r. 1603–1625
-m-
Anne of Denmark

Charles I
r. 1625–executed 1649
-m-
Henriette-Marie

Charles II
r. 1660–1685
(no legitimate heirs)

James II
r. 1685–1688

Henriette-Marie
-m-
Philip of Orleans

7 possible heirs to throne of Great Britain,
including the great grandchild of Louis XIV,
who became Louis XV, King of France

-m- **Anne Hyde**

-m- **Mary Beatrice of Modena**
r. 1685–1688

Mary II
r. 1689–1694
-m-
William III of Orange
(her first cousin)
r. 1689–1702

No children

Anne
r. 1702–1714
-m-
George of Denmark

No surviving children

James Francis Edward
("the Chevalier")
("the Old Pretender")
-m-
Clementina Sobieska

Marie Louise

Charles Edward
("Bonnie Prince Charlie")
(the "Young Pretender")

Henry
(last legitimate descendant of James II)

to the Throne of Great Britain

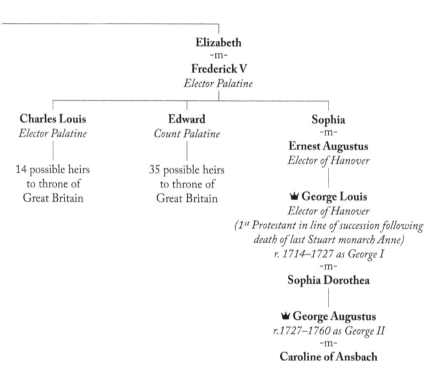

Elizabeth
-m-
Frederick V
Elector Palatine

Charles Louis
Elector Palatine

14 possible heirs
to throne of
Great Britain

Edward
Count Palatine

35 possible heirs
to throne of
Great Britain

Sophia
-m-
Ernest Augustus
Elector of Hanover

♛ **George Louis**
Elector of Hanover
(1ˢᵗ Protestant in line of succession following
death of last Stuart monarch Anne)
r. 1714–1727 as George I
-m-
Sophia Dorothea

♛ **George Augustus**
r.1727–1760 as George II
-m-
Caroline of Ansbach

♛ = ruled as king or queen

Appendix C

Timeline of Events Related to *A Noble Cunning*

Before the novel begins:

February 6, 1685 – King Charles II dies.

April 23, 1685 – Charles' brother is crowned King James II.

June 10, 1688 – James Francis Edward Stuart is born at St. James's Palace, causing fears among the populace of an ongoing Catholic dynasty.

November 5, 1688 – William of Orange invades England.

December 23, 1688 – King James II flees to France and sets up a court in exile at St.Germain-en-Laye near Paris.

April 11, 1689 – William of Orange and his wife Mary, Protestant daughter of James II, are crowned king and queen.

December 28, 1694 – Queen Mary dies of smallpox.

June 12, 1701 – Parliament passes the Act of Settlement which declares that henceforth no Catholic or anyone married to a Catholic can succeed to the throne.

March 8, 1702 – William of Orange dies. His sister-in-law Anne becomes queen.

Events occurring during the novel:

August 1, 1714 – Queen Anne dies, the last Stuart ruler.

October 20, 1714 – George, Elector of Hanover, the closest Protestant heir to Queen Anne, is crowned king of Great Britain as George I.

September 1, 1715 – King Louis XIV, longtime supporter of the young Stuart prince, dies.

September 6, 1715 – The Jacobite Rebellion begins at Braemar Castle in Aberdeenshire.

November 13, 1715 – The Jacobites are defeated at Preston in Lancashire.

December 22, 1715 – James Francis Edward Stuart, son of James II, lands at Peterhead In Scotland.

February 5, 1716 – James leaves Scotland, never to return.

February 9, 1716 – Leaders of "the '15" are tried and condemned to death.

February 24, 1716 – Several of the leaders are scheduled to be executed at the Tower of London.

Bibliography

Books

Ainsworth, William Harrison, *Preston Fight or The Insurrection of 1715*, London, George Routledge, 1875-1879, Project Gutenberg of Australia, May 2013. https://gutenberg.net. au/ebooks13/1302041h.html#ch9-11

Earle, Peter, *The Making of the English Middle Class: Business, Society and Family Life in London, 1660-1730*, London: Methuen, 1989.

Firth, Charles, *A Commentary on Macaulay's History of England*, ed. Godfrey Davies, London: Macmillan and Co., 1938.

George, M. Dorothy, *London Life in the Eighteenth Century*, reprint Chicago: Academy Chicago Publishers, 1984. First published by Kegan Paul, Trench, Trubner and Co. Ltd, 1925.

Hattersley, Roy, *The Catholics: The Church and Its People in Britain and Ireland, from the Reformation to the Present Day*, London: Chatto and Windus, 2017.

Hatton, Ragnhild, *George I*, New Haven: Yale University Press, new edition 2001, first published 1978.

Lees-Milne, James, *The Last Stuarts: British Royalty in Exile*, New York: Charles Scribner's Sons, 1984.

Lodge, Richard, *The History of England, 1660-1702*, originally published 1910, reprint First Rate Publishers, 2015.

Macaulay, Thomas Babington, *The History of England from the Accession of James II*, v. 1-2, reprint London: The Folio Press, 1985. First published in 1848.

Miller, Peggy, *James*, New York: St. Martin's Press, 1971.

Oman, Carola, *Mary of Modena*, London: Hodder & Stoughton, 1962.

Petrie, Charles, *The Jacobite Movement*, London & Spottiswoode, third edition, 1959, first published 1932.

Plumb, J. H., *The First Four Georges*, Boston: Little, Brown and Company, 1956.

Seton, Bruce Gordon, *The House of Seton: A Study of Lost Causes*, Edinburgh: Lindsay and MacLeod, v. 1, Digitized by the Internet Archive, National Library of Scotland, 2012. https://archive.org/stream/houseofsetonstv100seto/houseofsetonstv100seto_djvu.txt

Shield, Alice and Andrew Lang, *The King over the Water*, London: Longmans Green, 1907, reprint, no information.

Sowerby, Scott, *Making Toleration: The Repealers and the Glorious Revolution*, Cambridge, MA.: Harvard University Press, 2013.

Stuart, Flora Maxwell, *Lady Nithsdale and the Jacobites*, Innerleithen, Peeblesshire: Traquair House, 1995.

Szechi, Daniel, *The Jacobites: Britain and Europe, 1688-1788*, 2nd edition, Manchester: Manchester University Press, 2019.

Thomson, Katherine, *Memoirs of the Jacobites of 1715 and 1745*, v. 1-2, Project Gutenberg, digitally released March 31, 2007, London: Richard Bentley & Son, 1845. https://www.gutenberg.org/files/20946/20946-h/20946-h.htm and https://www.gutenberg.org/files/20947/20947-h/20947-h.htm#"

Tinniswood, Adrian, *Behind the Throne: A Domestic History of the British Royal Household*, New York: Basic Books, 2018.

Waller, Maureen, *Ungrateful Daughters: The Stuart Princesses Who Stole Their Father's Crown*, New York: St. Martin's Griffin, 2002.

Worsley, Lucy, *Courtiers: The Secret History of the Georgian Court*, London: Faber and Faber Ltd, 2011.

Articles

Barron, Denise, "Role of Anti-Catholicism in England in the 1670s," *Moya K. Mason, MLIS*, https://www.moyak.com/papers/popish-plot-england.html

Barton, Dennis, "James II and the 'Glorious Revolution' of 1688," *Church in History*, May 29, 2006, http://www.churchinhistory.org/pages/booklets/king-james(n)-1.htm

"Battle of Sheriffmuir," BTL17, *Historic Environment Scotland* with original documents and maps. http://portal.historicenvironment.scot/designation/BTL17

Cottrell-Boyce, Frank, "The Hidden History of Catholics in Britain," The New Statesman, April 29, 2017, updated September 9, 2021. https://www.newstatesman.com/culture/2017/04/hidden-history-catholics-britain

Hearfield, John, "Roads in the 18th Century," 2012. http://www.johnhearfield.com/History/Roads.htm

"Jacobite Rebellion of 1715: Rebels with a Cause?" National Archives, original Documents, with Introduction by Daniel Szechi. https://www.nationalarchives.gov.uk/education/resources/jacobite-1715/

McFerran, Noel S. "James III and VIII," *The Jacobite Heritage*, January 1, 2011. www.jacobite.ca/kings/james3.htm

Thompson, Ralph, "The Death of Queen Anne," *The National Archives* blog, August 1, 2014. https://blog.nationalarchives.gov.uk/death-queen-anne/

Worsley, Lucy, "How Glorious Was the Glorious Revolution?" *History Extra*, June 8, 2021, https://www.historyextra.com/period/stuart/how-glorious-was-the-glorious-revolution/. First published in *BBC History Magazine*, January 2017.

Acknowledgments

I must begin my acknowledgments by thanking the staff at Traquair House in the Scottish Lowlands, for telling my husband and myself the fabulous story of Winifred Herbert Maxwell, Countess of Nithsdale. I then read Flora Maxwell Stuart's excellent and exhaustive history of Winifred, *Lady Nithsdale and the Jacobites*, an essential source that gave me a much more detailed understanding of Winifred's challenging life and a blueprint for my novel. Ms. Stuart's lively portrait inspired me to try to do justice to Winifred in fiction.

My first draft of A *Noble Cunning* was 853 pages. It began with my protagonist "Bethan Carlisle," at the age of seven growing up in a Welsh castle, and followed her through a life that was filled with adventure long before her daring rescue of her husband at the Tower of London. Our dear friends Laure and Sébastien Larrea perused the original, War-and-Peace-sized manuscript, with relentless notes. Sébastien even prepared a *spreadsheet* for me with questions and suggested changes. They finished reading my tome while Laure was in labor giving birth to her second son. That, I would say, is going far beyond the customary obligations of friendship! The 853-page version was ultimately pruned down to less than 300 pages.

Jessica Cale at Historical Editorial provided a shrewd and probing analysis that helped me polish the manuscript further. Colin Mustful at History Through Fiction immediately saw the importance of this story and agreed to publish it, bless him. He was also incredibly patient through the entire process. Stephanie Barko, my publicist, has a deep understanding of the business and has been full of energy and great ideas.

I owe much also to other patient readers, Helen Mann, Julie Allison, Joyce Hansen, daughters Rebecca and Katherine, and my dear husband Alan, former newspaper reporter and editor, who was probably force-fed the entire story at least three different times. I am so grateful for all of their help.

About the Author

Native Texan Patricia Bernstein grew up in Dallas. After earning a Degree of Distinction in American Studies from Smith College, she founded her public relations agency in Houston.

In 2018, her third book was named a Finalist for an award from the Texas Institute of Letters. The *Austin American Statesman* named the book to a list of 53 of the best books ever written about Texas. Patricia's nonfiction was previously published by Simon & Schuster and Texas A&M University Press.

Patricia lives in Houston with her husband, Alan Bernstein, where she pursues her other great artistic love, singing with Opera in the Heights and other organizations. She also basks in the glory of her three amazing daughters. *A Noble Cunning* is her debut novel.

www.patriciabernstein.com

Other Books by History Through Fiction

Resisting Removal: The Sandy Lake Tragedy of 1850
By Colin Mustful

The Education of Delhomme: Chopin, Sand, & La France
By Nancy Burkhalter

The Sky Worshipers: A Novel of Mongol Conquests
By FM Deemyad

The King's Anatomist: The Journey of Andreas Vesalius
By Ron Blumenfeld

My Mother's Secret: A Novel of the Jewish Autonomous Region
By Alina Adams

If you enjoyed this novel please consider leaving a review. You'll be supporting a small, independent press, and you'll be helping other readers discover this great story.
Thank you!

www.HistoryThroughFiction.com

CPSIA information can be obtained
at www.ICGtesting.com
Printed in the USA
BVHW072030311022
650623BV00001B/35

9 781736 499054